WEDDING WIPEOUT

A Rabbi Kappelmacher Mystery

by

Jacob M. Appel

For information, email **Cozy Cat Press**, cozycatpress@aol.com or visit our website at: www.cozycatpress.com

COZY CAT
PRESS

ISBN: 978-1-939816-14-6
Printed in the United States of America

Cover design by Covershot Creations
www.covershotcreations.com

1 2 3 4 5 6 7 8 9 10

For my grandparents

Lillian and Leo Appel

CONTENTS

The Cast of Characters

FLORENCE EISENSTEIN—The elderly spinster whose sudden marriage shocked her family. Was her fatal asthma attack the product of foul play?

LORRAINE EISENSTEIN—Florence's sister and surviving heir to the Eisenstein egg cream fortune. If she was the intended victim, is her life still in danger?

ALFRED SHINGLE—Florence's suitor and mystery aficionado. What motive might he have to create a real-life whodunit?

AGATHA GROSSBART—The estranged cousin with a passion for single Jewish men. If she wouldn't kill for money, would she murder for a retired bachelor?

FRED EISENSTEIN—The ne'er-do-well nephew. Was Florence right to think him after her fortune?

LOUISE SINKOFF—The blind niece with the gambling habit. Did she murder the wrong aunt by mistake?

ANDREW SINKOFF—Louise's husband and bankroll. How far would he go to satisfy his upscale tastes?

GLADYS EINSENSTEIN—Florence and Lorraine's "other" niece. Could old family resentments drive her to homicide?

DR.HIRAM SCOTT—The family physician. Is he trying to conceal a tragic accident...or a brutal murder?

ART ABERCROMBIE, ESQ.—The Eisenstein family lawyer. Did he lie to Florence to trick her into marriage?

ANNIE PIERCE FINCHLEY—The voyeuristic neighbor. Is she an innocent bystander or the guardian of a deadly secret?

MARSHALL GREEN—The rabbi-turned-lawyer. Why is he so determined to prove that Florence Eisenstein was murdered?

JACOB KAPPELMACHER—An unlikely religious leader with a passion for cigars. Is he mistaking illusions for hallucinations?

RUDOLF STEINMETZ—Kappelmacher's "Man Friday." Can he talk his boss into letting sleeping dogs lie before the rabbi makes a laughing stock out of them both?

CHAPTER 1: THE CHALLENGE

Rabbi Kappelmacher had worked himself into one of those states where his eyes gleamed. He stood behind the podium in the small chapel, raking his bushy gray beard with one hand; he raised the other arm intermittently and pushed an imaginary button in the musty air to emphasize a point. Both Mrs. Conch, the cleaning lady, and I had seen him in this condition countless times before, and both of us knew better than to interrupt him, so Mrs. Conch continued to dust the pews and I pretended to remain unconvinced—even though, only a couple of minutes into the rabbi's lecture, I would have willingly sold my soul upon his say-so.

"So tell me, Steinmetz, are we to believe that Joshua stopped the sun in its path?"

"That's what the Torah tells us," I replied—knowing that I was stepping into a trap.

"Does it actually say so?" demanded Rabbi Kappelmacher. He paused to convey the impression that he was genuinely pondering the possibility. "Does it really say that the prophet Joshua halted the sun in the sky? But that cannot be. Because we both know that the earth revolves around the sun and not vice versa."

"I suppose you have to take it on faith," I answered. This happens to be my personal view as well as the reply that the rabbi sought to provoke. I'm a big believer in faith.

"On faith?" gasped Rabbi Kappelmacher. His cheeks suffused a deep crimson and from his expression one might have thought he'd swallowed an entire whitefish. *"On faith?* Don't be a *schlemiel*, Steinmetz. Children and animals take things on faith. Rabbis think rationally."

"I just thought—"

"No, Steinmetz, you didn't. You *didn't* think. If you'd thought about it, you would have realized that the Torah describes what *appeared* to happen. All we know is what the incident looked like—and it looked as though Joshua stopped the sun. Maybe it was an illusion."

"An illusion?"

The rabbi stepped around the podium and deposited both hands triumphantly in the pockets of his jacket. "Let's say I tell you I'm going to stop the sun, Steinmetz. What's the first thing I do? I send you over to the window and have you check the sun's position. Does that make sense?"

I nodded.

"And then I have you look at the clock, okay? That way you know exactly where the sun stood at three o'clock this afternoon."

I resisted the urge to point out that Joshua didn't own a clock.

"Now if we chat here for three hours and then I have you check the window and you find that the sun is in the same place, what would you conclude?"

"But that's not possible," I answered.

"Of course not, Steinmetz. But if it were, you'd naturally conclude that I'd stopped the sun. Am I right or am I right?"

"Well, yes, but in that case you would have stopped the sun."

"Not necessarily," said the rabbi. He removed his hands from his pockets and rubbed them together. "Maybe we chatted for three hours and then I drugged your drink. I let you sleep for another twenty-one hours, but moved the clock forward three hours, to six o'clock. Now, for a few moments at least, it will seem to you as though I stopped the sun. What do you say to that, Steinmetz?"

"But I'd figure it out pretty soon. When I checked my pocket planner, for instance. And my wife would be mighty upset if I didn't come home for supper. Not to mention that Mrs. Conch would find us when she locked up the sanctuary."

Mrs. Conch looked up and shrugged—as if to say, my job's cleaning, not philosophizing.

"All true, Steinmetz. But the ancient Israelites didn't have...what did you call it? A pocket planner. And if I drugged your wife too, then she wouldn't miss you. The larger the illusion, the easier it is to pull off."

"You don't really believe Joshua drugged the ancient Israelites?"

The rabbi retrieved his briefcase from the side table and sat down by the open window. "All I'm saying, Steinmetz, is that there's a rational explanation for everything. Forget about your silly faith. If you want proof of God, it's to be found in the miracle of reason. Only a divine being could create a world in which everything can be explained by careful analysis."

I was about to object when an unexpected visitor pushed open the doors of the chapel. He was a tall, thin man of about forty who walked with slight limp. His face, in contrast to his body, appeared broad and flat like a potato knish. Our visitor sported a three-piece suit and carried an attaché case under one arm.

"The prodigal son returns," announced the rabbi, rising to his feet.

"Hardly," our visitor answered. Color filled his cheeks.

"And to what do we owe this honor?" asked Rabbi Kappelmacher. "Maybe you've come to lead us in the afternoon prayers?"

The rabbi's tone puzzled me. As effusive and frenetic as he could be with me and Mrs. Conch, he usually adopted a degree of reserve with the congregants. He must have noticed my confusion, for he quickly revealed the identity of our unexpected guest.

"Rudolf Steinmetz, the assistant rabbi," he introduced me. "This is Marshall Green, the *former* assistant rabbi. Now junior partner at Abercrombie & Green."

So this was Marshall Green, rabbi turned lawyer. Or, as Rabbi Kappelmacher referred to him, the one that got away. Rumors abounded about Green—that he'd had an affair with a congregant and been asked to leave, that he'd gone to law school out of curiosity and then jumped at the six digit salaries. Some people even claimed that he now attended Episcopal services for political reasons. But the rabbi always referred to his former disciple with the utmost respect, and even if the rumors were true, Rabbi Kappelmacher certainly didn't believe them. Seeing my predecessor in the flesh, I tended to doubt the rumors. Green had too many premature wrinkles for a rich man or a philanderer.

"So to what do we owe this honor?" Rabbi Kappelmacher asked. He had taken Green by the arm and I feared he might examine his face with his hand like a blind man. "I thought you were too good for *our* law."

Green blushed again, wiping his forehead with a handkerchief. "Can we please go someplace private?" he asked. "Just the—the three of us." I admit that I was flattered by his decision to include me; he probably remembered what it was like to be the assistant rabbi. The slights come with the territory.

"So it's *that* kind of visit," said the rabbi enthusiastically as he led us out of the chapel and into the corridor. Five minutes later, we were ensconced in the rabbi's office: a small, dark chamber distinguished by exposed rafters and garish yellow paint. The rabbi leaned back in his chair and lit a cigar. For several moments, we sat in silence and listened to the hum of the air-conditioner.

"Well?" said the rabbi. "*Nu?*"

Green crossed and uncrossed his legs. "I have a legal problem," he said softly. "Or, rather, a legal puzzle."

"Then you should consult an attorney," suggested the rabbi. He let forth a full laugh that seemed to ripple down his beard into his chest.

"You know how you always said that there's a rational explanation for everything," continued Green. "Well, I have a case that seems to defy all logic. It's not even a case, really. Just an episode. And...well...I hoped maybe you might be able to help explain it."

"I thought *our* law wasn't good enough for you," teased the rabbi. "But possibly you're coming to your senses. There *is* a rational explanation for everything."

Green rummaged through his attaché case and removed a manila folder. "You may have heard of Irving Eisenstein?"

"Eisenstein's egg creams," said the rabbi. "I remember the shop on Delancey Street. Right next to Yonah Schlissel's knishes. The man must be in the earth forty years."

"Forty-three," answered Green.

"Forty-three," repeated the rabbi.

"Forty-three years this April. As you may or may not know, Irving Eisenstein died a very wealthy man. King of an egg cream empire. They marketed powdered drinks too— until shortly before he died, when the family sold the brand name to General Foods."

"Nu?" asked the rabbi. "And this has what to do with the price of *kugel* in Brooklyn?"

Green slid the folder across the rabbi's desk. "That's his will. He was one of Art Abercrombie's first clients. It's a strange document, you'll note. Even by legal standards. He disinherits the son outright. The boy—he's dead now too— married outside the faith, you see."

"You can say *shiksah*, Green. Steinmetz won't take offense."

"As I said," said Green, "he married outside the faith and, as far as I know, the old man never spoke to him again. Instead, he took out his anger on his daughters. Florence and Lorraine. He left trust funds for both of them. Annual stipends. If they both died unmarried, all of the money was to go to charity. For planting trees in Israel or whatnot."

"That's not so unusual," I offered. "He wanted his daughters to get married. He provided an incentive."

Green shook his head. "That's where you're wrong, Rabbi Steinmetz. He did precisely the opposite. If either daughter married, all of the money was to pass immediately to the other daughter. He particularly *didn't* want the daughters to marry. He thought the son had done enough marrying for the entire family."

"Is that legal?" asked Rabbi Kappelmacher.

"The courts prohibit most testamentary prohibitions against marriage," Green replied. "The one exception has been laid down by the First Circuit Court of Appeals in *Evans v. Dodge*. A parent may create a trust fund to provide

for the upkeep of a single child prior to his or her marriage.
Of course, the exception in the *Evans* case was designed for
circumstances in which the parent *wants* the child to marry,
but fears that, for one reason or another, such a marriage will
not occur. But the rule applies in this case too, even though
the intent was exactly the opposite."

Rabbi Kappelmacher scratched his beard. "Talmudic law
expressly forbids such an arrangement. You cannot place
restrictions on an inheritance. You either give it or you
don't. You can't half-give. *Our* law avoids all of these
complexities."

"Well, as you know, I don't practice Talmudic law," said
Green. "And neither did Irving Eisenstein. If he did, I
wouldn't have to come here in the first place."

The rabbi tamped out his cigar. "Well, why then, Green,
did you come here? So I drank the man's egg creams for
forty-five years. I can't imagine that can shed any light on
his last will and testament."

"I'm getting to that," said Green. He removed a
newspaper clipping from his attaché case and placed it on
top of the manila folder. "The Eisenstein sisters never
married. For forty-three years, they lived together in the
same old house in Pine Valley. Each year, they paid a visit to
Abercrombie and checked if there had been any change in
the status of the will, but there never was. I believe it was
more a matter of habit than hope. The trust funds themselves
were pretty generous, after all, and the sisters were already
well into their sixties when I joined the firm."

"I can't help but notice your use of the past tense," Rabbi
Kappelmacher interjected. "And since you've just placed a
newspaper clipping on my desk, might I venture to guess
that one—or possibly both—of them has recently left this
world? That's an obituary you have there, isn't it?"

"Please, rabbi," Green answered, clearly holding back his
frustration. "Just let me tell the story...."

"I'm no spring chicken," retorted the rabbi. "I thought
maybe I could cut to the heart of the matter before the sun
goes down and we have to celebrate the *shabbus*."

"But it's only Thursday."

"Precisely, Green. Now please tell me why one of the Eisenstein sisters dying is of such concern to you...or to me."

Green wiped his brow a second time. "As I was saying, about six months ago, the older sister—that would be Florence—started to socialize with a local man. A retired teacher. There's nothing wrong with socializing, of course, from the standpoint of the will. She just can't marry him."

"I take it that what you mean by socializing is *shtupping*."

"*Socializing*, Rabbi Kappelmacher," repeated Green. "I don't know what else they were doing. I found out about their relationship only this week. At the wedding."

"The wedding?"

"I received a call on Monday morning from Florence Eisenstein saying that she didn't care about the will, one way or the other, and that she intended to marry. And would I please come around the house on Tuesday afternoon to serve as a witness?"

"You'd have thought she'd have asked for Mr. Abercrombie," suggested the rabbi.

The tone of Green's voice changed without warning, and he spoke as though he were choosing every word with great care. "You would have, wouldn't you? But she insisted that it be me. In fact, she warned me not to tell Abercrombie at all, because she feared he'd try to talk her out of it."

All of a sudden, Rabbi Kappelmacher's eyes began to gleam again.

"And you believed her? About Abercrombie?" asked the rabbi.

"I had no reason *not* to believe her," replied Green. "But I did get the impression that...well...she didn't trust Abercrombie, for one reason or another. That's just a feeling I had, of course. I can't substantiate it."

"And let me see if I have this correct," said the rabbi. "After she called you, she got married and then she died—and that seems like a rather odd coincidence to you."

"There's more to it than that," said Green. "Much more. I went around the house Tuesday and both of her nieces and her cousin, Agatha, were there. Everybody was standing in the parlor, waiting. It seemed that her sister—Lorraine— wouldn't come downstairs for the wedding. They'd had an argument, apparently, about not inviting the nephew. First, Florence tried to reason with her sister, and then the groom went upstairs to talk some sense into her, but neither of them had any luck. So they got married anyway. Without her."

"And then Florence died?"

"Better than that. Then the nephew showed up and Florence ran upstairs and refused to come down again until he left the house."

"And the nephew?"

"Fred Eisenstein. He's the only one of the brother's children who ever paid any attention to the old women. He's also what you might call a ne'er do well. Squandered all of his money on some project to assist young artists. Anyway, he went upstairs to speak with his aunts, but Florence would have nothing to do with him. Finally, he managed to coax Lorraine downstairs, and she was all in tears—promising that she wouldn't turn her back on him like Florence had, and declaring that her sister had gone wrong in the head."

"If he wasn't invited, how did he come to show up?"

"He happed to phone his sister, Louise, and the babysitter told him that his sister and her husband had gone to spend the night at Pine Valley."

The rabbi scratched his beard. "That's not all, Green. You wouldn't come to me if that were all. What is it that's bothering you?"

"It's the will, rabbi. She told both of her nieces and her cousin that she'd broken the will—that she'd spoken to the firm and we'd told her that she could marry whom she pleased and still inherit."

"When did she do this?"

"On the phone, I guess. Maybe when she invited them to the wedding. It must have been after she'd spoken to me. The niece's husband—his name's Sinkoff—called yesterday afternoon. The cousin and the other niece phoned this morning, right after the funeral. They seemed convinced that they were to inherit a large sum of money."

"And they're not?"

"Not a dime. The will is air tight. They were the beneficiaries of Florence's will, of course. But as soon as she married, all of her father's money went to the sister. At the time of her death, Florence wasn't worth very much at all. They'll still inherit her small savings—but, quite frankly, that'll be a wash after the legal costs. Maybe they'll get a couple of thousand dollars a piece."

"Why did Florence believe she'd broken the will?"

"I haven't the faintest idea. Abercrombie denies telling her that the will had been broken and I certainly never did. And she knew nobody else at the firm would have the authority to tell her that, even if it were true. Which, I must emphasize, it wasn't."

"And what of the nephew?" demanded the rabbi. His eyes had retained their gleam, and I sensed that this meant trouble.

"Well, that's the clincher, rabbi. That's why I've come. When Florence called me early on Monday, she told me that she planned to disinherit the nephew. She did have some small savings of her own, you understand. She probably thought she had more than she actually did; she wasn't planning for the legal bills. Few folks do. Anyway, Florence said that she'd had a major row with her nephew, and that he'd always been after her money, but she was determined that he wouldn't receive a penny of it. She planned to leave the bulk of her estate to her new husband anyway, but she wanted to make sure Fred was written out as quickly as possible."

"And I imagine the nephew didn't take this news too well."

"You won't believe this," said Green. "But—"

"I'll believe anything, if it's true," interjected Rabbi Kappelmacher.

"Well, the nephew called me early this afternoon to inquire about the inheritance. So I said to him, probably with less tact than I should have, that it was a fortunate thing that his aunt had died before she'd had an opportunity to change her will. He demanded to know what I meant, and by way of explaining myself, I suggested that on account of their falling out, she'd intended to disinherit him."

"It must have taken some *chutzpah* to tell him that," suggested the rabbi.

"Do you want to talk about *chutzpah*, rabbi? Fred Eisenstein insisted on the phone today that he'd never had any falling out with his aunt at all and that he has absolutely no idea why she didn't invite him to the wedding. In fact, he says he visited her last Sunday and she didn't even mention it."

"He visited only Florence? Or both sisters?"

"Only Florence. Lorraine was out for her weekly trip to the beauty parlor. She had a standing appointment at the Paradise Salon. Now I'm a good judge of character, if I do say so myself. And I can tell you that young man is either telling the truth—or he's delusional. I've never heard anyone protest his innocence like that against such overwhelming evidence. You see, Florence seems to have made a point of telling everyone about their falling out. Her husband…her niece, Gladys…the Sinkoffs…and her cousin, Agatha. It was the very reason Lorraine wouldn't come downstairs for the wedding. Now don't you find it a bit odd, rabbi, that a woman would call all of her relatives to tell them that she'd broken a will that she hadn't actually broken and then inform them all that she'd planned to disinherit a nephew who claims that he was on the best of terms with her?"

Green's question weighed heavily in the dank air of the office. The rabbi lit another cigar and scratched his temple.

"And then she died?" persisted the rabbi.

"She had an asthmatic attack on Tuesday night. The husband drove out to the twenty-four hour pharmacy to fill a prescription. Her sister found her while he was gone."

"And the family stayed the night at Pine Valley?"

"All of them."

"Rather a strange coincidence, her dying on her wedding night," observed the rabbi. "That is indeed a troubling story. Almost inexplicable."

For my part, I didn't find the story particularly troubling at all.

"If I might venture a word, Mr. Green," I offered, "that's a fairly *odd* story, I admit. But not one that defies explanation. As Rabbi Kappelmacher always says, everything can be explained with reason."

"And what, pray tell," asked Rabbi Kappelmacher, "is your explanation, Steinmetz? Because I admit that I myself am absolutely perplexed."

"That surprises me," I continued. "It's really quite simple. The old woman didn't want her wedding to be a bitter-sweet affair. She lied about the will being broken so that nobody would feel bad about her losing her inheritance. Maybe she even convinced herself that she'd broken the will. Old women are capable of fantasies like that. My mother's sister persuaded herself that her husband had died a war hero in Europe when in fact he'd fallen off a ladder on a drinking binge. There's no telling what a person will convince herself to get through the day."

"And the nephew, Steinmetz?"

"His behavior is only natural under the circumstances. He feels badly that he argued with his aunt and he doesn't want to admit it. Pure denial."

The entire business struck me as rather straightforward.

"So you believe she was lying to make herself feel better, Steinmetz?" asked the rabbi. I could tell by his tone that he believed otherwise. "But then why did she get married in the first place? She stays single all of these years and then she up and marries on a lark? To a man who Green here says that she's been *shtupping* anyway. Why not just keep *shtupping* him and continue to collect her annuity?"

"I said socializing," Green corrected him.

"Yes, but you meant *shtupping*. You're the type who'll always say socializing, even at the expense of clarity. You and Mrs. Green probably 'socialize.'"

The former assistant rabbi's skin turned crimson.

"Now tell me, Steinmetz, even if you're correct about the will and the nephew, how can you explain Florence Eisenstein's decision to get married in the first place?"

I admit he had me there. I tried to avoid his gaze. His eyes were bulging like a child's with a new toy and it was a look that made me tremble. "Maybe she was a religious woman," I ventured. "Maybe she didn't believe in *shtupping* before marriage."

The rabbi laughed and dismissed my idea with a wave of his hand. "I doubt that, Steinmetz. And if you thought about it, you would too."

"Well, you must admit it's a possible answer," I insisted. "No matter how unlikely."

"Not at all possible, Steinmetz. I know for a fact that she wasn't a religious woman. Aren't I right, Green?"

Green appeared confused by the rabbi's sudden knowledge. "No, the Eisenstein sisters aren't religious. But how in the world did you know that? You yourself said that you'd never met them before."

"I never said I didn't know the Eisenstein sisters, Green. You inferred that. All I said was that I hadn't seen their father in forty-five years. I never said that I didn't know the daughters."

"Then you do know them?" I demanded incredulously. "You've been holding out on us all along?"

"Not at all," said the rabbi. "Far from it. I've never laid eyes on either sister in my life."

"Then how can you be certain that Florence didn't get married for religious reasons?"

"Because I use all the facts at my disposal, Steinmetz. I use the old rabbinic reasoning. Green here told us that the nephew went to visit Florence last Saturday, did he not? And that the other sister was at the beauty parlor at the time. Now I think it's safe to assume that if they've lived together all these years, it's highly unlikely that one sister is extremely religious and the other one isn't. So if Lorraine will go to the beauty parlor on the *shabbus*, don't you think Florence would probably *shtup* out of wedlock?"

I nodded reluctantly. It still amazes me that the rabbi can deduce so much from such small tidbits of information.

"So that's the reason why Florence Eisenstein *didn't* get married, Steinmetz," continued the rabbi. "Why she *did* get married—and we have it on good authority from Green here that she did—is a question that remains to be answered. Incidentally, Green, did the Eisenstein sisters get along with each other? I imagine the will might have made matters tense between them."

"Not as far as I know," answered Green. "They seemed to be the best of friends when they came by the office each year. They blamed their father for the will, not each other. Of course, they kept to themselves, so it's hard to be certain. But I think they were on excellent terms until the falling out over the nephew. Abercrombie knew them much better than I did, though. You might want to ask him."

The rabbi shook his head. "Puzzling, isn't it?"

"So you'll admit that this is one of those cases that seems to defy reason?"

"Aha, Green," exclaimed the rabbi. He jumped up from behind his desk, slapping his hands together in the process. "So that's why you've come. Now it all makes sense. You believe you have an example of human behavior that cannot be explained rationally. In effect, you're challenging me!"

"Well, I—"

"Your challenge is accepted, Green. When can we meet the deceased's family?"

"I'm actually on my way to make a condolence call. But there's really no need for you to come, rabbi. I just thought the case might intrigue you. It wasn't a challenge."

"All unexplained mysteries are challenges. It if weren't for the inexplicable, we wouldn't need rabbis. Come along, Steinmetz, we're going to make a *shivah* call."

Before I could adjust to this strange turn of events, Rabbi Kappelmacher had donned his evening coat and had charged off into the corridor.

CHAPTER 2: THE CONDOLENCE CALL

A thirty minute drive in the rabbi's vintage blue Cadillac took us to Pine Valley. It was one of those quaint, up-county hamlets where the wealthy had built country "cottages" in the pre-war era. The once-proud homes had seen better days, even better decades. Yet there was no masking the lost splendor of the sprawling lawns and stately mansions—even if the garden parties and debutante balls now existed only in the memories of the oldest residents.

"It's hard to imagine that people used to live in houses like these," I observed off-handedly as we passed a particularly impressive Victorian mansion.

"People *still* live here," answered Green. "Wait until you see the Eisenstein place."

I had to wait only a couple of minutes, for the former assistant rabbi soon instructed Rabbi Kappelmacher to pull off the road onto a tree-lined gravel lane. We followed the lane along a mesh fence for half a mile until the lawn gave way to heavy undergrowth. Whatever the state of the Eisenstein sisters' finances, they certainly weren't putting their capital into upkeep on the property. Once a stone bounced off the roadway and into the windshield; on several occasions, I feared we had burst a tire. When we finally emerged from the undergrowth, the road veered sharply to the right toward the grand chimneys of the Eisenstein estate. Immediately in front of us, a carefully-tended flower bed boasted row upon row of spring bulbs. Tulips, daffodils, hyacinths. They ran all the way up to the mesh fence. And on the far side of the fence, at a distance of maybe twenty yards, on a wooden porch attached to a modest structure, possibly a former carriage house, sat an elderly woman in a sun bonnet and pink taffeta gown.

When we passed, she waved to us and raised her glass. Rabbi Kappelmacher lifted one hand from the steering wheel and waved back through the open window.

"I take it that used to be part of the Eisenstein property," observed the rabbi.

"Until the early 1950s," answered Green. "One of the last things Irving Eisenstein did was to sell off the bulk of the estate. They carved four or five homes out of it."

"And that woman on the porch?"

Green motioned for Rabbi Kappelmacher to pull up behind a row of cars. "Just some neighbor. No relation, as far as I know."

We followed Green around the side of the Eisenstein house. He knocked on a small wooden door. "They don't use the main entrance anymore. They'd closed down most of the old place to save money. Even with the guests for the wedding, I imagine they were using only one third of the rooms."

"Do you really think we should be here, rabbi?" I asked, feeling suddenly out of place. "They've just had a death in the family. I'm not sure it's right to be crashing in on them during their mourning."

The rabbi frowned at me and crushed his cigar under his heel. "Don't be a *noodnik*, Steinmetz. There's a mystery to be solved."

I was about to object further when the door opened and a woman in a black dress and matching shawl welcomed us with a broad smile. Her face was coated generously with makeup. She had that late-sixties permafrost look that women of a certain age acquire briefly before they stumble into old age. "Mr. Green, from the lawyers," she said—as much to herself as to him. "How good of you to come."

"And I brought along Rabbi Kappelmacher and Rabbi Steinmetz," said Green. "Rabbi Kappelmacher knew Florence when she was a young girl."

Lorraine Eisenstein furrowed her brow and assessed us as though we were butcher's meat.

"From the store on Delancey Street," the rabbi explained. "I had a mighty big crush on your sister," he lied.

The frown quickly melted from Lorraine's face. "Well, come in then. You'll have to pardon my suspicions, but dear Florence wasn't well the last few weeks. There was no telling what element she might have befriended."

"Especially in this day and age," the rabbi consoled her. "It's a different world out there."

"Indeed, it is," Lorraine agreed. "Mr. Abercrombie was just telling me that he was involved in a lawsuit about a woman who used to be a man and now wishes to compete in the Women's Olympics."

"The Ingersoll case," Green explained as we followed Lorraine Eisenstein into a cozy 1950's-style kitchen.

"Imagine that, Mr. Green," said Lorraine. "A woman who used to be a man! It's no wonder Florence and I preferred to stay at home."

"Easily understandable," Rabbi Kappelmacher agreed. "Mr. Green here led me to believe that you two didn't get out much."

"Hardly ever. I drive into town once a week to visit the beauty salon and to pick up groceries. When Alfred wasn't around, we might go together to fill Florence's prescription. But other than that, we pretty much stayed put. Until a couple of months ago, we used to go to the library once every few weeks to take out books. That's where Florence met Alfred. But recently, poor Florence wouldn't even do that. Especially after what happened with Cousin Agatha."

"Cousin Agatha?" asked the rabbi as we removed our coats and hats, depositing them on a threadbare sofa in the corner.

"Oh, dear, yes. It was just dreadful—the beginning of the end, I think. After that, Florence just wasn't herself."

"The beginning of the end?"

"That's what I think," said Lorraine. "Florence woke up one morning and decided she wanted to have dinner with Cousin Agatha. Cousin Agatha, whom she hadn't spoken to in twenty-five years." She lowered her voice. "Cousin Agatha, whom neither of us could ever stand."

"And Florence wanted to have dinner with her?" asked Rabbi Kappelmacher, feigning disbelief.

"She wanted to introduce her to Alfred. So she called Cousin Agatha out of the blue and invited her to dinner. It's been over a month and it's still hard for me to digest."

We followed Lorraine through the dining room and across a wood-paneled library.

"And you must have joined them for dinner," the rabbi observed.

"Lord, no. I wouldn't dine with that woman if my life depended on it. You'll see. She's like a cat, stalking her prey. No man is safe with her around. Married men, single men—she'll take anything."

"Indeed," exclaimed Rabbi Kappelmacher. "It's a wonder Florence survived dinner with a woman like that."

"But that's just it. Florence didn't go. That was the evening of her first bout with the *asthma*." Lorraine Eisenstein lowered her voice to whisper the word asthma, as though the name of the disease itself might prove contagious. "She sent poor Alfred to town all by himself, the dear soul. I know *I* never would have trusted my beau alone with a woman like that. Knowing Agatha the way she did, in fact, I can't imagine why she would have allowed Alfred to dine alone with our cousin."

"Alfred must be a trustworthy fellow," suggested the rabbi. But before our host could answer, we emerged into a crowded drawing room.

The room itself was cluttered with souvenirs and artifacts that transcended any particular time period. To the right of the entryway, high-backed Georgian chairs surrounded a shiny new glass coffee table. To the left, a threadbare beige sofa sagged against the far wall. One of the antimacassars was missing and the sun had bleached the other a deep shade of cream. In the far corner, beyond the Eisenstein family, a grandfather clock stood watch over a baby grand piano. The atmosphere bespoke a lifetime—or several lifetimes—of haphazard purchasing.

The occupants of the room proved as diverse as the furnishings. Green introduced us. In addition to the man-happy cousin, Agatha, and the gaunt, bespectacled Art Abercrombie, we exchanged cursory greetings with the assorted nieces and nephews: mousy Gladys Eisenstein; Fred, whose winning smile and rugged good looks defied my expectations for the ne'er-do-well nephew; Louise Sinkoff and her husband, Andrew. Louise wore dark glasses and remained seated throughout our brief exchange. At first, I thought that she had been crying; yet when her husband, a short, stocky man of forty, helped her set down her drink, I suddenly realized that she was blind. This discovery made me nervous, as I always find myself uncomfortable around blind people, and I was relieved to escape into a corner with Rabbi Kappelmacher and Lorraine Eisenstein.

"When was the last time you saw Florence?" she asked the rabbi.

"It's been so long. I don't even know if I could tell you," Rabbi Kappelmacher replied. "Over forty years. When I was in school, the highlight of my day was an Eisenstein egg cream. It nearly broke my heart when your father closed down his store."

"The old store," said Lorraine nostalgically. "I haven't thought about it in years. What is it they say, rabbi? You can't go home again."

"Indeed," agreed the rabbi. "It's a different neighborhood now. A different world. But Yonah Schlissel's is still there. Nothing pleases me more than a Yonah Schlissel knish. Nothing."

"How about the blintzes at Sam Kaplan's?" asked Lorraine. She appeared to be warming up to the rabbi, which I gathered was his intent.

"I should be so lucky!" declared the rabbi. "Sam Kaplan's is long gone. Sam moved to Miami Beach."

"And Knobler's Delicatessen? They used to have the most indescribably delicious pastrami sandwiches. Florence and I would share one sandwich and we'd still have enough left over to bring home for dinner."

The rabbi patted his stomach. "Ah, Knobler's Deli. I haven't been there in years—not since they changed locations. But you're right about the pastrami. It was better than Levine's. Better than Burnstein's even. My mouth waters just thinking of it. I'll never forget how much your sister Florence loved Knobler's Deli."

Lorraine Eisenstein wiped a tear from her eye. "She did love those sandwiches. After all these years, I can still recall what she used to say about the pastrami. She'd say, 'Knobler, can you get me one of those sandwiches I like so much?' No matter how often she ordered pastrami, she could never remember what it was called."

"It must have been hard for you, losing her so unexpectedly."

"In a way, yes," answered Lorraine. "And in a way, no. I'll tell you the truth, Rabbi...."

"....Kappelmacher...."

"I'll tell you the truth, Rabbi Kappelmacher. Florence just wasn't Florence these last few months. Ever since the first asthma attack, she hardly left the house. Alfred was the only one who could coax her into going anywhere."

At that moment, a white-haired gentleman in his early seventies appeared in the doorway and made his way toward us. Even without introduction, I knew it was Alfred Shingle.

"Alfred, this is Rabbi Kappelmacher," said Lorraine. "And his assistant."

"I'm sorry about your loss," said the rabbi.

"I was just telling Rabbi Kappelmacher about how difficult Florence became over the last few months," Lorraine continued. "How she wouldn't go out and how she turned her back on poor Fred."

Alfred Shingle threw his sister-in-law a dirty look, but it melted quickly when he turned to face the rabbi. "Florence could be challenging," he said diplomatically. "But she hadn't gone wrong in the head, no matter what anybody might say to the contrary. She was only angry at herself."

"About getting sick," suggested the rabbi.

"Not at all," answered Alfred Shingle. "She was angry that she hadn't married sooner. She regretted letting her father's will influence her life. I trust you know all about the will."

"The lawyer told us," said Rabbi Kappelmacher. "A strange business. I guess we can be thankful that Florence started to enjoy life before the end."

Alfred nodded. "Death is a hard business," he said. "I read mystery novels, rabbi, but death never seems real in a book the way it does in life. I keep thanking the good Lord that Florence passed away in her sleep the way she did. As much as I miss her, I'm grateful that she died peacefully."

Alfred Shingle blinked his eyes several times. He was not the sort of man to shed tears in public.

"She died of asthma, I understand," said the rabbi.

"On our wedding night. Hiram Scott had put her on medication, but the prescription ran out. I'd never forgive myself for letting that happen, except Hiram assured me it didn't matter. She would have died anyway. She just stopped breathing...."

"You were with her when she died?"

"No," answered Alfred. "I'd gone out to fill the prescription. It was Lorraine here who found her."

I was starting to fear that the rabbi was pushing his amateur interrogation too far. He must have come to the same conclusion, for he changed the subject.

"Hiram Scott was Florence's physician?"

"He's been our doctor for years," replied Lorraine Eisenstein. "And before that was his father, Enoch. His father saved my life, you know. He brought me back from the brink when I had the scarlet fever."

"Modern medicine is an amazing thing," said the rabbi. "Which reminds me, Steinmetz, would you mind helping me put that ointment on my ankles?"

I was about to ask what ointment he was talking about when I felt the heel of his boot on my toe.

"Miss Eisenstein," he asked, "You wouldn't happen to have a bathtub I could fill with water? I'm supposed to soak my ankles before I put on the ointment. It reduces swelling."

"Up the far stairs and to the left," said Lorraine. "That's the only bathroom with a working bathtub in the house."

"The far stairs?" asked the rabbi. For indeed there were two staircases descending into the drawing room.

'The ones on the right," answered Lorraine. "The ones on the left lead to the old wing. There's no working bathtubs up there, just guest rooms. We don't use the old wing much nowadays. No need to, you understand. So we haven't bothered to modernize the plumbing."

Rabbi Kappelmacher thanked our host and trotted toward the left-hand staircase. I followed reluctantly. As soon as we'd reached the upper landing, I expressed my displeasure to the rabbi.

"What was *that* all about?" I asked. "You're not really going to soak your feet in the bath, are you? At a *shivah* call?"

The rabbi shook his head and rested his arm on the banister. We stood in a narrow hallway. The bathroom door at our left stood ajar; two other doors, further down the corridor, were shut. "Of course I'm not going to soak my feet, Steinmetz. I just needed an excuse to see the room where Florence Eisenstein died."

"But how do you even know it's up here? It's an enormous house."

"Rabbinic reasoning," replied the rabbi. "I'm certain it's up here. I figured that since the Eisenstein sisters don't seem to have put much money into fixing up the house, it's highly unlikely that they would have updated most of the bathrooms. However, I suspected that they would have added a modern bath—but, most likely, only one. And I assumed that since they're old women, the Eisenstein sisters would have preferred rooms *near* the working bath. In fact, Steinmetz, I'll bet you a fresh bagel that those two doors lead to their bedrooms."

"I wish you wouldn't lie to these poor people," I said. "If you keep doing this, eventually they're going to figure out that you didn't know Florence Eisenstein."

"Nonsense. These people have no reason to think I'm lying. Everybody trusts a rabbi. Besides, why in the world would I lie about something like this?"

"That's exactly what I've been wondering," I muttered.

The rabbi ignored me. He proceeded to examine both doors. "So which one do you think is Florence's room?"

"I don't know. But I'm sure it's simply a matter of rabbinic reasoning."

The rabbi laughed. "No, actually, Steinmetz, it's a matter of probability. We have a fifty percent chance of choosing the correct door. Of course, we have two chances—so I'll try this one." And with that, the rabbi gently pushed open the door nearest the stairs.

We found ourselves in a dimly-lit bedroom furnished with a double bed, a cherrywood bureau and a matching end table. A mirror was suspended above the bed and on either side of the mirror hung a framed photograph. I examined them while the rabbi stood in the center of the room, scratching his beard. One of the photos was a faded black-and-white snapshot: Two young girls, presumably Florence and Lorraine, arm-in-arm at the beach. The other was a recent photograph of Alfred Shingle. "We're in the right room," I called out. "There's a photograph of her husband."

"I already know that," said Rabbi Kappelmacher. "Look behind the door."

Once again, I found myself one step behind the rabbi. Suspended from a hook on the back of the door hung an old-fashioned wedding dress, one of the capped-sleeve lace creations that were popular in the 1920's. "I'll bet that belonged to her mother," I observed.

"Look here," replied the rabbi, expressing little interest in my thoughts on the subject. He'd stepped to the far end of the room and opened a door. "A walk-in closet, Steinmetz. An easy enough place to conceal oneself."

"Is this really necessary, rabbi?" I asked. "Aren't you taking this detective game a little bit too far?"

"I'm not playing detective, Steinmetz. I'm playing rabbi. How can I have faith in God if I can't explain Florence Eisenstein's behavior?"

"Just the same, rabbi, don't you think we'd best be going downstairs before somebody gets suspicious?"

"Don't be a noodnik, Steinmetz. Who'll become suspicious of a rabbi who needs to soak his ankles? Besides, I've just discovered something highly unusual. Look at that photograph of Mr. Shingle and tell me what you see."

I examined the photograph. "I see an old man in a sailor's cap standing in front of a flower bush. I think the flowers are bougainvillea."

"No, no Steinmetz," retorted the rabbi. "Look closer. Don't you see anything unusual about the photograph?"

I reexamined the photo more intently. For the life of me, I didn't see anything out of the ordinary.

"It's just a photograph, rabbi."

"No, Steinmetz, it's not just a photograph. It's the wrong photograph. Notice that it's a horizontal photo, but the impressions of a vertical photograph are still visible in the paint."

I shrugged. "That's not so highly unusual," I replied with frustration. "The woman just got married. It's only natural that she'd put up a photograph of her husband."

"To replace an old photograph, Steinmetz? I think not."

"If you'll pardon me, rabbi," I said, "I think you're grasping at straws. We'd better go downstairs."

"What if I told you, Steinmetz, that there's another photograph missing in the drawing room? You can still see the discoloration in the paint there too."

"I'd say," I answered, "that you'd had too much *schnapps* to drink with lunch. People replace old photographs all the time. If you're so curious about it, why don't you ask Miss Eisenstein?"

Rabbi Kappelmacher walked to the window and peered through the shades. "You can't see that neighbor's house from here," he observed. "There's a row of trees in the way."

"Is that highly unusual too?" I asked. "Do you think somebody planted the trees to keep Florence Eisenstein from seeing the neighbors?"

The rabbi shook his head. "That is a question to which I do not yet know the answer, Steinmetz. Of course, it is a possibility. Only a combination of time and rabbinic reasoning will tell us for certain."

I followed the rabbi to the window and pulled aside the blinds. He was right about at least one thing: All you could see from Florence's room was a thicket of trees that stood no more than twenty feet from the house. When I looked back into the room, I noted that the rabbi was untying his boots. "Just to allay your concerns, Steinmetz, I want to make it look as though I've bathed my ankles. How's that?"

"Can we please go home now?' I asked. "My wife will be waiting."

To my surprise, the rabbi agreed. "I'm ready whenever you are," he said. 'There's nothing like a good night's sleep to help the reasoning process."

Rabbi Kappelmacher, his laces untied, led the way downstairs. In the drawing room, we found that the mourners had divided into two groups. Near the tattered sofa, Lorraine, Alfred, Art Abercrombie and Green formed one circle. The remainder of the family had gathered around the coffee table where the portly Agatha Grossbart was in the process of relating a story. Her voice rang across the room, loud and grating.

"And then Uncle Irving said," she concluded emphatically, "that he manufactured egg creams, not cream eggs. Now *that* put the man from General Foods in his place."

Agatha grinned in pleasure at her own story. I noticed that her audience, save Fred Eisenstein, took the opportunity to excuse themselves. They joined us in bidding farewell to Lorraine and headed toward the door.

"I want to thank you, Miss Eisenstein," said the rabbi. "For your hospitality. And for the bath."

"You found it satisfactory?" asked Lorraine. "Sometimes it takes a while for the hot water to come up."

"More than satisfactory," answered the rabbi. "It was a pleasure meeting you. And you too, Mr. Shingle. And again, I'm sorry about Florence. Very, truly sorry."

Marshall Green then explained to us that he intended to catch a ride home from Abercrombie later that evening, and we headed out into the summer night. A soft breeze had picked up and added an air of romance, maybe even mystery, to the twilight.

"So do you have your rational explanation yet, rabbi?" I asked.

"Not yet, Steinmetz. Not yet. But I will soon enough."

"So you still don't believe that Florence Eisenstein was just a dotty old woman?"

The arrival of Agatha on the porch interrupted our conversation. Now that she was standing, I noticed that she walked with the assistance of a cane.

"Rabbi," Agatha called to us. "Could I trouble you for a ride back down to Haddam? That lawyer fellow led me to believe that we live in the same neck of the woods."

"Why, of course," agreed Rabbi Kappelmacher.

He opened the back door of the Cadillac for the woman and then took his place at the wheel. I hoped, momentarily, that we were done with this business for good. I'd had enough lying and deception for one day. My hopes, however, were quickly shattered.

"Rabbi," Agatha said, as soon as we'd pulled off the gravel path onto the main road, "I couldn't help overhearing your conversation with my cousin, Lorraine."

"A delightful woman," answered the rabbi.

"That's neither here nor there," said Agatha. "But I sensed that you were awfully interested in Florence's death."

I gritted my teeth. It appeared that the rabbi had gone too far.

"Such a tragic loss," said Rabbi Kappelmacher. "And Florence couldn't have been more than seventy. That's young, nowadays."

"I'll be blunt," Agatha continued. "I'm not one to mince my words. I share your suspicions."

"My suspicions?" inquired the rabbi. I noticed that he'd slowed down the Caddy and was eying our passenger through the rearview mirror.

"Your suspicions about Florence's death," explained Agatha. "As a matter of fact, if you'll buy a lady a drink, I'll be happy to tell you everything I know about the murder."

"The murder?" I interjected. "What murder?"

"Florence's murder," answered Cousin Agatha. "You do think that Florence was murdered, don't you, rabbi?"

"That's always a possibility," replied Rabbi Kappelmacher.

"Well, I do too," said Cousin Agatha. "When I heard you asking those questions about Florence, I told myself, 'Agatha, that's a man who knows there's more to this business than meets the eye.' You're a wise man, Rabbi Kappelmacher. Mrs. Kappelmacher must be proud."

"Mrs. Kappelmacher is no longer in the present world," replied the rabbi.

I noted the smile that instantly suffused across our passenger's face.

"Well, if Mrs. Kappelmacher were alive, I'm sure she would be proud of you. As it is, I guess we'll have to solve this caper together."

The rabbi, it seemed, had finally met his match. This woman was even madder than he was.

Agatha Grossbart fixed her lipstick with a pocket mirror. Then she instructed the rabbi to turn into the parking lot of the Six Star Bar & Grill.

"Have you ever solved a murder before?" she asked the rabbi.

"I'm afraid I haven't," he replied.

Agatha frowned with apparent disappointment. "Oh well," she said. "There's a first time for everything, I suppose."

"Indeed," said the rabbi.

"Of course, in this case," our guest continued, "We don't really need to solve the murder. All we need to do is catch the murderer. We need evidence. Proof."

"I don't follow you, my good lady," said the rabbi. "Assuming Florence Eisenstein was murdered, don't we need to figure out who the murderer is before we set about catching him or her?"

Agatha frowned again. "But we already do know who the murderer is," she said. "Or at least *I* do. I thought that part was obvious."

CHAPTER 3: THE EVIDENCE OF COUSIN AGATHA

We walked the short distance to the Six Star Bar & Grill in silence. Only once we were seated in a corner booth did the rabbi follow up on Agatha Grossbart's rather startling declaration.

"My dear lady," said Rabbi Kappelmacher, "You must excuse me for being so obtuse, but I confess that, for my part, I don't know who might have murdered your cousin. In fact, I don't as yet have any reason to believe that she was murdered."

"No?" asked Agatha, her voice heavy with disappointment. "But you suspect it, don't you? Why else would you ask all those questions about the night of her death?"

"I like to ask questions," said the rabbi. "It's in my constitution. But while we're on the subject, Miss Grossbart, you must tell me whom *you* think murdered your cousin. I admit that I am rather curious."

Agatha smiled with renewed enthusiasm. "First, you should purchase a lady a drink. Then, we can get down to business."

Three gin and tonics later, Agatha's tongue began to loosen.

"The way I see it, rabbi—by the way I never did catch your first name...."

"Jacob," said Rabbi Kappelmacher. "Like the fellow who wrestled the angel."

"I can call you Jacob then, can't I? The way I see it is that only one person had a motive to kill dear Florence. Only one person has despised Florence all these years."

"And who might that be?" asked the rabbi.

"It only makes sense if you understand our family, Jacob. Because we're not an ordinary family, not by any means. We make a point of not speaking to each other for years on end. Sometimes even for decades."

The rabbi sipped his coffee. "Lorraine led me to understand that you yourself had had a falling out with Florence, Mrs. Grossbart."

"Oh, that," she answered. "That was years ago. But we're going to be friends, Jacob, aren't we? So I might as well tell you the whole story. It must have been twenty-five years ago now. Florence had befriended a local businessman. He'd made his fortune in lawn chairs. One day, she invited me over for supper with her and the lawn chair magnate— what's his name—and halfway through the meal, she summoned me into the kitchen and accused me of trying to steal her man."

"I imagine she was being hypersensitive," said the rabbi.

"Of course, she was. I wouldn't have married that man for all the salt in the ocean. He was so dreadfully dull. All he could speak about was patio furniture. But Florence accused me of trying to lure him away. She could be jealous like that, you understand. And in the process of defending myself, I accidentally spilled a pot of tea on her. It left a dreadful scar. On her arm and her shoulder. She held it against me from then on. She acted as though I had intentionally scarred her. In fact, she refused to have anything to do with me after that. Lorraine, too. Would you believe that both of them shunned me on account of that ridiculous lawn chair fellow?"

"Until last month," prodded the rabbi. He'd removed a cigar from his pocket and twirled it between his fingers.

"That's correct," agreed Agatha. "Until last month. You know about my dinner with Alfred?"

"Miss Eisenstein told me. She said Florence had come down with asthma and she sent Alfred out to dine with you alone."

"And what a time we had of it, too," Agatha agreed. "We came here, in fact. They made a ham and cheese sandwich like you couldn't imagine."

"I couldn't imagine it," replied Rabbi Kappelmacher. "Really, I couldn't. But might I infer that you—how shall I put it best?—that you developed an interest in Mr. Shingle."

Agatha's face turned a deathly white. "Not at all, Jacob. I prefer younger men, successful men. Alfred's much too run-of-the-mill for my tastes. All he can talk about are those mystery novels of his."

"That was my perception as well," agreed Rabbi Kappelmacher. "But you do find it a bit odd, don't you, that after the incident with the lawn chair magnate, Florence would send her boyfriend out to meet you for dinner?"

Agatha smiled again and the color returned to her face. She sipped gingerly from her fourth drink.

"Florence and Lorraine could both be—'out there,' if you know what I mean," said Agatha. "Irrational. Even loopy. I take it you already know what happened at Florence's wedding."

"No, I don't," the rabbi lied.

Agatha laughed. "It was absolutely *un-be-lievable*. I wouldn't have believed it myself, if I hadn't seen it with my own two eyes. Florence Eisenstein getting married in her mother's wedding dress and her sister won't even come downstairs for the ceremony."

"Her sister, I take it, didn't approve of the match."

"Far from it," countered Agatha. "I think Lorraine was exceedingly pleased that Florence was getting married. There is the business with the money, remember. Overnight, my cousin became an extremely wealthy woman. What startled me was that they fought over poor Fred."

"The ne'er-do-well nephew."

"Fred's had his troubles, yes," agreed Agatha. "But he doted on Florence. She was always his favorite. I had the impression that Lorraine never particularly cared for him. So imagine my surprise to find that Florence planned to disinherit him and Lorraine was standing up for his fortunes."

"When did Florence tell you that she planned to disinherit Fred?"

"It's all that she could talk about," said Agatha. "She mentioned it on the phone that first night when she invited me to dinner. That was when the poor boy was still in Europe setting up those artists' colonies. And then she made a point of announcing it to all of us at the wedding. It was as though she was trying to justify herself."

"And did she give you a reason for her decision?"

"She said they'd had an argument before Fred left for Europe and that while he was away, she'd come to realize that he was only after her money. I believe they had another major altercation on the Saturday before the wedding. It's still hard for me to stomach, though. Florence must have really gone off the deep end. Anyone with half a wit could tell that the poor boy doted on her."

"I take it," observed the rabbi, "that you are fond of your cousin Fred."

"He's the only real family I've got," responded Agatha. "Fred comes to visit me every Friday. We play canasta or pinochle."

"And your other cousins? Louise and Gladys?"

"I have a lot of sympathy for Louise," said Agatha. "She's not a bad girl. She's just under the thumb of that no-good husband of hers. Fred tells me that monster's driven poor Louise nearly to the breaking point. She gambles, you understand. Fred says quite heavily. And Fred also says he hits her. I suppose it's hard being blind, Jacob. But you know that the sort of man who marries a blind woman is up to no good."

"Indeed," said the rabbi. He did not mention that the late Mrs. Kappelmacher had been blind.

"But I have nothing at all against Louise," Agatha continued. "Although for her sake, I do hope she files for divorce."

"And your cousin, Gladys?"

"Gladys Eisenstein is no cousin of mine!" declared Agatha with fury. She pounded her clenched fist on the tabletop and spilled water across the Formica.

"I take it that you're not a fan of Gladys's," observed the rabbi.

"Gladys Eisenstein is a selfish, ungrateful lout," Agatha pronounced with uncharacteristic acerbity. "The nerve of her showing up at the house after all these years. You do know that she hasn't spoken to any of us since she was a teenager. She ran away from home."

"I *didn't* know that," answered the rabbi.

Agatha wiped up the spilt water with a tissue she'd extracted from her sleeve. "That girl nearly broke her father's heart. She drove dear Isaac to an early grave, she did. And her mother too. Did you know that when she was nineteen, she hired a lawyer of her own accord to try to break the will? And that she slandered Florence and Lorraine in the local papers? It was a big to-do. She said that they'd duped Irving into disinheriting Isaac and that then they'd poisoned the old man. She even pressed criminal charges. The business only subsided when she ran off to San Francisco with some woman. I can't fathom what induced Florence to invite her to her wedding after all these years. We all know what good came of that!"

"So I take it that you believe Gladys murdered your cousin and Florence," observed the rabbi.

"Of course, she did," retorted Agatha. "In cold blood too. She's been after the inheritance all these years. To fund all of those foolish causes of hers, you understand. Asthma attack, my foot. She probably poisoned Florence as part of some deranged scheme. I just can't prove it yet."

"But I thought," objected the rabbi, "that when Florence got married, she lost all claim to the inheritance."

"Aha!" screeched Agatha. "So you *are* a detective, Jacob. That's rather clever of you. But what you don't know is that Florence told us all on the phone that she'd broken the will. Of course, it wasn't true, but Gladys didn't know that. Gladys didn't stand to inherit a thing after Florence's wedding—but she *thought* that she did."

"So let me see if I have this right," said the rabbi. "Florence led you all to believe that she'd broken the will."

"Yes, that's exactly how it was," answered Agatha. "Imagine my shock when I discovered that she'd been mistaken. I was kind of hoping, you understand, that Florence might have remembered me in some small way."

"And she didn't, I take it," said Rabbi Kappelmacher sympathetically.

"Oh, she did," replied Agatha. "She bequeathed me one fourth of her estate, with the rest to be divided equally among her nieces and nephew. But I understand from that lawyer friend of yours that one fourth of Florence's estate amounts to absolutely nothing. Even the house is in Lorraine's name now."

"But if something were to happen to Lorraine..." Rabbi Kappelmacher observed.

Agatha polished off her fourth gin and tonic, and let the glass reverberate against the tabletop. "In the first place, Jacob, I have an inkling that Lorraine isn't going to remember me in her will. I have an impression that she didn't want Florence to invite me to the wedding in the first place. Besides which, I imagine now that she's inherited Uncle Irving's millions, Lorraine will also get married. Probably to that Mr. Abercrombie. Your friend Mr. Green and I were discussing that very possibility tonight. He told me that the second Florence married Alfred, Lorraine became free to marry with impunity. You might say that the will has been broken of its own accord."

I noticed a rekindled gleam in the rabbi's eye. He asked the waitress for a refill on his coffee and offered Agatha Grossbart another drink. She eagerly accepted.

"Now that I've given you the background," announced Agatha, "I think it's time to lay a trap for that creature, Gladys. Maybe if we search her motel room, we'll find the poison. I heard her tell Fred that she's staying at the Bargain Motel in Cedar Springs."

The rabbi scratched his beard thoughtfully. "But I was under the impression that Gladys was staying with Miss Eisenstein."

"Not anymore," replied Agatha. "That was just for the night of the wedding. Florence wanted us all to stay over on the night of the wedding for one reason or another. But I can assure you that Lorraine cleared us out quickly enough after that. I guess that created more of a problem for Gladys than it did for the rest of us, seeing as she flew in from San Francisco for the wedding. If it were anybody else, I'd gladly put them up for a few days. But never, never that woman. I imagine Lorraine feels the same way about her, though I daren't ask. I don't think I've exchanged ten words with Cousin Lorraine since Florence died." Agatha swirled the miniature pink umbrella in her drink. "Anyway, the real question is, what are we going to do about exposing Gladys?"

"I'll have to think about that," said the rabbi.

"Why don't I give you my address and phone number," Agatha offered, "and you can give me a call tomorrow after you've slept on it. Maybe we can have another drink then too. I'd love to show you my place."

Rabbi Kappelmacher offered Agatha his note pad and his fountain pen. Agatha handed it back to him. "My arthritis," she explained. "You'll have to do the honors, Jacob."

"Fire away, my good lady."

She provided a Haddam address in the vicinity of the synagogue. Then the rabbi took care of the tab and we headed out to the Cadillac.

"I have one final question for you, Miss Grossbart," he said when we were back on the road. "I can't help wondering why you think that your cousin, Florence, was murdered in the first place. Isn't it possible that she did, in fact, die from an asthma attack?"

"Bah, humbug," replied Agatha. "Florence looked perfectly healthy when I saw her at the wedding. Healthy people don't die suddenly, as far as I'm concerned."

"There's no more specific reason for your suspicions?" asked the rabbi.

"I could just tell," Agatha answered. "Gladys was so unbearably sweet toward Florence at the wedding. It was out of character. And you should have seen how she cried tonight before you arrived. I'm certain she's faking it. When I heard you asking Lorraine about Florence's death, it came together for me all of a sudden."

"That's all, Miss Grossbart?" asked Rabbi Kappelmacher.

Agatha Grossbart paused for a moment. Her brow furrowed as though she were engaged in an internal struggle. "There's one more thing, Jacob," she said. "I occupied the room next door to Gladys on Tuesday night. On the evening of the wedding, that is. And around one o'clock, I heard someone moving about in her room. I'm a light sleeper, you understand. A few minutes later, I heard footsteps in the hall. I climbed out of bed to see what was going on, and…and when I peeked into the corridor, Gladys's door was open and her room was empty."

"Maybe she went to the kitchen for a glass of water," I suggested.

"She murdered Florence," Rabbi Kappelmacher agreed. Then he suddenly changed the subject. "You don't happen to remember the old Eisenstein shop, do you?"

"As clear as crystal. Those were the best egg creams in New York. Probably in the world. My life hasn't been the same since Irving sold out to General Foods. I can't imagine anything I'd enjoy more than an Eisenstein egg cream right now."

Except possibly another gin and tonic, I thought. But I held my peace. I'd had enough of Agatha Grossbart's drunken speculations for one evening.

"How about a Yonah Schlissel knish?" asked the rabbi, mimicking Lorraine Eisenstein.

Agatha beamed. "You know about Yonah Schlissel's knishes?"

"And the blintzes at Sam Kaplan's. And the pastrami at Knobler's Deli."

"You're making my mouth water just thinking about it," said Agatha. "Maybe one day this week, if you're not too busy, we could go down to the old neighborhood for lunch. I'd love a blintz at Sam Kaplan's."

The rabbi shook his head. "You're too late, my dear lady. Sam closed up shop and moved to Miami Beach. As it is, I believe this is the end of the line."

We'd pulled into a small complex with a sign out front designating it The Sunshine Enclave. With obvious reluctance, Agatha climbed out of the car.

"Goodnight, Jacob," she said and she waved enthusiastically from the curbside.

"Goodnight, my dear lady," the rabbi called back.

We then drove in silence for several minutes.

"You don't really believe Gladys murdered her aunt, rabbi?" I asked.

The rabbi didn't answer me. He veered into the parking lot of the synagogue. We both live walking distance from work and the rabbi often parks the Caddy in his reserved space overnight.

"You can't really believe that woman's story, rabbi. So she saw Gladys's room empty at one o'clock in the morning. That's not a crime. Didn't that Dr. Scott say that Florence had died of asthma?"

The rabbi turned to me and ran his hand through his beard. "I do believe," he said, "that our dear friend, Miss Grossbart, finds me attractive."

"But what about her claim that Gladys murdered her aunt," I persisted. "Why won't you give me a straight answer, rabbi?"

"I just did," the rabbi replied. "I told you that I think Agatha Grossbart finds me attractive. Your rabbinic reasoning should tell you the rest."

"I don't understand," I muttered. "I don't see what one thing has to do with the other. But in any case, I do hope you're willing to put this matter behind us, before you get in over your head."

The rabbi glared at me. "Why is it that you're always being such a noodnik, Steinmetz?" he demanded. "I'll put this matter behind us once it's settled."

"And when will that be?" I asked—already anticipating his answer.

"When we have a rational explanation," he replied. "In the meantime, we have some investigating to do. Don't you find it odd that Gladys Eisenstein's attitude toward her family would change so suddenly? Because for my own part, Steinmetz, I suspect she's crying much more over her lost millions than over her aunt. She didn't strike me as the type to take something like this very hard."

"You barely met her," I objected.

"That is true," the rabbi agreed. "I'll have to speak with her again before I know for sure. But if Agatha Grossbart is to be believed, Gladys was no fan of Florence Eisenstein."

"So you *do* think Gladys killed her," I said in disbelief. "You've really been taken in by that madwoman?"

"That, Steinmetz," observed Rabbi Kappelmacher, "is another question for another day. I'll see you at nine o'clock tomorrow morning in my office and we can discuss this business further. Right now, I need to get some shuteye."

And with that farewell, Rabbi Kappelmacher turned on his heels and headed off into the darkness.

CHAPTER 4: THE EVIDENCE OF THE PHYSICIAN

The next morning, at precisely nine o'clock, I passed through a dimly-lit basement corridor and knocked on the door of the rabbi's office.

Mrs. Billings, the synagogue secretary, called a greeting from the open door across the hall. "Rabbi Steinmetz," she called, "you're in for it today. I've never seen him in such a state. He called for the morning prayers an hour early. He insisted that I keep calling congregants until I found ten men willing to skip an hour of sleep."

"Thanks for the warning, Mrs. B," I replied and knocked a second time. A moment later, the rabbi poked his bald head—covered with only a crocheted yarmulke—into the corridor.

"You're late," he observed with a glance at his wristwatch. "It's nearly five minutes past nine. We're going to miss our appointment."

"Our appointment?"

"I'll explain in the car. You don't need to worry about the *minyan* either. We said our prayers at seven o'clock today."

The rabbi certainly *was* in a state. The fringes of his *tallis* hung out from underneath his vest and his eyes gleamed as never before. I momentarily feared that he was still under the spell of Agatha and her unsubstantiated suspicions.

"What in heaven's name is the meaning of this, rabbi?" I demanded as soon as we'd pulled out of the parking lot. "Is everything all right?"

The rabbi pushed an imaginary button in the air near the windshield. "It will be if we make it to Pine Valley by 9:45. I phoned Dr. Scott's office at eight-thirty and I convinced the receptionist that I needed an appointment for this morning. Urgently."

"So we're back to this again," I grumbled. "Can't you just let sleeping dogs lie?"

"As a rabbi," he answered, "I much prefer that they tell the truth."

I rode the remainder of the trip without speaking. As far as I was concerned, Florence Eisenstein was the only sane person around. Everyone else, from Agatha to the rabbi, had gone rip-roaring mad. Why else would Rabbi Kappelmacher have pushed up the morning prayers to visit a doctor when he was obviously in perfect health?

As it turned out, we arrived at Dr. Scott's office with ten minutes to spare. The waiting room was already crowded when we arrived—filled with elderly couples reading magazines, toddlers playing with toys, a middle-aged man with his arm in a cast. In other words, the usual suspects for a general practitioner's suburban office. Behind the front desk, a receptionist shuffled papers in a transparent effort to look busy.

"We have a 9:45 appointment," Rabbi Kappelmacher told the receptionist.

She looked up without interest. "Name?"

"Kappelmacher, with two p's."

"No," she said, matter-of-factly, with only a hint of spite. "I don't have any Kappelmachers listed. You'll have to reschedule."

"But I spoke to you this morning. At eight-thirty."

The receptionist shrugged. "Maybe," she said. "It can get awful busy here. How about an appointment for next Thursday at 8:45 in the morning?"

At that moment, Dr. Scott himself emerged from the back room. He was a red-faced man of about sixty-five in a white coat. His face resembled that of a Norfolk terrier and he exuded an air of untrammeled energy.

"Dr. Scott?" the rabbi asked without any heed to the receptionist.

"Yes?" The physician's voice was curt and unfriendly.

"I had a 9:45 appointment for my asthma and—"

"You'll have to take that up with Judy here," cut in the doctor. He deposited a clipboard on the counter and turned back toward the inner office.

The rabbi stepped after him. "Alfred Shingle assured me that you'd be able to see me," he said.

The doctor spun around instantly, smiling. "Why didn't you say so—?"

"—Rabbi Kappelmacher. Rabbi Jacob Kappelmacher—"

"Well, rabbi, I'm sorry about the misunderstanding," replied Scott with apparent sincerity. "It's just that I'm extremely busy. Especially over the past year or so. But any friend of Alfred's is a friend of mine. Incidentally, how do you know the old boy?"

"I was a childhood friend of his late wife," lied the rabbi. "Her father made the best egg creams in New York."

"So I've heard," Scott observed. "Never had the pleasure. I'm a Hudson Valley man by birth. It wasn't until I met Alfred that I ever tasted an egg cream."

"And how do *you* know Alfred?"

We followed Dr. Scott into a tidy exam room, where he instructed the rabbi to seat himself on an examination table.

"We went to City College together back in ancient times," answered Scott. "I must have been the only out-of-towner in the whole class. My real name's not Scott, of course. It's Schlansky. Harry Schlansky. But when I first started in practice, around here it was still much easier to pay off the mortgage with a name like Hiram Scott. Incidentally, did you see my new Town Car in the lot?"

"A beauty," replied the rabbi. I'm certain he couldn't have distinguished a Town Car from a Rolls Royce if his life depended upon it.

Dr. Scott slapped his leg and grinned through perfect teeth. "Best car in the world, as sure as I'm the best g.p. in Pine Valley. Of course, I'm the only g.p. in Pine Valley." The physician laughed heartily. "Now what seems to be the problem?"

Rabbi Kappelmacher frowned. "I hate to admit this, but I've been having trouble breathing these past few months.

Especially at night. Sometimes, I wake up and I just can't seem to get any air into my lungs."

"Do you smoke?"

"Only cigars."

"Well, quit," suggested Dr. Scott. "If I had a dollar for every smoker who comes to me and says he can't breathe, I'd have paid off the mortgage already."

"Actually," observed the rabbi, "I think I'm suffering from asthma. I remember what dear Florence was like at the end, and I think I'm starting to display some of the same symptoms."

"Could be," mused Dr. Scott. He applied a stethoscope to Rabbi Kappelmacher's chest and ordered him to draw several deep breaths.

When he was done, the rabbi coughed repeatedly.

"That's not a healthy cough" observed Dr. Scott.

"It sounds just like Florence, doesn't it?" asked the rabbi.

"Could be. I didn't see that much of her."

"But I thought you were treating her for asthma," observed Rabbi Kappelmacher.

"That, I was. I suppose I can tell you, seeing as she's gone now and you're a clergyman. Just keep this between us."

"Scouts honor," agreed the rabbi.

Dr. Scott grinned at the rabbi's remark. "Anyway," he said, "she only came in that first time with Alfred. It didn't seem too serious, so I told her to get some rest and wrote her a prescription. I thought she was making a nice recovery— and then she died."

"I imagine it shocked you when she died so suddenly," Rabbi Kappelmacher observed. "I didn't even know that asthma could be fatal."

"Oh, it can. Of course—and this is strictly between you and me—Florence didn't die of asthma."

"No?" asked the rabbi, his eyes suddenly aglow. "I could have sworn Alfred said she died of an asthma attack—that she just stopped breathing in her sleep."

Dr. Scott lowered his voice. "And for everyone concerned, I think it best that Alfred keep thinking that. But the truth of the matter is, rabbi, that the poor woman suffocated herself to death. She fell asleep face-down on one of those heavy goose pillows with her mouth and nose covered. It's a common cause of sudden death in infants, but it can happen to the elderly on rare occasions. But under no condition do I want you to share that with Alfred."

"He might blame himself,' agreed the rabbi.

"Might?" exclaimed Dr. Scott. "Of course, he'd blame himself. He'd say that he should have stayed with her that night and that he should have made certain that the pillows were safe. He beat himself up badly enough for letting the prescription on the asthma medication run out."

"I take it they called you as soon as they found her?"

'They did," replied Dr. Scott. "I tried to help over the phone, but it was clear that she was beyond assistance from the way Alfred described her."

"Did you go over and take a look at her?"

"You're a curious one, rabbi, aren't you," said Dr. Scott. "But since you ask. I drove down to the Eisenstein place around one-thirty, but there wasn't anything I could do. I'd been there only a short while when my answering service paged me with yet another emergency. It's been that sort of year, rabbi. With the new housing developments in the area, I have a hard enough time caring for the living, let alone the dead. Yet I did stop by again in the morning to check up on Alfred. That's when I made my determination regarding the cause of death."

The rabbi nodded with sympathy. "That was thoughtful of you. It must be hard on the old-timers like the Eisensteins though, having to compete for your time with all of these newcomers."

The physician made several notations on his chart. "I try to carve out an extra few minutes for my longtime patients, but it's a challenge. This isn't the same practice it was when my father started back in 1937. I have HIV cases up here, even Legionnaire's Disease. When I first took over, before there was a board certified pediatrician in town, ninety percent of the traffic was kids with scrapes or broken bones...."

"Lorraine said your father saved her when she had scarlet fever," observed Rabbi Kappelmacher.

Dr. Scott continued to scribble on his chart. "Could be. Scarlet fever was one of our biggest suppliers back then. Also mumps, German measles, a few residual cases of polio. It's a wonder anybody ever made it to adulthood." Dr. Scott finally looked up from the chart. "Now about your breathing. I can write you a prescription, if you'd like, but the truth is that your lungs don't sound so bad to me. If you lay off those cigars, you'll feel better in a couple of days."

Rabbi Kappelmacher coughed again and nodded emphatically. "I think I'll try that. I've been meaning to quit for years," he lied, "and I think this may be the perfect excuse. By the way, you don't think there's a chance that I might suffocate myself like Florence, do you? I wouldn't want to take such a risk."

The physician shook his head. "The odds are one in a million," he replied. "Florence's death was a fluke. You have absolutely nothing to worry about."

"Thank goodness for that," declared Rabbi Kappelmacher.

Dr. Scott walked toward the door. "One last question, doctor. When we were at the Eisensteins' place yesterday, Florence's cousin, Agatha, suggested that Florence's father had died under unusual circumstances. In fact, she said he'd been poisoned. Personally, I thought her remarks were utter bunk, but I imagine you can assuage my fears for certain…."

Dr. Scott's smile melted quickly, only to be replaced with an aggressive scowl. "*That* business, again. Don't these people ever learn. I have only a moment, rabbi, but I want to make this extremely clear to you—and to anyone who may have their own thoughts on the subject: Irving Eisenstein died of a massive heart attack."

"But some people thought otherwise?" pressed the rabbi.

"Not until much later. They dragged my father's name through the mud in the papers. Accused him of misdiagnosing Eisenstein's death. It must have been twenty-five years ago, but I remember it as clearly as yesterday. It was that girl—what's her God forsaken name?"

"Gladys?"

"That's right," said Dr. Scott. "Gladys Eisenstein. The son's daughter. She mucked about, accusing everyone of bloody murder. But I assure you, rabbi, there wasn't an once of truth in her accusations."

The mention of Irving Eisenstein's death had certainly changed Dr. Scott's tone quickly. He strode through the door without so much as a goodbye, leaving the two of us alone in the examination room.

I exchanged glances with the rabbi. He was scratching his beard nervously, and I could tell that something was bothering him. In the parking lot, I broached the subject.

"What's eating at you, rabbi?" I asked. "You can't possibly still think Florence Eisenstein was murdered."

Rabbi Kappelmacher leaned against Dr. Scott's dark blue Town Car. "I don't think it, Steinmetz," he observed. "I'm sure of it."

"But you have Dr. Scott's assurance that she died of self-suffocation."

"The odds against that are one in a million," said the rabbi. "You heard Dr. Scott say so himself."

"Then what? Somebody else suffocated her with a pillow and relied upon Dr. Scott's not wanting to hurt Alfred Shingle's feelings? Doesn't that seem farfetched?"

"Maybe," replied the rabbi. "In any case, somebody did indeed suffocate Florence. The circumstances—the alleged broken will, the unexpected wedding, the altercation with the nephew—all pointed in that direction. So I knew it was probable. I just had to make certain that it was possible."

The rabbi lit a cigar. So much for Dr. Scott's orders. He let the ashes fall on the hood of the Town Car.

"Let me guess," I ventured. "You think that madwoman, Agatha, is right about all this. Gladys Eisenstein sneaked downstairs in the middle of the night, waited for Alfred to leave Florence's bedroom, and then suffocated her."

"In the immortal words of Dr. Scott," replied the rabbi. "Could be."

"But that makes no sense at all," I argued. "There was no way that Gladys could have known that Alfred would leave his wife to run out and fill a prescription."

The rabbi frowned. "Don't be such a *dumkopf*, Steinmetz. Use your rabbinic reasoning. Gladys couldn't have known that Alfred would leave Florence's room in the middle of the night. Nobody could have until it actually happened. By the same token, nobody who entered Florence's room after Alfred left, if they hadn't actually seen him leave, would have thought it was Florence's room."

"Excuse me. You've lost me."

"It's the middle of the night, Steinmetz. You climb down the stairs from the guest wing and then up the stairs into that passageway where we were the other day. You see two doors. You choose one door randomly and enter a dark bedroom. By the light from the window, you see an elderly woman—alone—lying in bed. What do you instantly conclude?"

"I have no idea, rabbi. What do *you* instantly conclude, rabbi?'

"Think, Steinmetz, think. You'll never be able to take over for me if you don't use your rabbinic reasoning. Now if you intended to kill Florence and you entered a room in which one elderly woman was sleeping alone, what would you conclude?"

"I honestly don't know," I replied. "I guess I'd conclude that she'd had some sort of fight with her husband and that he'd gone to sleep somewhere else."

"No, you wouldn't, Steinmetz," countered the rabbi. "You'd conclude that you weren't in Florence Eisenstein's bedroom at all. In the darkness, you probably wouldn't notice either the wedding dress or the photograph of Alfred. So if you found that old woman sleeping alone, you'd think you were in Lorraine Eisenstein's bedroom. And you'd think that that the woman alone in the bed was Lorraine Eisenstein."

"And then I'd go out into the corridor and into the other room," I observed. But under your theory, our murderer killed the woman in the bed anyway. What exactly are you suggesting, rabbi? Your suppositions don't make any sense."

"On the contrary, Steinmetz, they make all the sense in the world," retorted the rabbi. He puffed on his cigar. "If I intended to kill Florence and I found a woman alone in the bed, I'd do exactly what you'd suggested—I'd leave as quietly as possible and go into the next room. However, what if my intention wasn't to kill Florence at all? What if I intended to kill *Lorraine* all along? Then I'd conclude that I was in the right bedroom and I'd mistakenly suffocated the woman in the bed, thinking it was Lorraine and not Florence."

I threw up my hands. "I don't know where you came up with that one," I stammered. "Do you mean to say that Lorraine was the intended victim? But in that case, what's the motive?"

"The same motive as for killing Florence," answered Rabbi Kappelmacher. "Money. Only possibly more of it. If any of the relatives discovered that Florence had not broken the will—that she was either mistaken or deluding herself—then they knew that all the money had passed to Lorraine when Florence married. That means Lorraine's heirs would have stood to inherit a large sum of money when she died. They'd receive barely anything if Florence died."

"And who, rabbi, are Lorraine's heirs?"

"Despite what Agatha Grossbart suggested, I imagine that they're the same as Florence's heirs. It has been my experience that elderly Jewish ladies leave money to their relatives, no matter how much they may dislike them personally. I'll bet that one fourth goes respectively to Louise, Gladys, Fred and Agatha."

A phone call to Marshall Green from the payphone across the street revealed that Rabbi Kappelmacher's suspicions regarding Lorraine's will were indeed correct.

"So where does that leave us?" I asked. "Do you think Gladys intended to kill Lorraine and accidentally killed Florence?"

The rabbi scratched his beard in silence.

"If that's the case, rabbi, don't you think we ought to warn Lorraine? Won't her life still be in danger?"

The rabbi shook his head decisively. "Not yet. I'm sure Lorraine can take care of herself. Besides, Gladys is staying at a hotel. We have more important business to attend to."

I waited for the rabbi to elaborate on his last remark, but he continued to scratch his beard without saying a word. Finally, my frustration got the better of me, and I broke the silence.

"What's eating you, rabbi?" I asked. "We've worked together for two years now. I can tell that you're worried about something other than the possibility that somebody intended to murder Lorraine and not Florence."

"Indeed, I am," agreed the rabbi. "Now you're using your rabbinic reasoning. Would you like to venture a guess as to what I'm worried about?"

"Once again, I admit you've baffled me," I concluded. "What's on your mind?"

The rabbi crushed his cigar under his heel. "I've been thinking about Gladys Eisenstein's behavior at the *shivah* call. Didn't it strike you as at all unusual?"

"Not in the least. Certainly not in comparison with *your* behavior. We barely spoke to her."

"I'm not talking about what she said, Steinmetz," replied Rabbi Kappelmacher. "I'm talking about where she sat. Do you recall how we came down the stairs and the guests had broken into two groups. There was the group we'd been part of. That would have been Marshall Green, Art Abercrombie, Lorraine and Mr. Shingle. And then there was the other group: Fred, Louise, Andrew Sinkoff, Agatha and Gladys."

"I remember," I agreed. "What of it?"

"It doesn't strike you at all odd that Gladys sat with the second group?"

"No," I said emphatically. "It doesn't. Maybe she sat down first and then the others joined her. In any case, I have no idea what you're driving at."

"What I'm driving at is this, Steinmetz," said the rabbi. "Mrs. Kappelmacher had a cousin, Bessie, whom she absolutely couldn't stand. They'd had a fight about their grandmother's jewelry when they were in their twenties, and they had barely been on speaking terms ever since. Inevitably, of course, we ran into Bessie at weddings and funerals and those assorted family occasions where attendance is essentially mandatory. And I can assure you that Mrs. Kappelmacher, rest her soul, never sat anywhere near her cousin. Even after they'd patched things up, it made her uncomfortable to sit near Bessie. And believe you me, Mrs. Kappelmacher cried like a baby when Bessie died. It was a combination of habit and a fear of awkwardness that drove them apart after they'd made up—and I think it's a universal feeling."

"I don't follow," I observed. "According to Agatha, Gladys was on bad terms with everybody there. Did you expect her to sit in the corner and not speak to anyone?"

The rabbi shook his head. "You must pay more attention to details, Steinmetz. Pretend our visit was a Biblical passage. If you were reading a Biblical passage, you wouldn't gloss over some of the words, would you?"

"Of course not," I answered. I hated Biblical interpretations that explained only a portion of the text.

"Then why do you ignore some of the details at the expense of others, Steinmetz?" asked the rabbi. "Gladys wasn't on bad terms with everyone there that night, at least as far as I know. She had no grudge against Marshall Green, for instance. Or Art Abercrombie. Or probably Alfred Shingle. Granted, she and Lorraine had a history of animosity, but given the choice between two siblings and a cousin you've fought with bitterly over many years, or one hostile aunt and three neutral figures, most people would choose to sit in the latter group, don't you think?"

"I think you've gone a little *meshugah*, rabbi," I answered. "So Gladys sat with her brother and sister. Is that supposed to convince me that she's a murderer?"

Rabbi Kappelmacher leaned against the phone booth and rested his hands in his pockets. "I'm not sure if it's supposed to convince you of anything, Steinmetz. I was just making an observation. Nothing more."

"In that case, can we please forget about this *mishegos* for now?" I asked. "Don't forget that I have to teach my Jewish history course at one o'clock."

"Cancel it, Steinmetz," the rabbi ordered. He was staring off across the street. I kept a tentative eye on him while I phoned Mrs. Billings and made arrangements to postpone my class.

"Now can we go, rabbi?" I pleaded. "We're loitering. People are looking at us."

"One moment, Steinmetz," he answered. "I'll meet you at the car."

Then, to my surprise, the rabbi marched across the street into the Paradise Beauty Salon. I waited outside the Cadillac for him to return.

"What was that about?" I asked. "Are you in the market for a pedicure?"

At this stage of the game, I thought anything might be possible.

"I was checking to see if Lorraine kept her appointment for last Saturday," explained the rabbi.

"And let me guess," I answered. "They have absolutely no idea who Lorraine Eisenstein is. Or, better than that, they told you that she and Florence helped murder their father."

The rabbi unlocked the door to the Cadillac; his expression betrayed no amusement. "Actually, they expressed a great deal of concern for Miss Eisenstein. They think she's a delightful woman and they were worried that I might have come bearing bad news. And for the record, Steinmetz, Lorraine did indeed keep her appointment."

"She must have wanted to look good in case somebody tried to murder her," I muttered.

"I heard that," the rabbi shot back. "You know, Steinmetz, I like you a lot. But if you thought a little more and complained a little less, you'd make an excellent rabbi someday."

Then the rabbi turned on the car radio, guaranteeing himself the final word on the subject.

CHAPTER 5:   THE EVIDENCE OF THE NEIGHBOR

We drove for twenty minutes to the sounds of the New York Symphony Orchestra. Outside, the early morning mist had burnt off entirely and the day promised to be a scorcher. As hurt as I was by the rabbi's remarks, I admit I was pleased to be on the road with the wind blowing in my face. I certainly found it preferable to the stuffy, un-air-conditioned room where I taught my Jewish history course to three retired accountants and the late cantor's wife. Almost a year had passed since Cantor Puttermesser's death, and the synagogue board had yet to find a permanent replacement.

"Any progress on the cantor search?" I asked the rabbi to break the silence.

"Yes, we've made much progress," he replied. "We've interviewed fourteen men we're assuredly *not* going to hire."

"And you call that progress?"

"The more candidates we eliminate," observed the rabbi, "the fewer we have to choose from. That's the process of elimination in action, Steinmetz. These decisions take time. You should have seen the *dumkopfs* we interviewed before we found you. Men who didn't know the first thing about rabbinic reasoning. Men who thought the Bible was like a cookbook where you could look up all the recipes for a good life."

"But you're always faulting me for my lack of rabbinic reasoning. I can't help wondering why you hired me."

"Because you're often a noodnik and a kibitzer, Steinmetz," answered the rabbi, "but you're rarely a dumkopf. You've got a solid head on your shoulders. You just seem to be afraid to use it."

I didn't know whether to take that as a compliment or as an insult. It's often difficult to tell with Rabbi

Kappelmacher. I decided to shift the conversation to a less personal topic.

"It must have been rough on you when Green left," I observed. "One can't help but notice that you viewed him as something of a protégé."

"At one point, I did," said Rabbi Kappelmacher. "But Green suffers from the exact opposite shortcoming that you do. You're afraid to take on your responsibility for rabbinic reasoning…and let's just say that Green is a bit *too* eager for additional responsibilities."

"Do you mean he thinks too much?"

"No, Steinmetz. I mean he wanted to become head rabbi. He figured I'd retire at fifty-two, and when that didn't happen, he figured I'd retire at fifty-five. When I hit sixty and showed no signs of slowing down, he jumped ship. Green isn't the type to wait in the wings. The funny thing is, Steinmetz, if he'd stayed on another year, I'd probably have retired when Mrs. Kappelmacher passed away. Now, of course, I have a duty to stick around to train you in rabbinic reasoning."

This was the first suggestion that the rabbi ever made that he was grooming me for his job. I was absolutely elated.

"So there's no truth to all the rumors about Green? That he was having an affair with a congregant and all that?"

"Not as far as I know," answered the rabbi. "Besides, Marshall is much too career-conscious for anything of that nature."

I glanced out the window of the Cadillac and suddenly realized that we were back in the Eisensteins' neighborhood. "So we *are* going to warn Lorraine," I said. "I suppose you really do believe she's in danger."

The rabbi sighed audibly. "We are *not* going to warn Lorraine. Why don't you ever believe me when I tell you something?"

"Then where are we going?" I asked.

The rabbi turned onto the gravel lane leading to the Eisenstein estate and then, to my surprise, steered the Cadillac onto the grass beside the roadway.

"We're going to make a new friend," said Rabbi Kappelmacher. "And I have a hunch she's not one of us, so try to look as rabbinic as possible."

I followed the rabbi on foot toward the Eisenstein home—into the dense wooded thicket and then out again on the other side. The spring bulbs appeared just as we'd left them the night before. A wheelbarrow filled with dirt rested beside the path and several bags of fertilizer stood stacked along the fence. I wondered if Lorraine Eisenstein had planted the flowers herself or if she employed a part-time gardener. She struck me as an indoor person. I couldn't imagine her on her knees in the dirt.

"Good morning," Rabbi Kappelmacher called out to the woman on the wooden porch, the same woman with whom he'd exchanged a wave the day before.

The woman raised her glass. But when the rabbi pushed open a small gate in the fence and walked towards the elderly woman, she immediately disappeared through the back door of the home.

"I don't believe we're welcome here," I observed. "Why don't we just warn Lorraine and leave?"

"Why don't we just use the Bible like a cookbook?" the rabbi retorted. "A woman has been murdered. It's our rabbinic duty to provide a rational explanation for her death. Now try to look as Jewish as possible."

"You have no evidence that Florence was murdered," I muttered. My protest fell upon deaf ears.

The rabbi climbed the steps of the porch and knocked. He waited for several seconds and then knocked again. After what felt like an eternity, the woman we'd encountered earlier appeared in the window and shook her head. The rabbi held up his index finger to symbolize one minute. The woman's brow furrowed. Finally, she opened the door a crack.

"I'm an Episcopalian and I'm quite happy being one," she declared before the rabbi could utter a word. "You're not going to convert me to anything, so you might as well be on your way."

So she thought we were trying to proselytize. The rabbi's head covering and exposed *tallis* must have raised her suspicions. No wonder she'd gone into hiding. Despite Rabbi Kappelmacher's warning, I found myself trying to look as un-Jewish as possible.

"I'm not attempting to convert you to anything," the rabbi pledged. "I'm a friend of the Eisensteins. Your neighbors."

The woman behind the door seemed to relax slightly. "Well, what do you want then? If it's about the property line, you'll have to speak with my son, and he's in Maine for the summer."

"It's not about the property line, I assure you," said the rabbi. "My name is Rabbi Kappelmacher and this is Rabbi Steinmetz. We were hoping to ask you a few questions about Miss Eisenstein."

"What sort of questions?" The woman behind the door peered at us warily over half-glasses.

"Questions about what sort of neighbor she is. You see, ma'am, Miss Eisenstein has been nominated for a great honor in the Jewish religion. An honor only available to individuals who have led extremely moral and upstanding lives. One of the requirements for the award is that the synagogue speak with her friends and neighbors. To put it politely, ma'am, a couple of years ago we gave this honor to a woman who turned out to be of questionable repute, so we don't want to take any chances."

The woman unlocked the door and stepped onto the porch. She was tall and slender, and there was no mistaking that her in youth she had been extremely attractive. "The name's Finchley, rabbi. Like the heroine in Theodore Dreiser's *An American Tragedy*. Annie Piece Finchley. You do read secular books, rabbi, don't you?"

"On occasion," the rabbi lied. He happens to be an avid reader. "I prefer my Bible."

"Well, I tell you, rabbi, you're missing out," said Mrs. Finchley. "But like the late Mr. Finchley used to say, *chaqun a son goût*. That's French for each to his own tastes. Live and let live. It's a philosophy worth considering."

"I couldn't agree more," replied Rabbi Kappelmacher.

Following Mrs. Finchley's lead, we seated ourselves around a card table. She poured us each a glass of pink liquid that turned out to be lemonade.

"Now what can I tell you about Lorraine Eisenstein?" Mrs. Finchley asked. "You were here yesterday, I remember, so you must be aware that the other sister died."

"You knew them well, Mrs. Finchley?"

Our host pondered the question for several seconds. "I knew them," she conceded. "I wouldn't say well. But I have some notions about the sisters, if you know what I mean. When you spend all day reading in front of somebody's house, you get a pretty good idea what their life is all about."

The rabbi lit a cigar and took pains to let the smoke blow away from out hostess.

"Let me get you an ashtray," offered Mrs. Finchley. "Mr. Finchley, may he rest in peace, was a cigar smoker. I'm so used to the smell, I've nearly forgotten how much I once disliked it."

Mrs. Finchley disappeared into the house and returned a moment later with a small bowl.

"That should do," she said. "Now what can I tell you about Lorraine Eisenstein? She's an excellent gardener, I can promise you that. She's out here nearly every day working on her flowers. But to tell you the truth, rabbi, she's not a very friendly woman."

"No?"

"Sometimes I stroll down to the property line and try to strike up a conversation, but she always answers with yeses and no's and I get the feeling she'd rather be left alone.

"Did her sister ever join her in the garden?"

"Not for as long as I can remember," Mrs. Finchley answered. "The other sister was into bird watching. She was always poking about the shrubbery with those binoculars of hers. If I didn't know better, I would have thought she was a peeping tom."

The rabbi pushed another imaginary button with his fingers. "You say Florence was an avid bird watcher?"

"Every morning for at least twenty years. That's when we moved into this place. Florence had a softer temperament than her sister does, rabbi. We hit it off quite well. Once in a while, she'd even come up to the porch and join me for a glass of lemonade."

"Did you see much of Florence the last few months?" asked the rabbi.

"Everyday until the day before she died," Mrs. Finchley answered. "Like clockwork. She was out before seven o'clock, which is when I get up, and then she'd head back into the house around nine."

The rabbi scratched his beard. "When was the last time you spoke to Florence, Mrs. Finchley?"

"Not for a while now. Probably late last autumn. I was in bed with multiple bouts of pneumonia through the winter. I got into the habit of sleeping late. It's only recently that I've broken it and returned to my old schedule. Say," Mrs. Finchley broke off suspiciously. "I thought it was *Lorraine* Eisenstein you were interested in."

"Indeed, it is. But her sister's death complicated matters. She was the person who nominated Lorraine for the honor, you see, and now that she's gone, it's hard to get a good feel for why she thought her sister deserved such a blessing. I've been trying to discover exactly what Florence thought of Lorraine."

"I believe they got along quite well," said Mrs. Finchley. "They each did their own thing. Lorraine gardened. Florence watched for birds. You would have thought they'd both continue to live in that old house forever."

"Death has a way of surprising us," observed the rabbi. "I understand that Florence's death was rather unexpected."

"That's what I hear," agreed Mrs. Finchley. "Something about trouble breathing. But I also understand that she married that nice man before she died."

"You mean Mr. Shingle?"

"Yes, that's his name. Delightful old gent. In many ways, he reminded me of Mr. Finchley. They were both avid readers. Of course, Mr. Finchley's tastes were slightly more respectable."

"You mean that Mr. Shingle reads popular fiction," said Rabbi Kappelmacher.

"That's one way of putting it." Mrs. Finchley poured herself another glass of lemonade. "He reads mystery novels. Absolute trash. But he has always been kind to me, the few times that he's stopped by for a drink."

"I understand he was a frequent visitor to the Eisenstein household," prompted the rabbi.

"Nearly every afternoon," Mrs. Finchley agreed. "He'd pass by around one o'clock in that old Buick of his. He liked to come for a late lunch after Florence had finished her bird watching."

"Understandably," said the rabbi. "Are there many other frequent visitors, Mrs. Finchley? We need to know what company Lorraine keeps, you understand."

Mrs. Finchley made a face as though she'd just bitten into a sour persimmon. "There's a nephew, rabbi. I think his name's Fred. He stopped by a lot last year and then disappeared for a while, but he showed up again....Let me see....It must have been last Saturday. I distinctly remember it because he always takes the final turn too fast. It's a wonder I don't suffocate from all the dust he churns up."

"I take it you're not a fan of Fred's," suggested the rabbi.

"Actually, I've never met him. But I imagine I wouldn't like him at all. I think you can tell a lot about a man from the kind of automobile he drives. Mr. Finchley, for example, drove an Edsel until the day he died. He wasn't the sort of man to stand by appearances or public opinion. The Edsel took him where he wanted to go, which is all he'd come to expect from a motorcar."

"He must have been a wonderful man," observed the rabbi.

"Best that ever lived. Not a day goes by that I don't thank my lucky stars for the time I had with him."

The rabbi smiled sympathetically. "If I may be candid, Mrs. Finchley, I hope to ask a few more pointed questions regarding Lorraine before we take our leave. These may be rather unpleasant questions, but you must understand that the synagogue can't take any chances."

'As long as they're not indecent," answered Mrs. Finchley.

I eyed the rabbi nervously. The idea of "unpleasant questions" made me nervous.

"You mentioned a dispute about the property line a few minutes ago," said the rabbi. "Could you tell us about that?"

Mrs. Finchley grimaced. "There's not much to tell. When we first moved here, Mr. Finchley and myself, there was a whole uproar about whether those flower beds over there were part of our property or part of theirs. Mr. Finchley insisted that they were on our land. He was a good man, but he could fight tooth-and-nail where his land was concerned. Maybe that was the Scotch-Irish in him or maybe it was the attorney in him. One or the other."

"Your husband was a lawyer?"

"Senior partner in Finchley, Abbott, Ingraham, Murray, Cavendish & Sandowsky for nearly thirty years. Saul Sandowsky happened to be a Jewish person. You aren't acquainted with him, by any chance, are you?"

"I've never had the honor."

"No matter. But he was a delightful man. A credit to your people."

"Indeed," said the rabbi. "We need more of those."

Mrs. Finchley accepted his words at face value. "Anyway, Mr. Finchley went to court and lost. It wasn't the first time, mind you, and it wasn't the last. He had a way about losing cases."

The rabbi toyed with his beard. "But that was twenty years ago. Why did you think I'd come about that matter today if it was all in the past?"

"Oh, that. Well, I saw the same fellow drive up to the house the other day. The Eisenstein sisters' lawyer. I believe his name's Abercrombie. There was no mistaking that face, even after all this time. I'm a very careful observer, rabbi. I never forget anything. Nobody will ever pull the wool over the eyes of Annie Piece Finchley."

"So you suspected that Mr. Abercrombie had come about the property line," prompted the rabbi.

"At the time, I figured he was here for a condolence call. It was only when you stopped by that I remembered the business about the property line."

"It's rather impressive that you could recognize Mr. Abercrombie after all these years," mused the rabbi. "Especially through the window of an automobile."

Mrs. Finchley grinned with pride. "I keep careful tabs on who goes up to the house, rabbi. You might call it a hobby of mine. For example, I can tell you there were nine visitors to the Eisenstein place yesterday evening. Mr. Abercrombie arrived around four o'clock, maybe four-thirty. Certainly before the sun reached the tree line. Then that nephew showed up with all his dust. Then a middle-aged couple I didn't recognize. He was driving. They seemed like they were shouting at each other, but the windows were rolled up, so I can't be certain. About twenty minutes later, a shrewish woman arrived in a rental car. I could tell it was a rental car because there was a Hertz tag around the license plate. Next came Mr. Shingle. It was already getting dark by that hour. Then there was an obese woman who walked with a cane. She arrived on foot. I imagine she took a cab and it dropped her at the curbside. Finally, you showed up with your friend here and a third man. Only the third man left with the lawyer, and you drove off with the obese woman. Now what do you think of that, rabbi? Impressed, aren't you?"

I, for one, was duly impressed. The rabbi seemed intrigued.

"I wish I had a mind like that," he observed after a pause. "I can hardly remember what I had for breakfast this morning. You know, Rabbi Steinmetz, I don't even remember which day Florence died. Was it a Monday night or a Tuesday night?"

"It was definitely Tuesday night," answered Mrs. Finchley. "I remember all the cars from the wedding on Tuesday afternoon. And then I remember hearing Mr. Shingle's Buick drive off in the middle of the night. I spoke to Lorraine this morning when she was wheeling those fertilizer bags around and she told me all about how he'd gone to fill some sort of prescription at the all-night pharmacy, but he'd arrived back too late. So I'm sure it was Tuesday. I'll never forget it. I don't sleep much and I had a night of it wondering what all of those motorcars were doing up at the house."

"Then you didn't know Florence was getting married?"

"I certainly did not," she said sharply. "I didn't dream of it. Of course, I hadn't spoken to Florence since the autumn, but common courtesy would have suggested an invitation. I found out Wednesday from the man who drove the hearse. Imagine that! I live here twenty years and my neighbor gets married and I find out from an undertaker. But I understand how the presence of—well—of an Episcopalian might have been unwelcome."

"Do you mean to say that you believe Florence didn't invite you to her wedding because you aren't Jewish?"

"I'm not offended," said Mrs. Finchley—although she obviously *was* offended. "It's just that we—Mr. Finchley and I—invited Jewish people to our wedding. I suppose I'm just ahead of my time, rabbi. Of course, as Mr. Finchley used to say, live and let live. I know you people have some fine traditions...."

The rabbi stood up and wiped his forehead with his handkerchief. I found Mrs. Finchley rather quaint—a woman entirely naïve to her own prejudices. The rabbi, I could tell, thought her a garden-variety bigot.

"Well, ma'am," he declared, "I appreciate your help. I'm sorry to have taken so much of your time. But if you do think of anything else I should know about Lorraine, particularly anything unusual, please let me know. As far as I know, Miss Eisenstein is a wonderful woman—our equivalent of one of your saints—but it's always essential to be on the look-out for surprises. Good day."

The rabbi rose from his chair and strode down the steps. I followed. "Rabbi," Mrs. Finchley called after us. "If you don't mind my asking, what is the name of the honor you're going to bestow upon Lorraine? I would like to congratulate her."

The rabbi turned toward the porch. "I guess I didn't make myself clear. The honor is to be a surprise." He threw me a surreptitious wink and then refocused his attention on the homeowner. "Between you and me, ma'am," he said softly, "were going to give Miss Eisenstein one of the greatest honors of the Jewish religion. We're going to make her an honorary '*noodnik*'s neighbor.'"

"Nude-niks neighbor," echoed Mrs. Finchley.

"But please don't say anything," cautioned the rabbi. "Sometimes, you understand, this process can take several years."

Rabbi Kappelmacher bid a second farewell to Mrs. Finchley and led the way back to the Cadillac.

"Did you hear that, Steinmetz?" he asked as soon as we were out of earshot. "That woman was absolutely insufferable. Ahead of her time, my foot. It's a wonder she didn't lean over and touch me out of curiosity."

"Calm down, rabbi," I said. "I happen to think she was rather endearing. She's perfectly harmless."

"That's what they said once about you know who," the rabbi retorted. He kicked the fender of the Cadillac and then his good cheer seemed to return. "Yet for an insufferable woman," he observed, "she certainly proved to be a gold mine of information. I can sense a rational explanation in the air, Steinmetz."

I wondered what had buoyed the rabbi's spirits. I hadn't found our meeting with Mrs. Finchley at all informative.

"Did you really learn anything from that old woman?" I asked.

"You would have too, if you'd been listening," replied the rabbi.

"May I ask what you learned?"

"I learned that Alfred did in fact go out to fill that prescription Tuesday night. I learned that Fred did visit his aunt on Saturday. I learned that Art Abercrombie was the first guest to arrive yesterday. I'd say I learned a great deal, Steinmetz."

"But those first two facts you already knew," I objected. "And as to the third one, you could have just asked Miss Eisenstein. I don't think it's much of a secret what order the guests arrived in."

"Steinmetz," said the rabbi. "You never cease to amaze me. Just because somebody tells you something doesn't mean that it's true. Yet you always seem to believe everything you're told. That is, except when I tell you something. Then you never believe it. We only had Alfred Shingle's word that he left the house on Tuesday night and we only had Fred's statement, second-hand through Green, that he visited the house on Saturday. Now we know for certain. As for Art Abercrombie's arriving first, yes I could have asked Miss Eisenstein. I still may. But that will be a difficult question to ask without raising suspicions. Not to mention which, we have no guarantee that Miss Eisenstein would tell us the truth. Mrs. Finchley, on the other hand, appears to be a reliable source on the subject."

The rabbi slid into the Cadillac. I climbed into the passenger seat. "We have to hurry," said the rabbi. "We still have two more visits to pay before the *shabbus*."

I glanced at my watch. It was nearly twelve o'clock. I wondered how much more sleuthing I would have to endure before the rabbi called it quits. I was about to ask him whom we were visiting, when he suddenly pushed another of his imaginary buttons.

"Steinmetz!" he cried. "I have it!"

"The rational explanation?"

'Not yet," he replied. "But I know what it was about Mrs. Finchley's story that bothered me."

"Well, what was it?"

"Mrs. Finchley said that Florence went bird watching on Monday. The day before her wedding. Doesn't that strike you as rather unusual, Steinmetz?"

So that was the big surprise! I slumped into my seat, disappointed.

"No, rabbi," I said. "It doesn't strike me as at all unusual. She went bird watching every morning."

"But on the day before her wedding, Steinmetz? Women aren't like that. Before our daughter got married, Mrs. Kappelmacher spent nearly a month obsessed with the preparations. If Florence went bird watching the morning before her wedding day, I imagine it wasn't just to look at birds."

"You mean she was looking for something else?" I asked. "But you have absolutely no evidence for that."

My patience was wearing thin. I'd had enough speculation for one morning.

"She might have been looking for something else, Steinmetz," observed Rabbi Kappelmacher. "It is a possibility. Only time and rabbinic reasoning will tell us for certain. In any case, I'm sure our rational explanation will reveal why Florence went bird watching on Monday morning. For any rational explanation must explain everything, Steinmetz. That's the only proof we have that God is watching over us."

CHAPTER 6: THE EVIDENCE OF THE BLIND
WOMAN

"So where to now?" I asked Rabbi Kappelmacher.

"Use your rabbinic reasoning, Steinmetz. You can figure it out rather easily."

"I can't, really," I answered. "I'm sure any guess I make will sound foolish."

"Well, what would you do if you were me, Steinmetz?" asked the rabbi. "Now that I have reason to believe that Florence Eisenstein was murdered, where would I go to find evidence to that effect?"

"I guess if I were you, I'd want to interview the suspects," I replied. "Since we've already spoken *at length* to Agatha, I imagine we're going to visit one of the nieces or the nephew."

"That, Steinmetz, is an excellent use of your rabbinic reasoning power. Now if you can deduce which of them we need to see this afternoon, then you'll truly have proven your mettle."

I concentrated on the choice. For the life of me, I couldn't see why it mattered which of them we visited first. My instinct was to guess Fred, because we still didn't know the details of his Saturday meeting with his aunt. At the same time, Agatha's story seemed to point toward Gladys as the most likely suspect. Yet I couldn't figure out why it mattered in what order we visited them

"I have it!" I finally exclaimed. "We need to visit Gladys Eisenstein today, because she's in from out of town and she'll be headed back to San Francisco soon."

The rabbi shook his head with disdain. "I had hoped that you might use your rabbinic reasoning more effectively than that. Did Gladys strike you as a particularly wealthy woman, Steinmetz?"

"Quite the opposite," I replied.

"Indeed, Steinmetz," continued the rabbi, "from everything we know of Gladys, I'd conclude that she's not terribly well off. If she were, she probably wouldn't be staying in the Bargain Motel in Cedar Springs. So let us assume that Gladys is not a rich woman. That means, in all likelihood, that she will stay in New York over a Saturday night for the reduced airline fair. She isn't going to leave town before Sunday. We can always visit her tomorrow night after the *shabbus*, if need be."

"Maybe she flew in early and stayed in New York *last* Saturday night," I suggested.

"Please use your rabbinic reasoning rather than speculating idly, Steinmetz," said the rabbi. "We know she stayed at the Eisenstein's on the night of the wedding. We can also deduce, with confidence, that she didn't stay at the Eisensteins' last weekend because she wasn't there when Fred stopped by on Saturday, and Mrs. Finchley didn't distinguish her presence from that of the rest of the wedding party. So while it is possible that Gladys checked into a motel last weekend, spent Tuesday night at the Eisensteins,' and then returned to the same motel, I find that unlikely. Too much inconvenience. On top of which, I imagine Gladys would postpone her departure in any case until the details of Florence's will are taken care of."

I bit my lip. I'd been so confident that I was using my rabbinic reasoning, I was now at a complete loss as to how to proceed. "I give up," I declared in exasperation. "If we're not visiting Gladys, who are we visiting?"

The rabbi pulled the Cadillac up in front of a nondescript suburban home. "Forty-four Maple Street," he announced. "This is our destination. I called information for the address when I ducked into the beauty parlor in Pine Valley."

A curbside mailbox had the name Sinkoff lettered on the side.

"For the record, Steinmetz," observed the rabbi, "we're visiting Louise Sinkoff. We'll have plenty of time to visit Gladys and Fred on Sunday. However, we definitely needed to visit Louise today if we're going to see her before Monday."

"I don't understand," I pleaded. "What difference does it make if we see Louise today or on Sunday, rabbi?"

"Because on Sunday," the rabbi stated smugly, "her husband will be home. And I have the hunch that if we want the truth out of Louise Sinkoff, we'd best speak to her alone."

I had to admit that the rabbi's reasoning made sense. From what Agatha had told us of Andrew Sinkoff, he didn't seem like the type to let his wife speak freely.

We walked up the slate path of the Sinkoff's home. Rows of begonias bordered the neatly manicured lawn. A cream-colored cat wandered about the neighboring yard. A teenage boy in a denim jacket appeared on the front porch of neighboring house and glared at us. I waved. He glowered at me and scooped up the cat in his arms, disappearing back into the house.

The rabbi rang the bell and a girl of about ten answered the door. She had her mother's high cheek bones and slightly upturned nose; it seemed that they both took after the *shiksah*'s side of the family.

"My mother's not home."

"She's not?" asked the rabbi. He appeared visibly disturbed. "Her aunt Lorraine assured us that she'd be in."

Now it was the girl who seemed upset. She tugged nervously at the sleeves of her dress. "My mother's out for the evening," the girl stated as if by rote.

"I'm a friend of your Aunt Florence's," the rabbi replied. "I saw your mom last night at Aunt Lorraine's house. Do you know when she'll be back?"

The girl thought for another moment and then disappeared into the interior hallway. She returned just long enough to shut the front door behind her.

"She's home," the rabbi said to me. "If she weren't home, there would have been a babysitter to open the door. Green told us that they hired a babysitter when they went up to Florence's for the wedding."

Rabbi Kappelmacher pushed the bell again.

We waited several more seconds and Louise appeared in the doorway. She carried a white cane in one hand.

"Who's there?" she demanded with more force than I imagined she'd had in her.

"I'm Rabbi Kappelmacher," said the rabbi. "And this here's Rabbi Steinmetz. We met you at your Aunt Lorraine's home last night."

"Good afternoon, Mrs. Sinkoff," I said to emphasize my presence.

Louise Sinkoff nodded. The tension melted out of her face. "I remember you. I was expecting somebody else. Well, rabbi, what can I do for you?"

She offered no indication that she intended to invite us inside.

The rabbi adjusted his hand-sewn *yarmulke*. "I was hoping I might have a word with you, Mrs. Sinkoff. It will only take a minute and it's rather essential for my peace of mind. It's about Florence, you understand."

Mrs. Sinkoff brought her hands up to her mouth and nervously tapped her lower lip. She appeared to be debating whether or not to invite us inside. "Please come in," she finally said. "I'll try to be of help, rabbi. But you must understand that my aunt and I weren't at all close. Fred's the one you should be speaking with. Or Lorraine. I'm sure they can do a much better job of answering your questions than I can."

"Maybe," said the rabbi. "But maybe not."

We followed Louise into a sparsely-furnished living room that seemed more like a lobby at a luxury hotel than a room in a home with young children. Several avant-garde sculptures stood at varied intervals on the hardwood floor. We seated ourselves on matching chairs whose futuristic design suggested high prices and high brow tastes. Mrs. Sinkoff settled opposite us in the sofa and crossed her legs.

"Now what can I do for you, rabbi?" she asked. "I have only a few minutes. You've caught me at a rather awkward moment."

The rabbi stared at Louise for several seconds without uttering a word.

"I guess I might as well tell you the truth, Mrs. Sinkoff," he finally said. "I'm not actually a rabbi."

This statement seemed to shock our host as much, if not more, than it did me. Her entire body went suddenly taut and I feared that the veins in her neck might burst. At the same time, I felt the butterflies rising in the pit of my stomach. Whatever the rabbi was up to, I anticipated that no good would come of it.

"If you're not a rabbi," Louise stated with forced composure, "Who are you?"

"Don't worry, Mrs. Sinkoff, I'm not here about whatever money you owe," observed Rabbi Kappelmacher. "I'm here about an entirely different matter."

Again the rabbi caught both Louise and me by surprise.

"How did you—?" gasped Louise. "If you're not from Atlantic City, how did you know about the money?"

The rabbi let forth a hearty laugh. "Relax, Mrs. Sinkoff. You have nothing to fear from me. I'm actually with the Federal Bureau of Investigation. I'm Inspector Kappelmacher. But your cousin, Agatha, mentioned that you had a—that you gambled—and I just put two and two together. But whatever you owe, I'm sure everything will work out all right. I have a business card, by the way. Inspector Steinmetz, what did I do with my cards?"

I was too dumbfounded to reply. My limited legal knowledge told me that impersonating an F.B.I. agent had to be a serious criminal offense. It took my concerted willpower and a stern glare from Rabbi Kappelmacher to keep me from exposing him then and there. As it was, Louise had begun to cry. Tears streamed from under her dark glasses and cascaded down her cheeks.

"Don't worry about the card, Inspector," she said through sobs. "Please just give me a second...."

She wiped her cheeks with a tissue and took several deep breaths.

"This is about Andrew, isn't it? It's about the money he borrowed from the firm. Please, Inspector, we'll pay it all back. With interest. We just need a couple more months, that's all."

The rabbi held up his hand to silence Mrs. Sinkoff. When that didn't work, he cleared his throat. "I assure you, Mrs. Sinkoff," he said, "the reason I'm here has absolutely nothing to do with your husband's business."

This declaration caught Louise Sinkoff entirely off guard. She blanched a deep white and ran her tongue across her lower lip. "Then you're here about the phone calls, aren't you? Andrew promised me he wasn't going to report the phone calls."

"I don't have the faintest idea what you're referring to, Mrs. Sinkoff," replied the rabbi. "I promise you I'm not here about any phone calls."

Louise seemed even more confused by this revelation. "I don't understand, Inspector. If you're not here about what I owe, and you're not here about the bank, and you're not here about the phone calls, what are you here about? Nothing has happened to Andrew, has it?"

"I'm here about your Aunt Florence's death," the rabbi stated in a somber tone. "To be forthright, I'm investigating the possibility that your Aunt Florence was murdered."

"Murdered? Aunt Florence?" renewed alarm appeared on Louise's face. "But that's preposterous. The doctor said Aunt Florence died of asthma. Besides, why would anyone murder Aunt Florence?"

"For her money, Mrs. Sinkoff," answered the rabbi. He appeared to be carefully assessing Louise's reaction to each of his egregious statements. She looked alarmed, but it was only natural to display alarm under the circumstances.

"But Aunt Florence barely had any money," said Louise. "Mr. Abercrombie said we'd probably receive a few thousand dollars—at most."

"Yes, Mrs. Sinkoff," said the rabbi. "However, none of you knew that at the time. I understand from Mr. Green that Florence let it be believed that she'd broken the will."

"Well, yes," stammered Louise Sinkoff. "But you don't think one of us—?"

The rabbi removed a hard candy from a bowl on the table, unwrapped it, and popped it into his mouth. "I'm not accusing anybody of anything," he said. "I'm just investigating. I have no conclusive proof that your aunt was even murdered. All I know is that Dr. Scott feared her death was suspicious, so the standard procedure is called for."

"I see," Louise said. "Wouldn't this be a matter for the local police, Inspector? Why the F.B.I.?"

Now, I feared, Rabbi Kappelmacher had been caught in the web of his own lies. Mrs. Sinkoff had proven shrewder than she appeared.

"Your grandfather was a very wealthy man, Mrs. Sinkoff," the rabbi replied smoothly. "He had many investments in different states. Since this case relates to his will, it's under federal jurisdiction. Now if I could please ask you a couple of questions, then Inspector Steinmetz and I will be on our way...."

Louise uncrossed and recrossed her legs. "Ask me whatever you want, Inspector," she offered. "I have nothing to hide."

"First, I'll need the basics, Mrs. Sinkoff. You have one daughter?"

"Two, Inspector. You met Samantha. The other is seven. She's at a friend's house."

"And I take it that your husband is a banker?"

"With First Consolidated. In the Commercial Division."

"Now Mrs. Sinkoff," observed the rabbi, "how would you characterize your relationship with your Aunt Florence?"

Louise frowned. "In all honesty, Inspector, I'd say we were distant. It wasn't that we didn't get along or anything, it's just that—well—my father was never close to his sisters, and he passed that distance along to me."

"So you'd say that you were distant with Lorraine as well?"

Louise nodded. "Before this week, I hadn't seen either of them...let me see...probably since my mother passed away....That's nearly thirty years ago."

"If you'll excuse me, ma'am, how old were you then?"

Louise reflected momentarily and made several calculations on her fingers. "I must have been about twenty-three then. It was the winter before I met Andrew."

"Your father passed away before your mother, I understand," pried the rabbi.

"June 5, 1982. It was a difficult time for the family, Inspector. My younger sister ran off to California and then my father died, and after that I pretty much lost touch with my aunts. We invited them to our wedding, but they didn't come. They did send a generous present though. Other than that, we'd exchange cards for the Jewish New Year, but that was about it."

"Until last week," prompted the rabbi.

"That's right, Inspector," Louise agreed. "It was roughly a week and a half ago that we received a call from Florence about the wedding. I have to admit, when Andrew told me that Florence had called, my first thought was that somebody had died. Either Lorraine or Cousin Agatha. It never crossed my mind that Florence might get married."

"Did Florence sound at all off-balance on the phone? Like she wasn't all there?"

Louise shook her head. "You'll have to ask my husband, Inspector. I didn't speak to her that night. I was so shaken up by the phone calls, you understand, and we'd just fought about whether or not to call the police—"

"What phone calls, Mrs. Sinkoff?" demanded the rabbi.

Our host rose from her chair and paced between the avant-garde sculptures. "I might as well tell you, Inspector. You're bound to find out about it anyway, if you want to, and it's really not a big deal. It just reminds me of all the calls we received back on the Lower East Side. Before my father died."

"You're not making yourself clear, Mrs. Sinkoff," observed Rabbi Kappelmacher. "Please do sit down and explain exactly what you're talking about."

Louise returned to her seat. She took a deep breath and then spoke in a determined, almost forced voice. "When I was maybe fifteen or sixteen, Inspector, I started receiving prank phone calls. The phone would ring and when I answered it, I'd hear a gasping, moaning sound. Like a man engaged in some sort of sexual activity."

"How awful," consoled the rabbi.

"It *was* truly awful. If anybody else answered the phone, the caller hung up instantly. At the time, I thought I'd been targeted because I was blind. I know that sounds irrational, Inspector, but that's how teenage girls think."

"And did they ever catch the perpetrator?"

Louise shook her head. "Never. My father changed our phone number and paid to keep it unlisted—and that was the end of it."

"Until recently," suggested Rabbi Kappelmacher.

"Exactly," agreed Louise. "About three weeks ago, I started receiving similar calls. The caller would gasp into the phone. Only it was more moaning than gasping. Andrew was out of town on business for the bank for a few days. By the end of the week, I was afraid to answer the phone."

"Where was your husband?"

"Chicago," Louise answered. "Then he stopped in Cincinnati on the way back. It was his first night home when Florence called. Andrew and I had just had a heated argument about whether to report the calls and I was upstairs in bed crying. This may sound strange to you, Inspector, but as much as the calls upset me, I felt awful for the caller. I figured he has enough trouble as it is without our involving the police. Andrew, of course, is a businessman. He sees things differently."

The rabbi nodded. Then he remembered that our host couldn't see him and he offered her verbal reassurance. "I understand exactly what you must have felt, Mrs. Sinkoff," he said. "That's a difficult decision to make. Incidentally, are you still receiving the calls?"

Louise shook her head. "That's the strangest part of it, Inspector. As soon as Andrew returned from his trip, the calls stopped. We haven't had one since. As odd as this sounds, the silence is kind of creepy."

Rabbi Kappelmacher scratched his head. "Do you have any ideas as to who the caller might have been, Mrs. Sinkoff?"

Our host uncrossed her legs for the second time. "Please don't tell any of this to my husband, Inspector. He wouldn't understand and he might not forgive me. He's under a lot of pressure at work and I don't want to cause him any more trouble."

"Mum's the word," replied the rabbi. "Your secrets are safe with me, Mrs. Sinkoff. It's a professional responsibility."

Louise sat for a moment in what seemed like deep reflection. "At first, Inspector, I thought the caller might be James, the boy next door. A woman can tell about these things, I think. I know he has a crush on me—although he'd never admit to it. He's a troubled kid, from what I hear. Left back a grade. Spent a couple of months in drug rehab. His parents are such nice people too, which is one of the reasons I didn't want to go to the police. He's a podiatrist. She's an elementary school teacher. Harry and Rita Garber."

"But I take it that you no longer think that James is your caller."

Louise shook her head and started to cry again. "No," she sobbed. "I don't." She wiped her face and leaned forward toward the rabbi. "I don't know how to say this, Inspector...."

"It can't be *that* bad," Rabbi Kappelmacher said. "Whatever it is, I'm sure that with God's help, you can work through it."

"I guess. I don't know. You see, Inspector, Andrew and I have been having problems. We've been fighting. Mostly over money. He has so much of it, you see, and he wastes it on these damn sculptures, when I have those men from Atlantic City breathing down my neck. I threatened to leave him last month if he didn't give me what I needed. Andrew didn't take well to that suggestion. And the long and the short of it is that I think Andrew may have been the obscene caller. To bring us back together. He knew about what happened when I was sixteen. It's the only explanation I can think of, Inspector. The calls started a couple of days after he left for Chicago and they stopped as soon as he returned. I think he may have wanted to call the police in order to throw suspicion off himself, especially since he knew I wouldn't let him. Andrew can be like that. So I hate myself for thinking this, Inspector, but it's the only explanation that makes any sense."

The rabbi ran his hand across his forehead. I could sense the gears churning in his mind. "Is it possible," he asked, "that the two callers are the same person, Mrs. Sinkoff? The one from the old neighborhood and the one from last week?"

Louise pondered the suggestion. "I suppose so. I considered that possibility, but it has been *such* a long time. More than three decades. And the timing seemed too strange. I really don't know, Inspector. I don't even remember what we were talking about when this came up."

The rabbi removed a cigar from his breast pocket, examined it between his fingers, and reluctantly returned it to his jacket. "I have only a few more questions, Mrs. Sinkoff. I just want to make certain I have this straight. Florence invited you and your husband to her wedding about a week and a half ago.   Do you remember the day precisely?"

"Not off hand," Louise replied. "If it's important, I can look it up in my diary. I keep very careful notes on my life. In Braille, of course. My therapist recommended it. She says it's therapeutic."

"There's no need for that, Mrs. Sinkoff. A week and a half ago is precise enough. At that time, did she tell your husband that she'd broken the will?"

"I believe so," Louise replied tentatively. "Wait, she must have. Because I remember that I wanted to offer her double congratulations at her wedding. Both on breaking the will and getting married. Of course, I never had a chance to do so, and now it turns out she hadn't broken the will at all."

Rabbi Kappelmacher nodded thoughtfully. "I understand that there was a dispute at the wedding. That Florence had a fight with your brother and stormed off."

"It was bizarre, Inspector," said Louise. "It was awful enough that Lorraine wouldn't even come downstairs for the ceremony. But Florence was just unbearable. She wanted absolutely nothing to do with Andrew and me. It's a wonder she even bothered to invite us! She shook my hand very cordially, but in a firm, almost indifferent sort of way, and then she spent nearly an hour in the corner with Gladys. You would have thought *I* was the one who'd slandered her in the papers." Louise paused and reflected for several seconds. "My sister, Inspector," she continued, "has always been the black sheep of the family. Before Tuesday, I hadn't seen her or even spoken to her since she was nineteen years old."

Louise then repeated virtually the same story about Gladys's attempt to break the will and her accusations against her aunts that we'd heard from Agatha.

"I tell you, Inspector," Louise concluded "both Florence and Gladys were acting pretty peculiar that afternoon. It almost seemed as though Florence was afraid of my sister, as though my aunt was trying to keep her from speaking to anybody else. Every time Gladys tried to walk across the drawing room, Florence followed her. And once, when I tried to join their conversation, Florence took Gladys by the arm—almost forcefully—and marched her off into the library. Of course, I can't imagine that Gladys would kill anybody, Inspector. Don't misinterpret me."

The rabbi stood up suddenly and offered Louise his hand. "Thank you for your time," he said.

"You won't tell my husband about this, Inspector?" she asked.

"I'll make you a deal. If you don't tell anyone I'm an F.B.I. agent, I won't tell anyone about our little meeting."

Louise agreed and escorted us to the door.

"One final question, Mrs. Sinkoff," said the rabbi.

"Yes?"

"Did you leave your room on the night of Florence's death?"

"No," she answered. "We didn't find out about it until the morning."

'And your husband, Mrs. Sinkoff? Did *he* leave your room?"

"Absolutely not, Inspector," replied Louise with a new edge to her voice. "My husband's a hard man, but he's not a murderer."

"Thank you, Mrs. Sinkoff," said the rabbi. He turned rapidly on his heels and strode up the front path.

Back in the Cadillac, he sat at the wheel for several minutes before he turned on the ignition. "Well, Steinmetz, what did you think of Louise Sinkoff?" the rabbi finally asked me.

"I don't know. She might be lying about her husband not leaving their room on Tuesday night. But whatever you may think, I can't imagine her trying to murder anyone. Although if you're right that the intended victim was Lorraine, then I must admit she seems pretty independent for a blind woman. She could easily have negotiated those stairs and murdered the wrong aunt by mistake, I suppose. But I don't know how she could have known there was only one person in the room when she entered. She would have had to feel around to see if there was one person in the bed or two—and if Alfred had been in the room, she'd have woken him. I don't see how she could have risked it unless she heard Alfred leaving and thought he'd departed from the other room. In any case, I don't think she's a murderer."

The rabbi lit his cigar and stared pensively into the dashboard.

"What did *you* think of Louise, rabbi?" I asked curiously.

The rabbi shook his head in despair. "I think, Steinmetz," he said, "that Mrs. Sinkoff is a woman who would be much better off in life if she attended synagogue regularly."

CHAPTER 7: THE EVIDENCE OF THE LAWYER

"Well, Steinmetz," Rabbi Kappelmacher asked when we were back on the road. "Where to now?"

I rolled down the window and let the summer breeze blow against my face. Then I glanced down at my watch. It was nearly three o'clock. Pretty soon we would both need to return to the synagogue for the *shabbus*. Rabbi Kappelmacher might be able to move the morning prayers to eight o'clock and arrange for me to postpone my Jewish history class, but there was absolutely nothing he could do about the Sabbath's coming at sundown. This pleased me to no end. After twenty-four hours of driving around the county lying to strangers, I was more than ready for my day of rest.

"You tell me, rabbi. All I know is that it can't be more than twenty-three hours away. In case you've forgotten, we have *shabbus* dinner with the Sisterhood scheduled for six fifteen."

"I haven't forgotten," said the rabbi. "My memory is not as poor as I led that Mrs. Finchley to believe. But you still haven't answered my question. Use your rabbinic reasoning and tell me where we're going next."

"Straight to jail," I answered. "I fear that impersonating an F.B.I. officer is a serious offense, rabbi."

"Don't be such a *noodnik*, Steinmetz. She won't tell anybody. In the first place, she thinks I'm aboveboard. She has no reason not to. On top of that, Louise is in no position to be accusing anybody of anything. Between her gambling problem and her husband's embezzlement, the last thing she'll do is check the credentials of a rabbi claiming to be an F.B.I. agent. Did you like that bit with the business card?"

I groaned. "That was really too much, rabbi," I replied. "What would you have done if she'd actually asked for the card? If she'd wanted to save it to show her husband, for instance?"

"I would have given her one of my real cards," he answered. "And if she or her husband called the synagogue, I would have told them that I must have given them one of my fake cards by mistake. But I was fairly certain it wouldn't come to that. Louise didn't strike me as the type of woman who'd want her husband to know that she'd been visited by an F.B.I. agent."

That was one conclusion, at least, that I could agree with.

"You still haven't told me where we're going," said Rabbi Kappelmacher. "You're never going to survive as head rabbi if you don't put your reasoning powers to work. Now where to?"

I thought for a moment. "You've already told me that we're in no rush to visit Fred or Gladys. So I'll rule both of them out for now. How am I doing?"

"So far, so good," replied the rabbi.

"By the same token, if you wanted to visit Lorraine, I imagine you would have stopped by her place when we visited Mrs. Finchley."

"Now you're thinking, Steinmetz. So where does that leave us?"

The answer seemed so obvious that I hesitated to offer it. "I guess, by process of elimination, we must be on our way to visit Mr. Shingle."

Rabbi Kappelmacher's face fell.

"When will you ever learn?" he asked in frustration. "You're not supposed to guess, you're supposed to reason. Leave the guesswork to the lay people."

"So we're not going to visit Mr. Shingle?"

"Not today. There's no rush. We can visit him on Sunday afternoon."

"Then where are we going?" I asked. "Haven't we eliminated everybody?"

Rabbi Kappelmacher frowned. "Not everybody, Steinmetz. You're forgetting that our primary goal isn't to interview potential murderers. Our primary goal is to obtain information. We need to know as much about Florence

Eisenstein as possible, Steinmetz. And who better to ask than her longtime lawyer? But we'd better get a move on, because I can't imagine Art Abercrombie stays at the office much past five o'clock on Fridays and I'm sure that at his age he doesn't come to work on the weekend."

Something in the rabbi's tone suggested that he had another reason for wanting to visit Abercrombie, but he seemed loath to share it with me. I knew better than to ask, so I closed my eyes and tried to sneak in a ten minute nap. Before I knew it, the rabbi was nudging my shoulder, and once I was awake again, we walked together through a set of glass doors into the oak-paneled lobby of Abercrombie & Green.

The rabbi paused in front of the desk marked RECEPTION. "So how do you intend to get an appointment with one of the leading lawyers in the country at 3:30 on a Friday afternoon?" I asked. I knew from the newspapers that Abercrombie was once again dabbling with the idea of running for the United States Senate, having backed out of two previous Senate primaries at the last minute. I was confident that he had little time for a meddlesome rabbi.

"Connections, connections," observed the rabbi. Then he informed the young woman behind the reception desk that Rabbi Kappelmacher was here to see Marshall Green. Several minutes later, we were directed to a corner office on the fifth floor where we were greeted by the former assistant rabbi.

"Rabbi Kappelmacher," Green declared. "Exactly the man I've been looking for. I must have phoned the synagogue five times this afternoon, but Mrs. Billings said you'd been gone all day. I believe 'vanished into thin air' was the expression she used."

"Mrs. Billings has a tendency to exaggerate," mused Rabbi Kappelmacher. We seated ourselves across from Marshall Green's mahogany desk while the lawyer quickly shoved several papers into an open drawer. "I've actually been looking forward to seeing you, as well. I have a couple of questions about this Eisenstein business that I'm hoping you can clear up. But first, what is it you so desperately needed to see me about?"

Green flexed a ballpoint pen between his fingers. He walked to the door, assured himself that it had been firmly shut, and returned to his seat. When he spoke, his voice was barely audible. "Rabbi," he said, "You'll have to pardon my caution, but word travels fast in a law firm. And under the circumstances, I think it best that this conversation stay between the three of us for now."

The rabbi grinned. "You're full of secrets these days, aren't you, Green?"

"Listen, rabbi," Green continued in his low voice. "This isn't a joking matter. Yesterday, on the drive back from the Eisenstein place, I mentioned to Art Abercrombie that I thought the circumstances surrounding Florence's death were unusual. He already knew about her claim that she'd broken the will, of course, but I hadn't told him about my conversation with Florence on Monday morning or her plans to disinherit her nephew. We were just having a friendly conversation. But when I suggested the nephew bumped the old lady off so she wouldn't have a chance to alter her will, Art exploded. He nearly drove off the road. He told me that he wouldn't have anybody dragging the Eisenstein family name through the mud and that the last thing he needed was a vicious lie like this interfering with *his* political plans. He went from Dr. Jekyll to Mr. Hyde in the blink of an eye. It was as though he was more involved in this business than an attorney ought to be. And I don't understand how, even if Fred had murdered his aunt, it would have any impact on Art's political ambitions."

Rabbi Kappelmacher ran a hand down his beard. "Very strange," he said, as much to himself as to us. "Very strange indeed."

"What's very strange?" I asked.

"I was only thinking," he muttered. "I'll level with you, Green. Steinmetz and I have been doing some sleuthing of our own, and we're not much closer to a rational explanation than we were yesterday afternoon. Yet the more I learn, the more I'm convinced that there's one simple explanation for *all* the peculiar events of the past week."

"I do hope so," said Green. "I've worked with Art Abercrombie for years, and he's never exploded at me like that. He's usually a very cool, calculating individual. A lawyer's lawyer. Did you know he backed out of the Senate race two years ago because he was afraid the press might find out that he cheated on an examination in law school?"

"I did not know that, Green," answered the rabbi. "What I do know is that I wish to see Art Abercrombie this afternoon."

"As easily said as done," said Green. "Only it's at your own risk. If you mention Florence, be prepared for him to explode at you."

"I'm warned, Green. But before we meet Abercrombie, I have to ask you a question. There's something that has been troubling me all afternoon. Ever since we visited Louise Sinkoff. Didn't you say that you spoke to Florence on Monday morning?"

"I did," said Green. "Probably around 9:30. Maybe ten o'clock."

"Right after she came back from bird watching," I suggested.

"And you told us," the rabbi continued, "that when you spoke to her, she didn't mention that she thought she'd broken the will."

"Not a word about it."

"Odd," said the rabbi. "Florence told Louise and her husband last week that she thought she'd broken the will. That was *before* she spoke to you."

Green furrowed his brow. "This *is* odd, rabbi. Do you think somebody told her not to mention to me that she'd broken the will?"

"That thought has crossed my mind, Green," said the rabbi. "I have a difficult question for you. Do you think it's possible that in your conversation on Monday morning, Florence didn't mention her belief that the will had been broken because she assumed that you already knew and the subject just didn't come up?"

Green shook his head. "Not possible, rabbi. I'm sure she said to me that she didn't give a damn about the will and she was going to get married anyway. I remember it vividly, because it really took me by surprise."

"I see," said the rabbi. "That means that either Florence intentionally misled you, or something happened between the time she spoke with Andrew Sinkoff and the time she spoke with you to make her think that the will had been broken and then that the will hadn't been broken. Puzzling."

Green shook his head. "But everybody at the wedding seemed to think that the will *had* been broken. I even heard Gladys Eisenstein congratulate her on it. You don't mean to suggest, rabbi, that she believed the will had been broken last week, and then didn't think it had been broken on Monday, and then did think it had been broken again on Tuesday? That's too complicated an explanation. She must have been told not to speak to me about the will."

"You think Abercrombie told her not to," suggested the rabbi.

"Who else?" asked Green.

The rabbi stood up. "Maybe Abercrombie can supply the answer."

Green made several phone calls and ten minutes later we were sitting across from the senior attorney in a spacious office whose walls were plastered with photographs of Abercrombie in the company of various celebrities. Abercrombie with Nelson Rockefeller. Abercrombie, in a tuxedo, with Congresswoman Bella Abzug on his arm. The lawyer leaned back in his chair and lit a cigarette, showing flagrant disregard for the conspicuous non-smoking signs posted throughout the building.

"What can I do for you, rabbi?" he asked in a deep voice marked by a slight British accent. "It was a pleasure meeting you last night, but I admit I didn't expect to see you again so soon."

The rabbi looked at Green, who was standing by the window. "Can we have a moment with you in private, Mr. Abercrombie?" he asked.

Green's face acquired a wounded look, but without further discussion, he walked rapidly through the open door and pulled it shut behind him. I felt bad for poor Green. I didn't understand what could possibly be so top secret that it couldn't be discussed in front of the former assistant rabbi.

"All right, rabbi, we're alone now," said Abercrombie. "Now what can I do for you?"

The rabbi lit a cigar. Abercrombie sniffed audibly, but didn't object.

"I'll only take a minute of your time, Mr. Abercrombie," said the rabbi. "I know you must be extremely busy these days. The papers say you intend to run for the Senate."

Abercrombie chuckled. "Never believe what you read in the papers, rabbi."

The rabbi smiled and puffed his cigar. "The reason I sent Green out of the room," he explained, "is that I'm worried about him. You must know that he used to work with me for many years."

"So I've been told," said Abercrombie. "He talks about you often."

I noticed a glint of pleasure in the rabbi's eyes upon hearing this news. "I'm a big admirer of Marshall's," he said. "That's why, when he came by the synagogue yesterday with this preposterous story that he thought one of his clients had been murdered, I was terribly distraught."

The seasoned lawyer's face betrayed a moment of shock when Rabbi Kappelmacher mentioned the word murder, but his relaxed smile quickly returned. "I've had similar fears myself, rabbi," observed Abercrombie.

"Now I'm ninety-nine percent sure that Florence Eisenstein was a dotty old woman who died of asthma," lied the rabbi, "but I wanted to speak with you to make absolutely certain. That's why I stopped by this afternoon. I told Green I wanted to ask you some questions about Florence Eisenstein, but I actually wanted your opinion about Green's suspicions."

This was a clever tactic on the rabbi's part, I had to admit

Art Abercrombie smiled the smile of a co-conspirator. He tamped out his cigarette and lit another. "I'm not sure what to tell you, rabbi," he said. "If you're asking me whether I think Florence was murdered, I think that's one of the most ridiculous propositions I've ever heard. Florence was a dear, sweet old woman who died of some respiratory problem."

"You're not at all troubled by this business of her thinking that her father's will had been broken or her plans to disinherit her nephew?" pressed the rabbi.

Abercrombie leaned forward across his desk with his hands clasped together. "Look, rabbi, since you asked, I'll tell you exactly what I think. I think Florence Eisenstein was a confused old lady. If I had a dollar for every old woman who comes into my office shouting disinheritance like there's no tomorrow, I'd be living in Ft. Lauderdale right now. Who knows why Florence decided to get married late in life, rabbi? Old people do that sort of thing. Everybody thinks I'm a confirmed bachelor, but maybe I'll tie the knot one of these days myself."

"So you didn't tell Florence that her father's will had been broken?" Rabbi Kappelmacher asked.

"*Me?*" responded Abercrombie. "Of course not. I don't think I've spoken to Florence since some time last year. Rest assured, rabbi, there's absolutely nothing to all of this. The sooner we put an end to all of these speculations, the better."

The rabbi nodded. "I couldn't agree more," he said. "Green's probably working too hard."

"I'll send him on vacation," said Abercrombie. "It'll do him good. Now if that's all, rabbi, I need to be at the Chamber of Commerce by five o'clock."

Rabbi Kappelmacher seemed lost in a trance. "One more thing, Mr. Abercrombie," he said. "You'll pardon my asking, but I just need to be certain."

"There's no need to ask for my pardon, rabbi," Abercrombie replied. "I'll be happy to tell you anything I can to put your mind at ease."

Rabbi Kappelmacher rose from his seat and strode over to the photograph of Abercrombie with Governor Rockefeller. "You've been practicing law for a long time," mused the rabbi.

"Forty-four years," said Abercrombie. He stood up and joined the rabbi by the wall of photographs. "That's me with Rockefeller in '71. And this here," he said, tapping another framed photograph, "is me with George Matesky. I helped his defense team. You may not recognize his name. He's more widely known as The Mad Bomber."

The rabbi pretended to admire the photograph. "I take it you've been the Eisensteins' lawyer all this time," he observed. "You must have known the father."

"Irving Eisenstein was one of my first clients. My practice is primarily in criminal and family law, but I helped negotiate the deal with General Foods that made Eisenstein egg creams a household name."

"So tell me," continued the rabbi, "is there any truth to the rumor that the Eisenstein sisters poisoned their father?"

The question was barely out of the rabbi's mouth when Abercrombie exploded. "That, rabbi, is a dirty, vicious lie," he shouted. He paused for a second to regain his composure. "I'm sorry," he said. "You'll have to excuse me. It's just that I don't take well to malicious slanders against my clients. It was just a vicious lie concocted by a kid because she couldn't get what she wanted. Did Gladys Eisenstein tell you that? I thought she'd gotten past that after all these years."

"Actually," said the rabbi, "it was Agatha Grossbart who mentioned it to me. The story sounded pretty fishy, but I had to ask you."

The lawyer seemed to relax slightly at the rabbi's expression of doubt. "I understand," he said. "If I were in your shoes, I probably would have asked the same questions. But you have to understand that you can only hear the same lie told so many times before it really gets to you."

"Don't think twice about it," said the rabbi. "I imagine there's also no truth to the rumor that the Eisenstein sisters sued their neighbors over the property line."

Abercrombie struggled to light a cigarette. "I'd nearly forgotten all about that, rabbi. It amazes me what nonsense you've managed to dig up in one day. But I have a surprise for you—for what it's worth. The Eisenstein sisters *were* involved in a legal dispute over the property line. But it was the neighbor who started it. An old-time lawyer named Bartlett Finchley. One of those people who was always out for himself. But I can't see what that has to do with anything. I don't even imagine Green knows about that business, unless this Grossbart woman told him."

The rabbi shrugged. "I imagine he doesn't," he said. "I only asked because Lorraine referred to it last night," he lied.

At the mention of Lorraine Eisenstein's name, Abercrombie's face glowed. He suddenly looked twenty years younger—like a man of fifty, not seventy. "Lorraine is delightful, isn't she? Both sisters were wonderful women, rabbi. That's why it disturbs me so much to hear any ill spoken of them."

"Understandably," agreed the rabbi. "Well, I do appreciate your time."

"My pleasure."

"And if you would be so kind, Mr. Abercrombie, not to mention the subject of our meeting to Green. I really like the boy a lot. I wouldn't want to jeopardize our friendship."

We shook hands all around and Abercrombie walked us to the elevator. It was already four-thirty when we pulled out of the parking lot and started toward Haddam. Rabbi Kappelmacher seemed to be uncharacteristically pensive.

"Well?" I asked.

"Well *what*, Steinmetz?"

"Well, what did you think, rabbi? Do you believe him about not speaking to Florence in almost a year? Or do you think Green is right that he's more mixed up in this than we first thought?"

"Than *you* first thought," Rabbi Kappelmacher corrected me.

"Do you mean you've suspected Abercrombie all along?"

"I never said that," answered the rabbi. "I just don't jump to conclusions the way that you do, Steinmetz. I take my time to think things through. In any case, I was glad to see you finally use your rabbinic reasoning powers back there."

I appreciated this unexpected compliment, but I had no idea how I'd merited it. I didn't think I'd said anything of significance during our entire visit.

"I hate to confess this, rabbi," I said sheepishly, "but I'm not sure what you're referring to."

Rabbi Kappelmacher laughed. "You never cease to amaze me, Steinmetz. Sometimes I think you're going to make an excellent chief rabbi, a real *rebbe*, and other times, I wonder. You don't even realize the importance of your discovery, do you?"

"What discovery?" I asked.

"Unbelievable!" exclaimed the rabbi. "You have no idea what I'm referring to. Back in Green's office, you made a crucial observation that I'd entirely overlooked up until then, Steinmetz. You reminded me that Florence went bird watching on Monday morning before she phoned Green's office."

"So? She went bird watching every morning."

"That is true," agreed the rabbi. "But it wasn't every morning that she decided to disinherit her nephew. Green indicated that Florence was determined to alter her will as quickly as possible. That being the case, don't you think she would have been on the phone at nine o'clock sharp, rather than thwacking about in the shrubbery for birds?"

I hadn't even thought about that. "So you *do* think she was looking for something else, rabbi," I said.

The rabbi shrugged.

"So what now, rabbi?" I asked. Against my better judgment, I was beginning to think that there was something odd about Florence's behavior in the period leading up to her wedding. "Who's next on our list?" I asked. "Fred or Gladys?"

Rabbi Kappelmacher glanced at his watch. "Now Steinmetz," he said. "We do exactly what we're supposed to do on Friday evening. We head back to Haddam for dinner with the Sisterhood and then we pray. As I always used to say to Mrs. Kappelmacher, all work and no rest makes the rabbi a bad Jew."

"Do you mean I have to wait until Sunday for your rational explanation?" I asked. I knew that it couldn't be any other way, yet still I found myself suffering from disappointment.

"That's exactly what I mean, Steinmetz," said the rabbi. "God wouldn't want it any other way."

CHAPTER 8: THE EVIDENCE OF THE NEPHEW

The *shabbus* passed uneventfully. Despite my worst fears, there was nothing to distinguish that Saturday from any other. Agents from the Federal Bureau of Investigation didn't charge into the synagogue during the *kaddush* prayers to arrest the rabbi for impersonating one of their own. Gladys Eisenstein didn't sneak into my bedroom in the middle of the night and try to suffocate me with a pillow. The rabbi made no mention of Florence Eisenstein's death when I saw him at the *kaddush* on Saturday morning or at the *hafdalah* service later that night. In fact, by breakfast the next day, the events of the preceding week seemed like a distant memory. Yet when my wife answered the door on Sunday and informed me that Rabbi Kappelmacher was waiting for me on the porch, I knew that I was in for another adventure.

"Good morning, Steinmetz," he greeted me when I stepped out into the morning air in my bathrobe and slippers. "Go inside and put on some clothes. I don't think you'll make a good impression on Fred Eisenstein if you show up dressed like that."

"I thought Sunday was my day off," I grumbled. "What ever happened to, 'On Saturday He rested and on Sunday He slept in?'"

The rabbi laughed. "A rabbi is always on duty, Steinmetz. If you wanted to sleep in, you should have become a priest."

"You're telling me," I muttered. I went quickly into the house and changed into a sport jacket and slacks.

Half an hour later, we pulled up in front of the Greenwich Village address of Fred Eisenstein that Rabbi Kappelmacher had obtained from Green. It was an old brownstone, badly in need of repair. Across the street, a handful of teenage girls giggled at us. One of them, I noted, had bright purple hair.

"Can you imagine Louise and Andrew Sinkoff living in this neighborhood?" the rabbi asked me as he pushed the buzzer marked "F. Eisenstein."

The very thought made me chuckle. It amazed me that a brother and sister could grow up in the same home and choose such different lifestyles.

After the rabbi made clear to Fred through the intercom that we weren't the landlord, and that we had no interest in collecting the previous month's rent, the nephew buzzed us in. We climbed six flights of stairs and found Fred waiting for us in the last doorway at the end of a narrow passageway. His hair was still wet and he was barefoot.

"Rabbis," Fred greeted us warmly. "This is a surprise."

"Life often brings the unexpected," observed Rabbi Kappelmacher. "May we come in?"

"By all means," agreed Fred.

We followed him into a spacious studio apartment. Several expressionistic paintings covered the walls and several others, presumably new acquisitions, leaned against the wainscoting. A large futon lay underneath the window across the kitchenette. Several boxes stood in one corner. Otherwise, the apartment was bare.

"You'll have to excuse the absence of chairs," Fred explained, "but I only moved in last December and I've been in Europe for the past six months. Please feel free to make yourselves at home."

Fred Eisenstein removed three heavy boxes from the stack in the corner and arranged them like chairs. He seated himself and we did the same.

"I understand you were in Europe on business," said the rabbi. "Your cousin Agatha told us you're establishing artist colonies."

"Artistic communes," Fred corrected him. "Places for promising artists to go paint or draw without distraction. I'm an art dealer. It helps me to have access to the brightest young stars in the world of art. Of course," Fred added with a mournful shake of the head, "all of this costs money. The Amsterdam Commune is going strong, but we've had a difficult time locating affordable space in Munich and Copenhagen. That's why I went on this trip."

"And you were successful?" the rabbi inquired.

"Yes and no. When you showed up this morning, I feared you might be the city marshal. I'm afraid that I'm a month behind on the rent."

"Dear me. In that case, we won't take too much of your time."

Fred laughed heartily. Although he must have been in his early forties and his hairline showed signs of retreat, he reminded me of an overgrown child. I found his sincerity and warmth disarming.

"Time is the one thing I have plenty of, rabbi," he said. "That's the plight of the art dealer in the modern era. Too much time, too little money. I imagine there's much more security in serving as a clergyman."

"I imagine so too," said the rabbi. "But the truth of the matter is, Mr. Eisenstein, that I'm not actually a rabbi. I'm only posing as a rabbi for the time being."

Fred Eisenstein looked quizzically at Rabbi Kappelmacher. I believe he was trying to figure out if the rabbi was pulling his leg. "Let me guess," he finally said. "You're actually a Borscht Belt talent scout. You're scouring for promising comedians."

I couldn't help smiling at the suggestion. Rabbi Kappelmacher wouldn't recognize comedic talent if it jumped off his plate during breakfast.

"I'm glad you find that funny, Inspector Steinmetz," said the rabbi coldly. "Actually, Mr. Eisenstein, I'm a field inspector with the Federal Bureau of Investigation."

Fred Eisenstein looked as though he didn't know whether to laugh or to cry. "You're for real, aren't you? I knew there was something about you I couldn't place. You didn't seem stodgy enough to be a rabbi."

"Indeed. I imagine rabbis must be a pretty stodgy lot."

"It's too bad, isn't it?" said Fred. "You'd think they'd be more dynamic and outgoing. They have so much potential to do good, and they waste their time with outdated rituals. At least, all the rabbis I've met. Though the truth of the matter is, Inspector, I don't run into too many rabbis in my line of work."

"Your aunt Florence was married by a rabbi, I imagine," said Rabbi Kappelmacher.

"Funny you mention it," said Fred. "He fit the bill to a T. Even stodgier than that other rabbi who used to come around when the sisters went through their religious phase. I thought they would have called him for the ceremony. His name was Stern. Rabbi Stern. And he looked sterner than you could possibly imagine. The one redeeming feature about Aunt Florence's wedding was that they didn't drag in that old geezer, although I understand that he still has a congregation. But the fellow they found in the phone book wasn't much better."

"They hired a rabbi from the phone book?"

"That's what Aunt Lorraine told me. I wonder what kind of rabbi advertises in the yellow pages, but I didn't have much of a chance to find out. As soon as things became...well...complicated, the guy too off. It was probably for the best though. It was hard enough trying to talk my aunts out of their rooms without that old windbag wandering the house citing Old Testament passages about domestic tranquility. But I'm sure this doesn't interest you in the slightest, Inspector. Now what can I do for you? I can't imagine what I could possibly have done to bring the wrath of the F.B.I. down upon me. The works I deal in are much too abstract to be obscene."

The rabbi removed a cigar from his pocket. "Do you mind if I smoke, Mr. Eisenstein?"

"Actually," the nephew objected. "I'd prefer that you didn't."

"Quite all right," the rabbi answered without sincerity. His tone changed from warm to chilly. "Inspector Steinmetz and I are investigating the murder of your Aunt Florence, Mr. Eisenstein. We have reason to believe that her death did not result from natural causes."

Fred Eisenstein stared at his hands. "Are you serious, Inspector?"

"Dead serious, Mr. Eisenstein. This is not a joking matter."

"I guess not," said Fred. "May I ask why you think my aunt was murdered? You must appreciate that this is all coming at me from left field."

Rabbi Kappelmacher returned his cigar to his pocket. "I'm not at liberty to tell you that, Mr. Eisenstein. However, if you'll answer a handful of questions for us this morning, we'll be on our way."

"Don't I have a right to consult a lawyer?" Fred asked. I couldn't tell if he was joking or seriously considering seeking the advice of counsel. Under the circumstances, the prospect terrified me.

"Not unless you're a suspect," the rabbi replied suavely. "And as of now, you're not, Mr. Eisenstein. If you do become a suspect, at that time I will inform you of the fact, and you may call your attorney."

"I see," said Fred. "Well, I have nothing to hide. Ask me anything you wish. Only don't expect me to believe that my aunt was murdered."

"Please, Mr. Eisenstein," said the rabbi. "All I need from you are the answers to a handful of questions. Nothing more. Now could you please describe for us your relationship with your Aunt Florence."

Fred paused and then the smile returned to his face. "I'd say we were close, inspector. Not *very* close, but close. I visited her and my Aunt Lorraine fairly often. Maybe once a month. I'm not sure what else I can tell you."

"You said that you were out of town for the past six months. Did you see your aunts before you left?"

"The day before I left, in fact, inspector. I had an evening flight, so I stopped by in the morning. I believe it was a Thursday."

"And how did your visit go?"

"Nothing out of the ordinary, inspector. I believe that Florence was out bird watching when I arrived. It was in the middle of December and she liked to walk down to the small pond behind the house to watch the winter ducks. I chatted with my Aunt Lorraine for a while and when Florence returned, we all had lunch. And no, inspector, I can't tell you what we had for lunch."

I was quite dumbfounded by the playful animosity that had so quickly developed between Fred and Rabbi Kappelmacher. It was as though they were taunting each other.

"So you went to Europe," observed the rabbi.

"To Amsterdam, Copenhagen and Munich. I have the receipts to prove it if you'd like to see them. I returned to town last week."

"And you called your aunts to let them know?"

"On Wednesday night."

"You spoke to both of them?"

"Yes, I did. I told them I might stop by the house on Sunday or Monday."

"But you actually stopped by on Saturday," the rabbi observed.

Fred nodded. "That's not a crime, is it? It turned out that a prospective investor called on Friday and we made plans to meet on Sunday, so I thought I'd see my aunts sooner rather than later."

"Why not wait until Monday? Wasn't that the original plan?"

Fred threw up his hands in exasperation. "I don't know. Because I decided to go on Saturday—it's as simple as that. It wasn't a calculated decision."

The rabbi nodded. "I see. When you spoke to your aunts on Wednesday, did anything about your conversation strike you as particularly unusual?"

"No, it didn't. In fact, our conversation was as usual as it possibly could be. Lorraine told me about her plans for the garden and Florence said she'd seen a sparrow hawk on the Finchley property next door. That's a bird, by the way."

Rabbi Kappelmacher scratched his beard again. "Did either of your aunts mention to you on the phone that Florence intended to get married the following week?"

"They did not. Lorraine told me that she needed to speak with me in private, but she couldn't with Florence around. I guess, by your standards, that would be suspicious."

"And did you ever get to speak to Lorraine in private, Mr. Eisenstein?"

"Never had a chance to. I dropped by on Saturday, but Lorraine was at the beauty parlor. And then I didn't see her again until the wedding. But it doesn't matter anymore. She told me all about the matter on Tuesday night—about how Florence had made her promise not to mention the wedding to me under any condition."

"And you don't find that odd?"

Fred rolled his eyes. "In hindsight, yes, I do, inspector. But at the time I didn't know about it, so obviously I couldn't have. Needless to say, Florence didn't mention her plans when I saw her on Saturday."

"Did you argue with Florence on Saturday, Mr. Eisenstein?

"Absolutely not."

"Did your aunt tell you that she'd broken her father's will?"

"No, she didn't. I only heard about that for the first time at the wedding—from Louise."

"Did she tell you that she planned to disinherit you?"

"No."

"Did she accuse you of being after her money all of these years?"

Fred jumped up from his box. "What's the meaning of this, inspector? Are you accusing me of murdering my own aunt? Because if you are, by your own admission I have a right to have an attorney present."

The rabbi smiled genially. "Calm down, Mr. Eisenstein. I'm not accusing you of anything at all. In fact, I can tell you that right now you are certainly *not* a suspect. I just wanted to know whether you would stick to your story under pressure. You see, Mr. Eisenstein, for one reason or another, your aunt told other people that you'd have a terrible row on Saturday and that she planned to disinherit you."

Fred Eisenstein sat down again. "So I've heard, inspector. But I assure you that I left my aunt's house on the best of terms with her. We were even planning a trip to the Museum of Natural History for later this month. My Aunt Florence loved the room with the stuffed birds. She was always begging me to take her to visit."

"Did you plan on taking Lorraine and Alfred Shingle with you to the museum, Mr. Eisenstein?"

"Of course, I planned on taking Lorraine. We always did everything together. But I didn't plan on taking Mr. Shingle, because I didn't even know he existed. I understand my aunt met him in January, when I was already in Europe, and she didn't even mention him on Saturday." Fred Eisenstein frowned. "I have to say it hurt me very badly, inspector, that my aunt would lie to me like that. It was a lie of omission, but it was a lie. Of course, I only stayed for twenty minutes or so, so I imagine it might have slipped her mind. I guess. I really don't know."

"You only stayed for twenty minutes?" the rabbi asked. "You didn't even wait for your Aunt Lorraine to return home?"

"I was nervous about the meeting with my potential investor and I wanted to get home to prepare for my meeting the next day. I can give you his name, if you'd like. But if at all possible, I'd prefer to keep him out of this. I don't want to scare him off. Okay?"

"We'll see," said the rabbi. "But there's no need to involve your investor *at the moment*, especially if you're forthright. Now you said you only stayed at your aunts' house for twenty minutes. What precisely did you do during that time?"

"We talked, inspector," replied Fred. "We sat in the drawing room and I told my aunt about my trip and then she talked about that sparrow hawk she'd seen on the Finchley property. I think she planned to go searching for it again Sunday. We didn't talk at all about wills or weddings or anything out of the ordinary."

"So let me see if I have this straight," said Rabbi Kappelmacher. "When you showed up at your aunt's wedding on Tuesday, you didn't know that Florence planned to disinherit you and you have no reason to believe that she'd broken the will."

"That's what I said."

"Incidentally, Mr. Eisenstein, how did you find out about the wedding?"

"I called Louise's house and the babysitter told me that they'd gone up to Pine Valley for a relative's wedding. I thought that sounded fairly odd, so I drove up to my aunts' place."

"You didn't think to call ahead?"

Fred shook his head. "I feared something must have been terribly wrong. I raced straight out the door and sped all the way to Pine Valley."

"And what happened when you arrived?"

"It was the strangest thing, inspector. I had absolutely no idea what to expect. I certainly didn't expect to interrupt my aunt's wedding. Yet I understand that she and the groom had just exchanged kisses when I arrived. I walked into the drawing room and asked Louise what in God's name was going on. The next thing I knew, Florence was charging past me up the stairs."

"That must have all been quite a shock to you, Mr. Eisenstein," the rabbi observed.

"I'll say it was. Alfred and I tried to coax her back down, but she'd locked herself in her bedroom. She wouldn't even speak to me. It was the same with Lorraine. I finally went downstairs to talk to Louise and she told me that Lorraine had also refused to return. When she heard my voice, however, Lorraine finally came to the kitchen to explain what was going on."

"And she told you about the disinheritance and the broken will?"

"She told me that I was being disinherited. She didn't tell me a thing about the broken will. I'm pretty sure she didn't even know about it. It was only later that Louise mentioned it to me. Over dinner, I believe. We went out for Chinese food with her husband. But anyway, I've never seen my Aunt Lorraine so upset. Apparently she'd been arguing with Florence all week long because Florence had gotten the notion into her head that I was after her money and had refused to invite me to the ceremony."

"You have no idea where she might have gotten that idea, Mr. Eisenstein?"

"Absolutely none."

The rabbi suddenly pushed an imaginary button in the air with his index finger. "Didn't you call Mr. Green's office on Thursday to ask about the inheritance, Mr. Eisenstein?"

"I might have."

"But why would you have done that if Lorraine had already told you that you'd been disinherited?"

Fred Eisenstein leaned against the window sill. I could see the frustration mounting in his features. "My Aunt Lorraine didn't say that I'd been disinherited. She said that Florence had announced that she planned to disinherit me. I told Green exactly what I'm telling you, inspector. I never had a fight with my aunt and I don't know why she planned to disinherit me or even if she actually would have gone through with it."

"But you admit that it was rather convenient for you that Florence died when she did," stated the rabbi. "Before she had an opportunity to alter her will."

"Florence didn't have very much money, inspector," said Fred. "You can't really believe I would murder my aunt over a few thousand dollars."

"I didn't say that, Mr. Eisenstein. As I told you, you are *not* a suspect—yet. However, by your own admission, you thought that you stood to inherit a large sum of money from your aunt. After all, at dinner your sister told you that Louise had broken the will."

"I guess," said Fred. "I really don't know."

The rabbi's third degree tactics were starting to frighten me. What would he do if Fred did consult a lawyer and subsequently discovered that there was no Inspector Kappelmacher at the F.B.I. posing as a rabbi in Haddam?"

"Do you know of anyone who might want you to be a suspect in your aunt's murder?" Rabbi Kappelmacher asked. "Any reason that someone might want it to look at though you killed your aunt?"

Fred looked confused. "So that's what this was all about, inspector?" he finally said. "You think somebody is trying to frame me?"

"I'm sorry I had to put you through that, Mr. Eisenstein," the rabbi apologized. "But I needed to hear your story in your own words. And yes, since you asked, I do believe it is possible that somebody is trying to frame you. Now please tell me if you can think of anyone who'd have a motive for doing that."

The rabbi's suggestion left our host looking distraught. "I can't imagine," he muttered. "Look, I wish I could help you. But I don't have the faintest idea who would want to frame me."

"I assume you're on good terms with your sisters, Mr. Eisenstein," said the rabbi.

Fred rubbed his face with his hands. "I'm very close to my sister, Louise, inspector. Gladys and I have had our differences. The truth of the matter is that I hardly even recognized Gladys on Tuesday. I hadn't seen or spoken to her in twenty-five years and, quite frankly, I don't particularly like her."

"And does she like you?"

"She was friendly enough this week, inspector. Yet I imagine not. We had a terrible falling out around the time that my father died, as I'm sure you already know. She ran off to San Francisco. I think with another woman. In any case, she said a lot of nasty things about my aunts and about Louise and me."

"You'll have to pardon me, Mr. Eisenstein," the rabbi interjected, "But what sort of things in particular?"

"Gladys said that Florence and Lorraine had murdered my grandfather, and that Louise and I were afraid to challenge Irving Eisenstein's will because we couldn't come to terms with the fact that our aunts were cold-blooded killers."

"And do *you* think your aunts murdered your father?"

"Are you out of your mind? Gladys was a screwed up kid. I imagine it wasn't easy for her being gay in our family. I know it wasn't easy for me. On top of that, she was into all sorts of drugs. Not just marijuana, but the hard stuff. I think she made up all that hogwash about my aunts for the attention."

"I see," observed the rabbi. "I have only a few more questions, Mr. Eisenstein. I promise. Then we'll get out of your hair. Could you tell me exactly what happened on the night that your aunt died?"

Fred returned to his box and rested one knee upon it. "Not much, in all honesty. When we returned from dinner, almost everyone had gone to sleep. Alfred and Cousin Agatha were sharing a snack in the kitchen, as I recall. Alfred apologized to us for Florence's behavior. To his credit, he didn't pass judgment on me despite all of Florence's accusations. He seemed to hope that she'd be more receptive to my presence in the morning. Then Agatha kissed me on either cheek, like she always does, and we all went to bed. It wasn't until the next morning that Louise woke me with the news. I'll never forget the scene in Florence's bedroom. Poor Alfred was on his knees at the foot of the bed crying and Dr. Scott was trying to console him. Lorraine was sitting in the corner, staring into space. And Florence's body was lying on the bed, just as they'd found it. I'll remember that moment for the rest of my life, inspector. Yet in the midst of all the chaos, Florence looked so peaceful...."

Fred Eisenstein brushed back his tears with his hand.

"I have only two more questions," said the rabbi. "First, did you leave your room between when you retired to bed and when Louise woke you in the morning?"

"As a matter of fact, I did," answered Fred. "We went up to bed around ten o'clock. Maybe twenty minutes later, I decided to go downstairs for a glass of warm milk. I drank my milk and then I went back upstairs and went to sleep."

"Did you encounter anybody else when you went down to the kitchen?" the rabbi asked. "Did you see your sister, Gladys, for instance?"

Fred shook his head. "I didn't see anybody."

"One final question. It appears that you knew your Aunt Florence rather well. Did she strike you as the sort of woman who would go bird watching the day before her wedding?"

"If you'd asked me two weeks ago, inspector, I would have said no. But I also would have laughed at the suggestion that Florence would get married. So I really can't tell you. I know she rarely missed a morning. She liked to stand across from the Finchley place and watch the birds on the neighbors' back porch."

"I see," observed the rabbi as he stood up. "Thank you very much for your time, Mr. Eisenstein. I'll ask you not to mention this conversation or my true identity to anyone. If you think of anything else, please don't hesitate to contact me at the Haddam Jewish Center. Just make certain you ask for Rabbi Kappelmacher or they might put you through to the real rabbi by mistake."

The rabbi smiled and shook Fred's hand.

"I can't imagine I'll think of anything, inspector," said Fred. "But if I do, you'll be the first to know."

When we were back outside, I noticed another glimmer in the rabbi's eyes.

"I liked him," I observed. "Did you really have to give him the third degree?"

"I had to figure out if he was telling the truth," answered the rabbi.

"And was he?"

"Use your rabbinic reasoning, Steinmetz," he urged.

"That's all you have to say?"

The rabbi led the way back to his car. "For your information, I happened to like Mr. Eisenstein too. Very much. But something is bothering me. I can't shake the feeling that there's something our friend, Fred, didn't tell us."

"Do you know what that something is?" I asked.

"Don't be a *dumkopf*, Steinmetz," replied Rabbi Kappelmacher. "If I knew what it was, it wouldn't be bothering me, now would it?"

CHAPTER 9: THE EVIDENCE OF THE BANKER

On the trip back to Haddam, we stopped for lunch in the Bronx at one of the rabbi's favorite Kosher delis. I ordered the brisket platter and the rabbi selected the tongue and pastrami combo. He took one bite of his sandwich and frowned.

"Life is strange, isn't it, Steinmetz?" he observed.

"How so?" I asked.

"Last week, if you'd asked me, I would have told you that this was the best sandwich in the entire world. A gift from God. Because in my limited world view, this was the best that I could think of. But when I started talking to Lorraine Eisenstein about the old neighborhood, I remembered how good the sandwiches are at Knobler's Deli. And now this sandwich just doesn't taste as good anymore. We should really go to Knobler's for lunch one of these days.

I smirked. "Maybe this is your punishment for lying to those poor people, rabbi. There's a commandment about lying, you know."

"There are different types of lying," retorted the rabbi. "Small lies are permissible if they expose a larger truth. That's in the Talmud, Steinmetz. In any case, it will please you to learn that we're done playing F.B.I. agents for the day."

Thank goodness for small favors, I thought. I took a bite out of my sandwich and watched the rabbi picking at his food. "Might I surmise, rabbi," I asked, "that we're on our way to see Gladys Eisenstein?"

"You may surmise as much as you wish," said the rabbi. "But if you used your rabbinic reasoning, you wouldn't have to surmise at all. We'll visit Gladys tomorrow. Today, we have more pressing matters to attend to. If we want to find

Andrew Sinkoff at home, we have to do it on the weekend. Besides, I also want to pay a visit to Mr. Shingle, and according to Green, he lives in a retirement development in the same neighborhood as the Sinkoffs."

The rabbi paid our bill and, twenty minutes later, we found ourselves at the home of our first victim. Ironically, the boy next door was throwing rocks at squirrels as we arrived. For the second time in three days, Rabbi Kappelmacher knocked at the Sinkoffs' door. This time, however, Andrew Sinkoff himself greeted us.

"You're the rabbis from Florence's funeral, aren't you?" he asked in surprise. "Is there something amiss?"

So he believes we're rabbis, I thought. Not F.B.I. agents. Rabbi Kappelmacher had been right that Louise wouldn't tell her husband about our visit.

The rabbi extended his hand. "Jacob Kappelmacher," he reintroduced himself. "This here's Rudolph Steinmetz. There's absolutely nothing amiss, but I was hoping I could borrow a moment of your time."

Andrew eyed us suspiciously. "This is rather a bad time, rabbi. My wife isn't feeling well today. Maybe if you came around later in the week, I'd have a few minutes."

The rabbi leaned forward. "Listen, Mr. Sinkoff. I'm here to help you, okay? I know all about your—shall we call them 'borrowing endeavors' at the bank. Now if you give me a moment of your time, I'm confident you'll want to hear what I have to say."

The banker's jaw tensed up when the rabbi mentioned the embezzlement. His attitude toward us underwent a one hundred eighty degree reversal. "Please come in, rabbi," he said, the confidence suddenly drained from his voice. "I'm sure we can clear up whatever misapprehensions you may have acquired about my work at First Consolidated."

The banker led us across the living room and through a set of French doors into a cozy, book-lined study. There were additional sculptures of a smaller dimension than the ones out front, displayed on a shelf under the window. A bear rug covered much of the floor and the head of the carpet seemed to be snarling at us.

Rabbi Kappelmacher held up a cigar and looked at our host for approval. To my surprise, Andrew Sinkoff retrieved a cigar case from his desk and opened it for the rabbi. "Cuban," said Sinkoff.

Now it was the rabbi's attitude that shifted: He thanked Sinkoff twice and then sniffed the Cuban cigar as though it were a fine wine. "Cuban indeed," said the rabbi. "And fresh."

Andrew Sinkoff lit a cigar of his own. "I have my sources," he said. "Now what can I do for you? I'm very concerned about what you mentioned earlier. Lies like that can destroy a man's career."

"I imagine so," said the rabbi.

"May I ask you, man to man, where you heard that lie?"

"You may ask all you wish," answered the rabbi. 'But I'm afraid that I'm not at liberty to tell you. You see I'm not actually a rabbi, Mr. Sinkoff. This is just a cover. I'm a private investigator."

Sinkoff nearly choked on his cigar. For my part, I couldn't believe that the rabbi was at it again—lying to these people without shame. I was also amazed, once again, at how easily people accepted his falsehoods.

"I think this is highly unreasonable," declared Sinkoff. "I let you into my home on the understanding that you were a rabbi and a friend of my aunt's."

"And also on the understanding that I knew about a certain problem you've had at the bank," replied the rabbi. "But please rest assured that I'm not here about whatever you've been up to at work. At least, not directly. That was just a pretext to steal a moment of your time"

"Well, you have it," said the banker. "Now what it is you want?"

The rabbi paused a moment to savor his cigar. "Let's just say that I believe my client and you may share the same interests."

"I doubt that," said Sinkoff. "What do I call you, by the way? You're not a rabbi...."

"I go by many names," answered the rabbi. "My real name isn't important to you. You might as well call me Rabbi Kappelmacher in case your wife overhears us."

Sinkoff nodded. "Well then, Rabbi Kappelmacher, I'd like to know who your client is and what his interests are?"

The rabbi shook his head. "I'm afraid I'm not at liberty to reveal the identity of my client. She—I mean my client—has her reasons for keeping her identity secret. What I can tell you is that my client has hired me because my client intends to try to break Irving Eisenstein's will, and my client suggested that you might have an interest in doing so as well."

Sinkoff appeared visibly more relaxed after the rabbi's explanation. "So Gladys hired a private dick," he mused. "You're working for Gladys, aren't you?"

The rabbi remained suggestively silent.

"So that's what this is all about," continued Sinkoff. "And here you have me hot around the collar worrying that you're going to expose me at the bank. Well, I tell you, Kappelmacher, I have bad news for both you and Gladys. That will is solid as the Rock of Gibraltar. When I first found out about it, I phoned a friend of mine at the trusts and estates division of a major law firm. He told me on good authority that Irving Eisenstein's will is constructed to fit precisely within the letter of the law. If you'll give me a moment, I can even look up the name of the case for you."

"*Evans v. Dodge*," stated the rabbi. "First Circuit Court of Appeals."

"Exactly," said Sinkoff, apparently impressed with Rabbi Kappelmacher's legal knowledge. "But if you already know about that, I don't see what I can do for you."

"My client knows that the will itself is legal. However, she believes that it was produced under duress. To put it in plain terms, Mr. Sinkoff, my client believes that Florence and Lorraine tricked their father into setting up those trust funds when his original intention had been to disinherit them entirely. My client also believes, and I must emphasize that she has significant new evidence to substantiate her claim, that Irving Eisenstein was murdered by his daughters."

Sinkoff took this lie in stride. "So Gladys is up to that old game again," he observed. "Louise has told me the entire story. As far as I'm concerned, Kappelmacher, I think it's a load of bunk. And even if it's true, what new evidence could possibly have come up after all these years?"

"I'm not at liberty to tell you that, Mr. Sinkoff. Not yet, at least. But I can assure you that it's highly favorable to my client. And to you, as well, if you're interested."

"You mean you need money," Sinkoff replied coolly. "Well, I'm sorry to disappoint you, Kappelmacher, but I'm overextended as is. Did you know that each of those bronzes," he added, pointing to the statues on the shelf, "sells for a hundred grand. In the long term, they're promising investments. In the short term, however, they're not easy to liquefy. So I hate to break it to you, Kappelmacher, but you're barking up the wrong tree."

Rabbi Kappelmacher tamped out his cigar in an ashtray and slid the remaining two thirds into his pocket. "I'm not after money, Mr. Sinkoff.   What I need from you is information."

"Information?"

"About the Eisenstein family. Fred and Louise have a vested interest in protecting their aunts, I suspect, even if it means withholding information from me and my client. Might I suggest that you're a man more likely to look out for your own best interests."

Sinkoff smiled. I believe he thought that the rabbi had paid him a compliment. "If all you want is information, I'll be glad to provide what I can. But I must warn you, Kappelmacher, that I hardly know the Eisensteins. Fred stops by now and again, but usually when I'm out. My wife's brother and I don't see eye to eye on very many things."

"You probably know more than you realize you do," observed Rabbi Kappelmacher.

"Maybe."

"People always know more than they think they do," said the rabbi. "Besides, I just want to confirm some details that I

already know. For starters, how long have you been married
to your wife?"

"Twenty-four years this coming April."

"And when did you first meet your wife's aunts?"

Sinkoff shook his head, as if to say, I told you so.
"Honestly, Kappelmacher. Last Tuesday, around one o'clock
in the afternoon."

"Do you mean to tell me that you'd never even met them
before that?"

"Never. We invited them to our wedding, but they didn't
come. Like I said, I won't be very helpful."

"*All* information is helpful," declared the rabbi.
"Sometimes, what somebody doesn't know is more
important than what somebody does know."

"I know what you mean, Kappelmacher," said Sinkoff.
"That's the way it is in business."

"So can I infer that you and your wife weren't
particularly close to your aunts?"

"You could say that. I'd nearly forgotten all about them."

"It must have surprised you when Florence called to
invite you to her wedding," suggested the rabbi.

"I admit it caught me off guard. I understand that
Florence wasn't in the best of health. Maybe she wanted to
make peace with her family before she died."

The simplicity of Sinkoff's explanation for the wedding
struck me as perfectly plausible, and I kicked myself for not
thinking of it. "You know," I said, "I think there's a lot to be
said for Mr. Sinkoff's explanation. I had an aunt of my own
who used to complain that she was on the verge of death all
the time. And every year, around her birthday, she gathered
her family together for one last reunion. As it turned out, she
lived to be ninety-four years old."

Rabbi Kappelmacher glowered at me. "I'm sure Mr.
Sinkoff has better uses for his time than to hear your
memories of your *meshuggah* relatives."

To my relief, Sinkoff interjected on my behalf. "That's
quite all right," he said. "I had an aunt of my own who could
be the same way. My father's sister.   The way she
complained, you'd have thought she was going to die on the

spot. And you know what? She lived well past one hundred."

"Anyway," the rabbi interjected irritably, "none of this is relevant to the business of my client. What I do need to know is exactly what your wife's aunt told you on the phone, Mr. Sinkoff. I understand that she told you that she'd broken her father's will."

"Correct. She said she'd broken the will, so she'd decided to get married. And would we be free to come around the house on the following Tuesday afternoon?"

"Now think hard, Mr. Sinkoff. Did Florence tell you *how* she'd broken the will? Or who had told her that she'd broken the will?"

Sinkoff shook his head. "I really don't remember. I think she might have said that she'd heard from her lawyers. That's Abercrombie and Green."

"She didn't happen to say if she'd spoken directly to Mr. Abercrombie or Mr. Green, did she?"

"I can't recall."

"And you didn't ask her about breaking the will? Weren't you at all curious?"

"No, I didn't. I'd just returned from out of town, and Louise wasn't feeling well that night, so the last thing I had time for was a conversation with some distant relative I couldn't have cared less about."

"You said your wife was sick, Mr. Sinkoff," observed the rabbi. "Sort of like she is today?"

Sinkoff clenched his jaw. "That's exactly right, Kappelmacher. I resent your tone. Are you accusing me of lying?"

The rabbi shook his head. "Of course not. I'm not in a position to accuse anybody of anything. But I was hoping you'd be more forthright with me. I am on your side, after all. You had a fight with your wife that night, didn't you, Mr. Sinkoff?"

"It had nothing to do with this, Kappelmacher," retorted Sinkoff. "It was about some prank phone calls we'd been receiving. I don't see what business that is of yours."

"Probably none at all, Mr. Sinkoff. But I have no patience for half truths. Yet you're quite right, Mr. Sinkoff. We have more significant matters to discuss—such as why you took off from work Tuesday for Florence Eisenstein's wedding."

"My wife insisted. We went up to that macabre old house around lunch time and we returned the following morning around eight. I had to go into the office early on Wednesday."

"You stayed the night at the Eisenstein place?"

"That's the way they wanted it, I believe. In any case, it was what Louise wanted. You probably know about Fred showing up and the commotion that followed."

"I do," said Rabbi Kappelmacher. "Did you leave the house at any time that night?"

"We had dinner with Fred at some restaurant in the area. It was Chinese food. I'll never forget it. Nothing sticks out in one's mind like bad Chinese food. It's a wonder people can live like that up in the suburbs. Personally, I'm a big fan of Harry Wok's. In Midtown. It's pricey, but it's worth it."

"I imagine so," said the rabbi. "After you returned from dinner, did you leave the house again until the following morning?"

"No. We went straight up to bed."

"And did you leave your room after that? To go to the bathroom maybe, or to fix yourself a snack?"

"No, I didn't. As I said, Louise and I went straight to sleep. What are you driving at, Kappelmacher?"

"You didn't hear anyone in the hallway later that night?"

Sinkoff scratched his head. "Come to think of it, I did hear something. We had a room at the top of the stairs, so everybody had to walk past us to go down. It was around ten thirty, maybe a little later. I heard footsteps in the passageway. I remember it because Louise said to me, 'Fred's probably raiding the kitchen for milk.' But I don't see what any of this had to do with breaking the will."

"Please bear with me," pleaded the rabbi. "I'm not at liberty to tell you that, but I assure you, it's important. For your sake as well as that of my client. Did you hear anything else that night?"

"Well, we heard Fred's footsteps headed in the other direction about twenty minutes later."

"You're certain they were Fred's?"

"No," Sinkoff replied irritably. "I'm not sure they were Fred's. I was half asleep as it was."

"Did you hear anything else?"

"Not a sound. I'm a light sleeper too, and those stairs creak terribly, so I imagine I would have heard if somebody else had headed downstairs."

"I see." The rabbi rubbed his beard, deep in thought. "How did you learn that Florence had died?"

"I think we found out when we went downstairs to leave. That fat woman, Agatha, was in the kitchen eating her breakfast and she told us. Then Louise insisted on breaking the news to Fred. We left half an hour later than I'd wanted to."

"You didn't stay longer on account of Florence's death?"

Sinkoff shook his head. "To what purpose? Louise wanted to, but we would have just been in the way."

"Did you know that Lorraine and Florence were involved in a legal dispute over their property line a number of years ago?"

"I can't say that I did."

"Did you know that Florence had dated a lawn chair magnate?"

"I think I might have known that, Kappelmacher. I really couldn't say for sure." Sinkoff folded his hands across his lap. "Are we almost through with this? I can't see how this is helping you or your client in any way."

"Very well," said the rabbi. "We won't take up any more of your time. Only one more question and we'll be on our way."

"Shoot."

"Mr. Sinkoff," the rabbi said, "my last question is about those crank phone calls you were receiving. Did you ever report them to the police?"

"No, we never did," the banker replied. "Louise was opposed to it. Now, if that's all, you'll have to excuse me. I have a golf date for three o'clock."

"Please give my regards to Mrs. Sinkoff," said the rabbi. "I hope she feels better. And on behalf of my client, I must ask you to keep our meeting a secret. As a quid *pro quo* for other secrets, if you understand my drift."

"I understand your drift very well," said Sinkoff.   He escorted us through the living room to the front door and closed it firmly behind us.

As soon as we were back in the car, I expressed my displeasure to the rabbi. "Was that really necessary?" I demanded. "You weren't dealing with Fred or Louise back there. That man's as shrewd as they come."

The rabbi ignored me. He sat at the wheel of the Cadillac staring straight ahead, oblivious to everything I had just said. Knowing his moods, I waited patiently while he immersed himself in thought. Ten minutes elapsed.   Suddenly—when I was starting to worry that he might be ill—he jumped up in his seat and pushed an imaginary button.

"You're an absolute genius, Steinmetz!" he exclaimed. "An absolute, first-class genius. I didn't know you had that in you."

"Had *what* in me, rabbi?" I asked. "What *are* you talking about?"

"I can't believe I didn't think of that."

The rabbi turned to me and I feared for a moment that he might kiss me to express his gratitude. "Now I understand what bothered me so much about our conversation with Fred.   I   think   we're   rapidly   approaching   a   rational explanation."

"What did I do, rabbi?" I asked. "Aren't you going to tell me what it was that you realized about Fred Eisenstein?"

The rabbi shook his head. "Not until I have more time to think it through. It is possible that I'm mistaken, after all. It has been known to happen on occasion."

I sunk back into my seat, highly disappointed at the rabbi's sudden secretiveness. Yet I knew there was nothing I could do to loosen his tongue until he was ready to share. I glanced at him periodically on the drive to Alfred Shingle's. When he saw me looking at him, he smiled and said, "You know, Steinmetz, I think you may make a satisfactory head rabbi after all."

CHAPTER 10: THE EVIDENCE OF THE HUSBAND

I was still wondering what I'd done to merit the rabbi's praise when we arrived at the retirement community where Alfred Shingle lived. Chateau Gardens was one of those self-contained communities where narrow lanes curved past identical bungalows in endless circles.

"So what are our secret identities now?" I asked. "You promised no more F.B.I. agents for the day, so are we still private investigators or do you have another surprise up your sleeve?"

"Steinmetz," answered the rabbi, "I have good news for you. I know this may come as a shock to you, but with Mr. Shingle, we're going to assume the most unlikely roles possible. We're going to be rabbis."

This news surprised me. I'd become so used to watching the rabbi in various guises that the thought of him actually identifying himself as a rabbi struck me as unusual. At the same time, I found myself more relaxed.

We walked up Alfred Shingle's front path and rang the bell. Several moments later, Florence's widower opened the door. He wore a three-piece suit and a bowtie, and he carried a paperback book under one arm.

"Oh, dear me," he said. "Rabbi Kappelmacher, right? And Rabbi Steinberg?"

"Steinmetz," I corrected him.

"That's right. Like my Cousin Esther's second husband. Well, this is a very unusual coincidence, I must say. I was just thinking about you, Rabbi Kappelmacher."

"Only good thoughts, I hope," answered the rabbi. "May we step inside for a moment?"

Alfred Shingle seemed genuinely delighted at the suggestion. "Why sure," he said. "Please do. You'll have to excuse me though, if the place needs some tidying. I wasn't expecting company and...well...Florence..." He swatted an imaginary fly with his hand to complete the sentence and led us into a stuffy parlor. Bookcases lined three of the walls; additional volumes were stacked on the coffee table. I glanced at some of the titles. *The Case of the Overzealous Undertaker. What the Cantor Knew.* All mysteries.

"As I said, rabbi," Alfred continued once we were ensconced on the sofa. "I was just thinking of you. Are you familiar with the Harry Kemelman mysteries?"

"Indeed, I am," declared the rabbi. I sensed that he was lying. "There's nothing like a good mystery novel to pass the afternoon."

Alfred Shingle beamed with delight. "I couldn't agree more. So few people feel that way these days, I fear. Everyone's reading true crime stories and legal thrillers. But give me an old-fashioned mystery any day, I say."

"And you said you were just thinking of me," the rabbi prodded him.

"Why, of course," answered Shingle. "Because of the Kemelman mysteries. I'm halfway through *Tuesday, the Rabbi Saw Red.* I've read all the other Rabbi Small mysteries, but the library acquired this one only last month. The new librarian also enjoys Jewish-themed mysteries."

I watched the rabbi's eyes widen as he realized that Harry Kemelman had written mystery novels about a rabbi. "I've always said that the job of a rabbi is very similar to that of a detective," he observed. "Both occupations involve solving puzzles. Of course, rabbis solve them for a higher purpose. But I must say, Mr. Shingle, that I share your fascination with mysteries. In fact, that's why Rabbi Steinmetz and I stopped by."

"A mystery aficionado is welcome in my home any day," Shingle replied warmly. "We have a club here at our complex, you know. We're small—only six of us, and that's if you include Mrs. Metzger, who has health problems of her own. I was always trying to talk Florence into joining us, but group discussions weren't for her. Maybe you'd like to join us one of these days. Every Thursday from noon to four.

Usually, we discuss books, but sometimes we have guest speakers. Rabbi Steinmetz is welcome too."

"I'd like that," said the rabbi. "I can't promise anything though. I look forward to the day I can retire, so I can read the whole day through without interruption. I imagine your late wife must have been an avid reader of mysteries too."

Shingle shook his head. "Poor, dear Florence," he said. "I miss her terribly. We all knew she was ill, but it happened so quickly. Yet the truth of the matter, rabbi, is that Florence didn't particularly care for mysteries. She preferred nature books. In fact, that's how we met. I was in the science section of the public library doing research on poisons because I thought I'd found a mistake in *What the Cantor Knew*. The author gets the symptoms of methyl-iodide poisoning all wrong. As soon as I saw Florence—she was carrying a stack of books—I knew she was the woman for me. It's funny how life works, rabbi. If I hadn't found that mistake in that book, I never would have gone to the nature room—and I never would have met my dearest Florence."

The rabbi smiled sympathetically. "I imagine Florence had other hobbies as well as reading. If I recall correctly, she always had an interest in birds."

"She did," Alfred replied dreamily. "Up with the dawn every morning. I used to make fun of her about it. I told her I hadn't planned on falling in love with a rooster."

"Her loss must be devastating," the rabbi observed. "I lost Mrs. Kappelmacher several years ago and I still haven't fully recovered."

"It's the mysteries that save me, rabbi," Shingle replied. "They keep my mind occupied. In any case, may I offer you a cold drink?"

I was about to accept when the rabbi answered no for both of us. "That's very kind of you, Mr. Shingle, but Rabbi Steinmetz and I must be on our way soon."

Shingle seemed mortally wounded by the thought that we might leave. "Please call me Alfred," he said. "And stay as long as you'd like."

Rabbi Kappelmacher leaned back in his seat. "As I was saying, Alfred, Rabbi Steinmetz and I stopped by because there are several small real-life mysteries we hoped you could clear up for us."

"Real life mysteries?" Shingle asked.

"Small puzzles," Rabbi Kappelmacher continued. "Regarding your late wife."

"Puzzles regarding Florence?" asked Alfred. "I'm not sure I understand you."

"I realize this is a difficult time for you, Alfred," Rabbi Kappelmacher said diplomatically. "I knew your late wife when she was younger and she was truly a marvelous woman. I can still picture her behind the counter at Eisenstein's egg creams. Even after I lost touch with her, I still thought about her—all these years. So, for my own peace of mind, I guess I hoped you could answer a few questions for me."

Shingle seemed to be on the verge of tears by the time the rabbi finished his eulogy. "Florence had that effect on many people, rabbi," he said. "When she agreed to marry me, I was the happiest man on the face of the earth."

The rabbi scratched his beard. "If I may speak plainly to a fellow mystery fan, Alfred, I can't help wondering how Florence decided whom to invite to your wedding. I guess I would have hoped that she might have invited me. I sent her a note shortly after Mrs. Kappelmacher passed away," he lied, "so I know she knew where to find me."

The widower's tone turned highly apologetic. "It was a very small affair, rabbi," he said. "Florence only agreed to marry me two weeks ago. On Tuesday afternoon. I'd been asking her since our second date, but there was that silly business about her father's will. As if my pension weren't enough to support us both. I didn't think she'd ever come around."

"I thought the will had been broken," said the rabbi.

"You're not the only one. Florence told all of her relatives that she'd broken the will as a way of convincing that to come to the ceremony. I guess she believed more people would want to attend to the wedding of a rich woman than a poor woman—or maybe she feared they'd try to talk her out of it. It really saddens me that the world has come to this. That a woman as wonderful as Florence had to lie to convince her own family to be present on the most important day of her life."

"I only wish I could have been there," said the rabbi. "So you don't believe that Florence actually thought she'd broken her father's will?"

Shingle shook his head decisively. "If she thought so, she never mentioned it to me. In fact, I was there when she made the phone calls and she rolled her eyes when she told them about breaking the will. That lawyer friend of yours called me to ask about all of this. I know he's a friend of yours, rabbi, so I'll hold my tongue. But would you believe the man didn't even offer his condolences?"

"I'd believe it," said the rabbi. "Green has a *gute neshome*, a good soul, but he can be thoughtless at times. I understand that *he* was invited to the wedding."

"Please don't take it personally, rabbi," pleaded Shingle. "It all happened so fast. Florence called up a handful of her relatives. I'm sure if we'd had a larger affair, she would have thought to call you. As it was, we didn't even invite my cousin Esther and her new husband. You don't happen to be related to him, do you, Rabbi? Marvin Steinmetz from Queens?"

"Not that I know of, Mr. Shingle," I said. "Probably at some point in the distant past."

"Most likely," Shingle said enthusiastically. "I should put you in touch with him, Rabbi Steinmetz. He's the only family I have left. My sister passed away last autumn. All of the other cousins died in the war."

"So it was only Florence's family at the wedding?" the rabbi prodded.

"That's right," answered Shingle. "The two nieces and Florence's cousin, Agatha. The nephew showed up uninvited."

"I understand that the late Mrs. Shingle had had a falling out with her nephew, Fred," said Rabbi Kappelmacher.

"Poor Florence," Shingle replied. "She wanted so much to have a peaceful wedding. Her nephew is a decent fellow, rabbi, don't get me wrong. But somehow Florence got it into

her head that he was after her money. She was an extremely
open-minded woman when making decisions, yet once she
decided upon something, she could be stubborn as a herd of
mules. I tried to reason with her. Her sister tried to reason
with her. But she was dead set against inviting him. To be
candid with you, rabbi, I don't know if I can forgive her
sister, Lorraine, for refusing to attend the wedding. A
nephew is family, but a *sister* is a *sister*. It nearly broke
Florence's heart."

"Don't be too hard on your sister-in-law," urged the
rabbi. "Surely, she must be suffering too."

"I know. And Florence did forgive her. She told me that
night before we went to sleep. But just because Florence
forgave her doesn't mean that I have to."

The rabbi waited while Alfred wiped his eyes. "There
are a couple of other things that I've been wondering about,
Alfred. You don't mind if I ask you, do you? I imagine it's
difficult for you to talk about."

"I like talking about it," Shingle replied. "I wish
Florence's family wanted to talk about it as much as you
do."

Rabbi Kappelmacher leaned forward to within inches of
the widower. "It would mean a great deal to me to know that
Florence still thought of me after all these years. Maybe not
often, but at least from time to time…."

"I'm sure she did," said Alfred. "We didn't talk much
about the past though. We tried to live our lives in the
present, especially after Florence took ill."

"Of course, of course. But I couldn't help
wondering….There was a photograph of you in Florence's
bedroom, Alfred. I noticed it when I came upstairs to bathe
my feet the other day. I wanted to see her room, you
understand. For closure. I couldn't help noticing that the
photograph had replaced another photograph. The one of
you was vertical. The previous photo had been horizontal. It
left an impression on the paint. I hate to ask you this, Alfred,
especially at a time like this, but the previous photograph
didn't happen to be a photograph of me, did it?"

Alfred smiled apologetically. "I really couldn't say. I remember the photograph of me, but I can't recall what was there before that. You're probably better off asking Lorraine. You really admired Florence, didn't you?"

"All these years," the rabbi lied. "There's only one other matter that has been troubling me, Alfred. It's the strangest thing too, but I have to ask you about it—mystery fan to mystery fan."

I shifted uncomfortably in my seat, fearing the worst. I'd noticed that Rabbi Kappelmacher had a tendency to save the least tactful questions for near the conclusion of our visits.

"The matter is this, Alfred," said the rabbi. "I shared a drink with Florence's cousin, Agatha, last Thursday on the way back from the Eisenstein house, and she told me—I know this sounds preposterous, but she insisted upon it—that she believed Florence had been murdered. Poisoned in such a way as to make it look like asthma."

"Murdered?" Alfred gasped. He appeared stunned. "That's the craziest idea I've ever heard….Hiram Scott said she died of asthma…."

"I told Agatha that Florence had died of asthma. Yet she insisted that your wife had been murdered by her niece. That is, by Gladys Eisenstein."

The widower slowly regained his composure. "Why would Gladys murder dear Florence?" he asked. "If anyone had a motive to murder my wife, it wouldn't have been Gladys. Why, they hardly know each other, rabbi. You can tell Agatha Grossbart to mind her own business. Murder! And I'd thought Agatha was such a delightful woman, too."

The rabbi seemed to sense Shingle's discomfort and he retreated quickly. "Maybe the mystery fan in me took over there for a second, Alfred. I'm sorry. Yet it was such a strange claim that I had to ask."

Shingle still seemed to be disturbed by the thought that his wife had been killed. "If anyone had a motive to murder Florence, it wouldn't have been Gladys. Maybe if you told me Fred had killed my wife—but Gladys?"

"Something about a grudge from the past," the rabbi explained. "Agatha said Gladys disliked Florence. Even hated her, as hard as that is for you and me to believe. Personally, I can't accept that anyone would think anything negative of the dear woman. But Agatha insisted that Gladys despised Florence and was after her money."

Alfred Shingle stared down at the coffee table. I believe that he was seriously reflecting on the possibility that his wife's niece had murdered her. "Can't be," he finally said. You learn a lot reading mystery novels, rabbi. You know that as well as I do. Gladys can't have poisoned Florence with a poison whose symptoms would be mistaken for asthma, if there actually is such a substance, rabbi. I'm certain of it. Can you use your mystery aficionado instincts and tell me why?"

The rabbi paused for a moment of thought. He rubbed his beard and he appeared to be in deep concentration. "I'm not sure," he finally said. "You're much better at this than I am, Alfred. Why?"

Shingle glowed at his own supremacy. "Why, rabbi? It's rather apparent. Because Gladys didn't know that Florence suffered from asthma. I was there when Florence phoned her niece and I'm sure she didn't mention it. In all fairness, *you* didn't know that—and I guess you couldn't have been expected to. So if this were a real murder mystery, rabbi, Gladys couldn't be a suspect. In fact, the only two guests who must have known about the asthma were Florence's nephew, Fred, and Agatha herself. Possibly your lawyer friend too, although I can't see what motive he would have had to kill my wife. So, even hypothetically, Gladys couldn't have poisoned Florence because she couldn't have known Florence was sick until she actually showed up at the wedding. My wife hadn't spoken to her in many years. She had to call information in San Francisco for the phone number."

Shingle seemed genuinely zealous in proving that Gladys hadn't murdered his wife. Yet after he finished his argument, an impressive one, I might add, he slumped back in his chair. "Forgive me, rabbi," he said. "I keep wishing this were a whodunit, but this isn't. Like I was telling you the other night, death doesn't seem as real in fiction as it does in life."

"How true," agreed Rabbi Kappelmacher.

Alfred Shingle had started to sob. "Please excuse me."

"That's quite all right," the rabbi replied. "Rabbi Steinmetz and I should be going now, in any case. But I promise we'll stop by again. Or at least I will. We'll have an opportunity to discuss happier matters, like the rabbi mysteries."

Alfred Shingle composed himself. "Please do stop by again," he urged us. "Remember Thursdays from noon to four. You're welcome any week. If I tell Mrs. Metzger you're coming, she might even bake us a cake...."

"Soon," replied the rabbi. He expressed his sympathies to the widower once again and we departed.

"So what did you make of that?" I asked the rabbi when we were back on the road, headed toward Haddam. "An odd old fellow, isn't he?"

The rabbi nodded. "Indeed he is."

"He does have an endearing quality to him though, doesn't he? And I have to admit that he really impressed me with that bit about how Gladys couldn't have poisoned her aunt."

Rabbi Kappelmacher scowled at me. "That impressed you, Steinmetz? I would have expected better from you. Reasoning like that may work in mystery novels, but it doesn't do any good in real life."

"You mean you think he's wrong about Gladys? You think she did poison her aunt?"

"I didn't say that either," said the rabbi. "Why can't you ever listen to me when I tell you anything. All I said was that Mr. Shingle's reasoning didn't make any sense. It was predicated on an entirely false premise: Namely, that the phone conversation Alfred was present for was the only phone conversation that took place between Florence Eisenstein and her niece. Did you ever consider that Gladys might have called back the next morning to solidify her travel plans? That she might have told Florence about her asthma then?"

I had to admit that the thought hadn't crossed my mind— and yet it sounded perfectly plausible. I was somewhat disappointed. For a short while, I'd believed that the rabbi had met his match.

"Are we going to visit Gladys tonight?" I asked the rabbi. "It seems that she's at the center of this mystery. If it is, in fact, a mystery—and not a wild goose chase."

"Not unless you want us both to get fired," the rabbi answered. "I still have to write my sermon for next week if I want Mrs. Billings to type it up on the computer in time. Tomorrow, we'll pay a visit to Gladys and see what we can learn. For tonight, I'm ready to go home and play rabbi for a while. I'd suggest you do the same. That lovely wife of yours is probably wondering what you've been doing with yourself all week."

For the first time in days, I now found myself wanting to proceed with our detective work. I guess I'd been bitten by the mystery bug. Although I didn't relish the lying or the risk of exposure, I was starting to enjoy the thrill of the chase. Comparatively, I feared, the life of an assistant rabbi was relatively mundane.

CHAPTER 11: THE EVIDENCE OF THE BLACK
SHEEP

That night I found myself unable to sleep. As much as I wished to fight it, the circumstances surrounding Florence Eisenstein's death were truly beginning to intrigue me. Some of the rabbi's so-called clues seemed far reaches to me—the photographs, for example, and Gladys Eisenstein's choice of seating at the *shivah* call. Yet other facts now appeared to me in a new light. I couldn't help wondering why Gladys left her room in the middle of the night or what Florence had been looking for when she went bird watching on the previous Monday morning. From the rabbi's questions, I inferred that he thought the case related in some way to events from the distant past, namely circumstances surrounding the death of Irving Eisenstein. That being the case, I couldn't wait for our meeting with Gladys. Whatever the rabbi's rational explanation might ultimately be, my instincts told me that this mousy woman would be at the center of it.

On Monday morning, after the *minyan*, we drove out to the Bargain Motel in Cedar Springs. It was exactly what I'd come to expect in discount motels: A concrete horse shoe surrounding a swimming pool, smack in the center of an interstate strip-mall. I had little difficulty imagining Gladys plotting her aunt's murder from within a sterile motel room. Cedar Springs struck me as just the sort of place to drive one to homicide.

"You're right about one thing," I observed to the rabbi. "Gladys is probably strapped for cash."

"As a young man, my father shared a bed in a tenement on Hester Street," Rabbi Kappelmacher replied. "He had the bed from eight a.m. to four p.m. Then one of the other tenants replaced him."

The rabbi left me to ponder his wisdom while he inquired at the front desk for Gladys. The desk clerk appeared reluctant to give out her room number, but the rabbi laid his religion on thick—made references to a fictitious ceremony, in fact—and the young man finally relented. We were soon standing in front of room 203.

Gladys answered the door wearing a sweat suit. The outfit added to the effect of her short-cropped hair and beak nose, creating the impression that she actually was a human mouse. If this was a cat-and-mouse game, I was thankful that I was on the rabbi's side.

"Yes?" Gladys asked. "Can I help you?"

She didn't appear to recognize us.

"I'm Rabbi Kappelmacher," replied the rabbi. "This here is Rabbi Steinmetz. We met last Thursday night at your Aunt Lorraine's."

Gladys nodded. "I believe we did," she said. I expected her to follow up on this statement, but she merely stood in the doorway and sniffed several times.

It was Rabbi Kappelmacher who finally broke the silence. "Rabbi Steinmetz and I were hoping we could have a word with you, Miss Eisenstein. It's rather important."

Gladys's expression remained impenetrable. "I don't think that's possible," she said. And then she shut the door in the rabbi's face.

"So much for the old rabbinic charm," I joked with the rabbi. "I don't think she likes us. So what do we do now? Do we sneak in through the window or do we tell her that we're F.B.I. agents and arrest her for concealing evidence?"

The rabbi did not find my remarks nearly as amusing as I did. He frowned at me. "Don't be a *kibitzer*, Steinmetz," was all that he said. He knocked on the door again. After an interminable wait, Gladys opened the door a crack and peered through the crack. She did not unlock the chain.

"I'll have to ask you to leave," she said, her voice icy and level. "If you don't, I'll have to ask the front desk to summon the police."

This time, before she could slam the door, the rabbi shoved his boot into the crack. "My good lady," he said in a friendly tone, "we've come about the will."

"The will?" Gladys Eisenstein's eyes narrowed.

"Your grandfather's will," the rabbi explained. "I have the evidence that can break your grandfather's will. Please give me twenty minutes of your time and I assure you that it will be worth your time."

"What sort of evidence?" Gladys demanded.

"You'll have to trust me. If you give me twenty minutes, I'll be glad to explain."

The mousy woman scowled. She drew her head back into the motel room and I heard her unlocking the latch. "Twenty minutes," she said. "But let me make myself clear. I don't like rabbis and I don't like organized religion and if you so much as mention a word about your damn God, you're out the door faster than you can say 'Jumping Jesus on a pogo stick.'"

"I will take that under advisement," replied the rabbi.

We entered Gladys's single room and I waited for my eyes to adjust to the dimly-lit interior. She motioned for us to seat ourselves in the two chairs by the window, settling herself on the bed and wrapping her arms around her knees. "Explain," she said, looking down at her watch. "Your twenty minutes have already begun."

The rabbi squandered one of our precious minutes scratching his beard. Then he rose and stood in the thin beam of light peeking around the window shades. "Miss Eisenstein," he said, "What I tell you now, I tell you in the strictest confidence. Rabbi Steinmetz here will deny that I ever said it and so will I. That being said, I've come to tell you that you were correct about the death of your grandfather."

"Excuse me?"

Gladys's indifference faded rapidly and the rabbi now appeared to have her full attention. He must have realized this, for he paused strategically.

"You'll have to explain yourself, rabbi," said Gladys.

The rabbi lit a cigar. Gladys Eisenstein sniffed, but she did not object. "As you may know, Miss Eisenstein," the rabbi lied, "I was your aunt's rabbi for many years. You may recall that she became quite religious for a period of time several years ago."

"I didn't know that," said Gladys. "What does that have to do with Irving Eisenstein's—my grandfather's—will?"

"It has come to my attention," Rabbi Kappelmacher continued, "that years ago, in an attempt to break your grandfather's will, you publicly accused your aunts of murdering your grandfather. You claimed that they tricked him into disinheriting your father and then poisoned him before he could change his mind."

"I was an angry kid," Gladys objected. "Those were groundless suspicions. I can't substantiate any of that."

"But *I* can," the rabbi retorted. "I can, and with your help, I will."

"Excuse me?" Gladys leaned forward and sniffed in the direction of the rabbi. It took all the forbearance I could muster not to offer her my handkerchief.

"You heard what I said, Miss Eisenstein. Florence called me on the morning of her wedding. After extracting from me promises of the strictest confidentiality, she confessed to me the entire plot. She told me that she and her sister had conspired to murder your grandfather and that they had indeed poisoned him. She feared that she was quite ill, you understand. She wanted to die with a clear conscience."

"You cannot be serious."

"I'm as serious as I could possibly be. Of course, I couldn't keep a secret like that, but I didn't have any proof other than her confession. I planned to pay her a visit on Wednesday and to implore her to go to the police. Of course, your aunt died before I ever had the chance."

Gladys appeared unsettled by the rabbi's lie. She pulled nervously at the cuffs of her sweats. "So you mean that my grandfather didn't intend to disinherit my father. Or me. Unbelievable! I never dreamed that day would come, rabbi. I only wish Amy had lived to see it."

"Amy?"

"My roommate, rabbi. In San Francisco. She was killed in a motorcycle accident earlier this month. But you can't imagine how happy this news would have made her. She always said that she'd thought we'd be rich someday."

The rabbi held up his hand. "Hold on a moment, Miss Eisenstein. I hate to put a damper on your enthusiasm, but you're not rich yet. You see, I have no way of proving that your aunts murdered their father. I have only Florence's word for it—and now she's dead."

"I thought you said that you had evidence," said Gladys.

"I deceived you somewhat, Miss Eisenstein," explained the rabbi. "I don't exactly have any tangible evidence—like a smoking gun. But I do know who can provide that evidence. In other words, I know who we can go to for proof that your aunts murdered your father."

"Who?" Gladys demanded. "Speak plainly, rabbi. I don't enjoy playing games."

"The person who can provide the evidence," the rabbi lied, "is the only other person who knows firsthand that your grandfather was murdered. Lorraine."

Gladys looked exceedingly displeased. "And how are you going to convince my Aunt Lorraine to confess to murder? I'd think she has every incentive not to—like the prospect of life in prison."

Rabbi Kappelmacher's eyes gleamed and I knew he was up to something out of the ordinary. "Miss Eisenstein," the rabbi observed, "I have reason to believe that your Aunt Lorraine didn't poison only your grandfather. I believe that she also murdered your Aunt Florence to keep her from confessing, only she did it one day too late."

For the first time in our encounter, Gladys appeared genuinely surprised. She twitched her nose from side to side nervously, as though unable to scratch an itch. "You think Aunt Florence was murdered?" she asked. "That's hard for me to believe."

"I have indisputable evidence."

"What evidence?"

The rabbi frowned. "That, Miss Eisenstein, I'm afraid I am not at liberty to share."

"May I ask why not?"

"You may ask," said the rabbi. "But once again, I'm afraid I cannot answer you. What I can tell you is this. If you'll let me, I'd like to ask you a few questions about the night Florence was murdered. You don't have to answer them, of course. You can tell me my time is up—what was it?—twenty minute?—and send me away. In that case, I'll forget about this whole business and go back to my synagogue. But if you'll cooperate, I think I may be able to prove that your aunts murdered your grandfather and that your Aunt Lorraine killed your Aunt Florence to keep her from revealing their secret. If I do, I'm sure Green can break Irving Eisenstein's will. And that, Miss Eisenstein, will make you a very wealthy woman."

It didn't take long for Gladys to make up her mind. "I'll make you a deal, rabbi. If you let me ask two questions of my own, then I'll let you ask me anything you'd like. Of course, I reserve the right not to answer—but I'll try to be as cooperative as possible."

"Very well," agreed the rabbi. "Ask away."

'First, what do you get out of this? I know enough about the world to know that nobody does anything for nothing."

The rabbi smiled. "Indeed, Miss Eisenstein. I understand that people exist who feel that way. For my part, there are still some puzzling aspects of your aunt's death which intrigue me. I dislike unsolved mysteries, my dear lady. Our ability to explain all phenomena rationally is the only proof of an omniscient and omnipotent God. So that's one reason why this matter interests me....Of course, I also have more worldly interests to consider. Maybe a few thousand dollars to the synagogue if you do succeed in breaking the will?"

Gladys nodded. "Okay, okay. One more question. Why me? Why not Fred or Louise or Agatha?"

"Why, Miss Eisenstein? Because I knew you'd believe me—and I doubted they would. Agatha told me all about your earlier attempt to break the will and how the family reacted. Incidentally, she believes *you* poisoned your Aunt Florence."

"Does she?" mused Gladys.

"She thinks you held a grudge against Lorraine and Florence all these years and, believing the will had been broken, you poisoned your aunt on the night of the wedding. We, of course, know better. Which leads me to my first question, Miss Eisenstein. Where did you come up with the idea that your grandfather had been murdered?"

"What do you mean by that, rabbi?"

"Let me put it a different way. What exactly happened twenty-five years ago that led to your rupture with your family?"

Gladys gritted her teeth. "I'd really rather not talk about this, rabbi."

The rabbi stood up. "Come along, Rabbi Steinmetz," he said. "We can tell when we're not wanted."

The rabbi had already opened the door to the room when Gladys called us back.

"All right. I'll tell you. But it was a long time ago, so I may not get all the details right. Dates and places and such. It was actually my friend Amy who suggested the idea to me. We were talking one day—it must have been in the neighborhood of my grandfather's shop, maybe at Ratner's or Knobler's Deli—and she said that she couldn't believe my brother and sister and I had taken our father's disinheritance sitting down. She wanted me to hire a lawyer."

"You needed money?"

"Who doesn't? But yes, we were involved with certain organizations desperately in need of funding. The Radical Education Project of Students for a Democratic Society was our primary concern that year. We were going to send missionaries to Guatemala to organize the peasants. Eventually, we did raise the money—nearly $30,000—but the missionaries vanished into the countryside and were never heard from again."

"So you decided to try to break your grandfather's will," Rabbi Kappelmacher suggested.

"Exactly. As I said, it was Amy's idea. I hired a lawyer on contingency and tried to recruit Louise and Fred into the effort. I knew my parents wouldn't want to rock the boat— even if the money were rightfully theirs. As it turned out, my brother and sister were afraid of offending my aunts. Why, you ask? Because that was back when it still seemed likely that either Florence or Lorraine, or possibly both, would marry. When one sister married, the other one became a very rich woman. Or, to be more precise, a woman likely to leave a hell of a lot of money to her nieces and nephew. So I went after the will on my own, rabbi."

The rabbi nodded. "You still haven't told me where you came up with the notion that your grandfather had been murdered."

"It's hard to say," replied Gladys. "I believe it was Amy who first suggested the possibility as a joke. But I started thinking about that strange will and his sudden death—and I connected the dots. You know my grandfather died only two weeks after he wrote that will."

"Indeed," said the rabbi. "I did *not* know that."

"They said it was a heart attack, but they said everything was a heart attack back then. So I asked Aunt Florence. I didn't accuse her. I just suggested the possibility that my grandfather's death hadn't been the result of natural causes. And there was something in her response that convinced me. I can't explain it. Just something in the way she told me to forget about it that made me know for certain. Of course, I couldn't prove it. The lawyer I hired on contingency turned out to be practicing law without a license. He'd been disbarred or something. So I threw it all to the wind and moved out to San Francisco with Amy—and that was that."

"And all this time you believed that your grandfather had been murdered?"

Gladys shook her head. "After a while, I didn't think much about my family at all. Amy was my family. I found a job at the Arts Center and I blocked out all thoughts of egg creams and Pine Valley and even the will. Life goes on, so they say."

"It must have shocked you when your aunt called to invite you to her wedding," said the rabbi.

"Very much so. I don't even know how she tracked me down."

I wondered where the rabbi was headed with these questions. I couldn't understand why he'd given Fred the third degree and was now treating Gladys with kid gloves. I looked tentatively at the rabbi and said, "May I ask a question?"

"Sure," Gladys agreed.

The rabbi emitted an unnatural cough. I could tell that I'd made a mistake, but it was too late to retreat. I didn't want to lose face. "Miss Eisenstein, if you disliked your aunts so much, why did you fly all the way out here from San Francisco for Florence's wedding?"

Our host suddenly grew defensive. "What do you mean by that?" she demanded.

The rabbi came to my rescue. "Rabbi Steinmetz can be abrasive, Miss Eisenstein, but he didn't mean any harm. He does raise an important question. When you came out here for the wedding, did you still believe, in the back of your mind, that your grandfather had been murdered? Because if you did, you may have inadvertently hinted as much to your Aunt Florence. In other words, you may have prompted her confession to me."

Gladys bit her lip. "I hate to admit it, rabbi, but I don't think I was the impetus for her confession. In the first place, I'm sure I didn't mention her father's death to her. I was trying especially hard not to stir up old troubles. Besides, I didn't show up at the house until lunch time. You said Aunt Florence called you in the morning."

"Indeed," said the rabbi. "You're one hundred percent correct. What could I have been thinking? Anyway, where were we? So you came to the wedding because you knew Florence was sick and—"

"I never said anything of the sort," Gladys retorted. "I hadn't the faintest idea that Aunt Florence was ill until she told me on Tuesday. I came to the wedding because Aunt Florence told me she'd broken the will. That's the only reason. I wanted my fair share of the money and I expected that, despite what had happened in the past, I might still inherit if I coddled up to my aunts. That's the real reason I came, rabbi. The *only* reason. Of course, it turns out that

Florence hadn't broken the will and that I'll be lucky if I make two grand. And you know what, rabbi? I don't think Lorraine likes me very much. I'm not even sure if I'm going to get anything when *she* dies. Unless I can break that will, I'm probably out of luck."

I wondered whether Gladys was lying or whether she really didn't know that she was a beneficiary of Lorraine's will.

"I assure you that we can break the will," said the rabbi, "and that we *will* break the will. Now I want you to try to remember exactly what happened on the day of Florence's wedding."

"Well, like I said, I arrived around noon. My plane landed at nine thirty, but it took forever to arrange for the rental car."

"Did you stop to check into your motel?"

"No, I didn't. I didn't plan on staying at a motel. I planned to stay in Pine Valley for my entire trip. But after Florence died, Aunt Lorraine made it clear that she couldn't handle having all of us falling over each other, by which she meant that she wanted me to leave—because everybody else intended to leave anyway. But I was gracious about it. I moved in here on Wednesday afternoon and now it looks like I'll be here at least through next weekend on account of the will. My original plan was to leave yesterday, but I had to change my ticket."

"Certainly," observed the rabbi. "Did you speak to your Aunt Florence at the wedding? Did she say anything to you that indicated she thought her sister might be trying to kill her?"

Gladys shook her head. "We must have talked for three hours, but she hardly mentioned Lorraine. As difficult as it was for me to believe, she was much more interested in hearing about my life in California. Of course, Lorraine wouldn't come downstairs for the wedding. That was a bit suspicious, I think."

The rabbi took several puffs on his cigar. "I have a difficult question for you, Miss Eisenstein. Did you have the impression that your Aunt Florence didn't want you to speak to the other guests at the wedding? Think hard."

Gladys tugged at her shirt cuffs. "Not at the time. But now that you mention it, she did corner me when I first showed up and she dragged me away when I tried to speak with Louise. Why? I'm not sure how that can matter?"

"Nor am I," said the rabbi, "but we'll find out soon enough. Now I understand that your sister and brother-in-law dined with your brother that night. Did you join them?"

"No. I'd had enough socializing for one day. I stayed back at the house and read a magazine. *Modern Photography*. That's my thing these days. I took a class last year at a local college and now I'm getting pretty good at it."

"Did you experience anything out of the ordinary that night, Miss Eisenstein?" the rabbi asked. "Perhaps you went down to the kitchen for a snack and heard something unusual?"

Gladys sniffed and poked her nose forward. "I can't say that I did," she said. "I fell asleep reading in bed and I didn't wake up until Louise came in to tell me about Aunt Florence. I'll be glad to lie about it on the stand though, if you think it will help out case."

"That won't be necessary," Rabbi Kappelmacher assured her. "As a religious man, I wouldn't be able to condone that sort of lie. In any case, I'm confident we'll have the truth soon enough."

"When will you present your evidence to the lawyers?" asked Gladys. "I'm hoping to leave town by next weekend. I need you to set a date, rabbi. Soon enough isn't good enough where this much money is concerned."

The rabbi stood up and walked toward the door. I followed. "I'll be in touch," he said curtly. "Sometime next week. You have my word upon it. Maybe we can even have lunch at Ratner's or Knobler's Deli. My taste buds have been craving the old neighborhood all week."

Gladys Eisenstein seemed on the verge of responding, but she didn't say a word. Not even good bye. Yet her mousy face was still visible at the crack in the door when we drove off.

"Well?" I asked the rabbi.

"Well, what? I'm a rabbi, not a mind reader."

"Well, what did you think? Did she suffocate her old aunt or didn't she?"

The rabbi scratched his beard. "I think, Steinmetz, that was one of the strangest women I've ever encountered."

"At last, something we can agree upon," I said. "She reminded me of a mouse."

"Did you notice how she kept stalling when I asked her why she first thought her grandfather had been murdered? It was as though she didn't want to tell us the real story, and she needed time to make something up."

"She did stall a lot," I concurred. "Do you think there's something she's not telling us?"

"Time will tell," muttered the rabbi. He appeared to be lost in thought again and I dared not interrupt him.

"That was a great story you made up," I finally said to break the silence. "About Florence's confession and Lorraine's killing her to keep her quiet."

The rabbi didn't answer me.

"You did make that up, didn't you?"

Rabbi Kappelmacher turned and flashed me a look that conveyed the impression that he thought I was out of my mind. "What kind of *dumkopf* are you, Steinmetz? Of course, I made that up. Why is it you believe everybody except me? I already told you that I'd never seen the woman in my life. Now if I'd never seen the woman in my life, how could I have been her rabbi? And as for Lorraine murdering her sister to keep her from confessing, that's one of the stupidest ideas I've ever heard. Only a woman like Gladys Eisenstein—a woman already predisposed to suspicion and hatred—would believe it. Think it over. On top of all that, the cock-eyed story I provided to that strange woman doesn't offer a rational explanation for anything. We still don't know why Florence suddenly decided to get married or what prompted her to decide to disown her nephew or what happened to those photographs. So stop being a *noodnik*, Steinmetz, and start thinking."

I could tell that the rabbi was angry. He often pokes fun at me, but he rarely lets forth his wrath at me like that. I hoped that he wasn't upset about the question I'd asked Gladys Eisenstein.

"I'm sorry, rabbi," I said. "I can tell you're mad. I didn't mean to interfere with your questioning back there."

To my surprise, the rabbi smiled at me. "No big deal, Steinmetz," he said. "I should apologize for snapping at you just now. It's only that I hate being deceived."

"Who deceived you?" I asked. "Do you think mouse woman is lying to us?"

The rabbi shrugged. "I don't know. But somebody is lying to me, Steinmetz. Because either Gladys Eisenstein left her bedroom in the middle of the night on Tuesday or she didn't. Either Gladys or Agatha is lying."

I hadn't thought of it in just that way, but I had to concede that the rabbi had a point. One of these two women was lying. I suspected that when Rabbi Kappelmacher figured out which one, then he'd have his rational explanation—and possibly his murderer.

CHAPTER 12: THE EVIDENCE OF THE SISTER

The rabbi remained in an irritable mood as we headed north on the now familiar route to Pine Valley. "Steinmetz," he said, "I have a terrible feeling about all of this. Call it rabbinic instinct, but I can't help feeling there's a rational explanation right under our noses. I just hope we find it before our killer strikes again."

"Again?" I asked. "You don't think that's really going to happen, do you?"

The rabbi frowned. "Once a killer, always a killer. If you're willing to murder one person, you're probably willing to murder several more if it suits your interests. That's why God punished Cain for slaying Abel. I only wish the Eisenstein family would take this matter more seriously and stop lying to me. One of them is liable to get killed."

I digested this sobering prediction. "You still think that Lorraine was the intended victim, don't you?" I asked.

"I think, Steinmetz," replied the rabbi, "that if any of those relatives found out that the will hadn't been broken, then they had every motive to murder Lorraine and none at all to murder Florence. I can only hope that Lorraine takes my concerns more seriously than her nephews and nieces."

Rabbi Kappelmacher's somber tone sent a shiver down my spine. I could easily imagine the mousy Gladys returning to the house to murder Lorraine. I could also picture the blind niece murdering the wrong aunt by mistake. Even Fred, behind his good-natured bohemian charm, struck me as a fellow capable of treachery. In any case, my own instincts told me that the rabbi was right and that Lorraine's life was still in danger. I was lost in these fears when we pulled onto the gravel lane leading to the Eisenstein estate.

Mrs. Finchley raised her glass of lemonade as we passed. The rabbi waved in response. Then, for the second time in five days, we walked around the side of the Eisenstein house and the rabbi rapped on the kitchen door.

"Coming!" a voice called from inside. We heard the creaking of floorboards and the shuffling of feet. "I'm coming!" The door opened inward all of a sudden and we stood face to face with Lorraine. She wore mud-caked overalls and a sleeveless blouse—a far cry from the more formal attire of our previous visit. It was clear that she'd just returned from the garden.

"Rabbi," she said in apparent surprise. "Oh, it's so good to see you."

"I'm sorry to disturb you," responded Rabbi Kappelmacher. "We were in the neighborhood...."

"I was actually just thinking about you," said Lorraine. "It was so nice of you to come the other evening and I never had a chance to thank you."

She beckoned us into the house.

"I can't help but wonder what brings you up to Pine Valley," Lorraine observed once we were seated around the coffee table. "This isn't exactly the center of the universe."

The rabbi removed his cigar from his pocket and glanced at Lorraine for approval. She disappeared into the library and returned with an ashtray. "My father used to smoke," she explained. "You remind me a lot of Rabbi Stern, rabbi. He's such a wonderful man. Do you know him?"

"I have not had the honor," said Rabbi Kappelmacher. "I imagine Rabbi Stern must be the man who performed Florence's marriage ceremony."

"No, no," Lorraine replied. "For some reason, Florence wouldn't hear of it. She wasn't right in the head those last few days. She insisted upon calling up some rabbi she found in the phonebook. I didn't meet him, of course. But my nephew told me all about him—how he took fright when Fred showed up and made a quick exit. I can't imagine Rabbi Stern abandoning a family like that in a time of crisis. Nor can I imagine you behaving with such indecency. I guess they don't make rabbis like they used to."

"I guess not," the rabbi agreed. "But I have to level with you, Miss Eisenstein. I'm not a rabbi."

"Not a rabbi?" Lorraine drew her fingertips to her mouth in surprise.

"That's correct, Miss Eisenstein. I'm not a rabbi, although I sometimes wish that I were. I'm actually an F.B.I. agent. Inspector Jacob Kappelmacher. And this here's Inspector Steinmetz with our Undercover Division."

"Dear me," muttered Lorraine.

"I've come to speak with you about a very serious matter, Miss Eisenstein," the rabbi continued. "A matter of life and death. It is my belief—or rather, the agency's belief—that your sister, Florence, may have been murdered."

"Gracious," exclaimed our host. The color drained from her face. "Murdered? But Dr. Scott said...."

"I know what Dr. Scott said," said the rabbi. "I also know that your sister didn't die of asthma. I believe she was suffocated with a pillow."

"Dear, dear me," Lorraine repeated.

"Your sister may have had an asthma attack on Tuesday night," noted the rabbi, "but it wasn't fatal. It is my firm belief that after her husband left to fill her prescription, somebody—one of your guests, I'm afraid to say—sneaked into her room and suffocated her to death."

"Good heavens, rabbi. I mean, inspector. I don't think I understand. Why would anyone want to murder Florence?"

The rabbi combed his beard with his fingers. "Do *you* have any idea why somebody might have wanted to murder your sister?"

"I can't imagine. You don't think—? On account of the money...But that can't be, inspector. You do know, don't you, that Florence gave up her portion of the inheritance when she married Alfred."

"But your relatives didn't know that, Miss Eisenstein. They thought she had broken your father's will."

"I just can't believe that, inspector. We're not a very close family, by any means, but we're also not the sort of people who would kill one another...."

Rabbi Kappelmacher sighed. "There is another possibility, Miss Eisenstein. I regret having to share this with you, because I know you're experiencing some difficult times. Yet under the circumstances, there is no alternative. Miss Eisenstein, prepare yourself for a shock. I believe it possible that one of your relatives murdered your sister by mistake."

"By mistake?"

"Yes, by mistake. I believe that *you* may have been the intended victim and that the murderer mistook your sister for you in the dark. And if that is the case, Miss Eisenstein, I fear that your life may still be in danger."

Lorraine stared at the rabbi as though he had lost his mind. She repeatedly opened her mouth as though to speak and then shut it again. Finally, her voice wavering, she said, "It's hard to believe that somebody would want to kill me."

"I'm not sure of anything yet, Miss Eisenstein, but it certainly is a strong possibility. I assure you that if this is the case and one of your relatives was trying to kill you, I will do everything in my power to prevent them from succeeding in the future."

"Dear, dear me," was the only reply from Lorraine.

"Now, Miss Eisenstein," the rabbi continued, "I'm hoping that Inspector Steinmetz and I can ask you a handful of questions that may aid us in our investigation."

Lorraine nodded.

"I want to emphasize that your honesty is absolutely necessary, my dear lady. Lives are at stake. Please don't try to protect anybody and don't hold anything back."

"Of course," she agreed.

"Now, Miss Eisenstein," the rabbi proceeded, "I need you to tell me candidly about the events leading up to Florence's death. About her marriage, about her plans to disinherit her nephew, basically about anything that she did in the last six months that struck you as being out of the ordinary."

The spinster offered a thin smile. "I'll try, inspector. As best as I can. But there was so much out of the ordinary and it's all so confusing....I'm not even sure where to begin."

"Take your time," Rabbi Kappelmacher soothed her. "Begin at the beginning. You told me that your sister met Mr. Shingle at the library about six months ago."

"That's right," Lorraine agreed. "He walked up to her and told her that she was the most beautiful woman in the library and asked if she'd like to join him for a cup of coffee. Of course, I was there with her, so he took us both out to lunch at the Pine Valley Café—but from the outset, it was clear that he had his eye on Florence."

"He wanted to marry her, in fact," prodded the rabbi.

"So Florence told me. But there was the will to consider, you understand. Florence and I tried not to discuss the will. It was the only point of contention that ever existed between us. Not that we actually argued about it or anything like that, but it made us both uncomfortable. I thought we should make a pact that if one of us ever married the other would agree to share the inheritance—outsmarting the will, I liked to call it—but Florence was vehemently opposed. The law was the law as far as Florence was concerned—although I honestly think that was partially an excuse on her part...either to avoid marriage or because she was superstitious about challenging Papa's wishes. If I'd been able to break the will legally, I would have—but Florence was always more reluctant, especially when we had more than enough money to live on. As you must know, our stipends only continue until we marry. Florence was nervous about marrying Alfred and losing her allowance, even though I'd pledged to support her out of the inheritance."

"But she did marry him," said the rabbi.

"Yes, eventually she gave in. Alfred doesn't know about my promise to support her if his pension didn't prove enough, so please don't tell him. My brother-in-law can be a fiercely proud man and I'm sure he wouldn't have tolerated such an arrangement. But maybe Florence did tell him. She was acting so strangely at the end, I suppose anything is possible."

"What do you mean, Miss Eisenstein?"

"It was dreadfully odd, inspector. First, there was that business with our Cousin Agatha that I told you about. That was right around the time Florence took ill. And then there was her decision to disinherit poor Fred. You should have seen her on Saturday afternoon when I returned from the beauty parlor. She wasn't herself. She kept cursing Fred for wanting her money and cursing our father for writing the will—and I imagine you know about the business with the photographs."

Now we seemed to be making progress. The rabbi punched another imaginary button with his index finger. "What photographs?" he asked.

Lorraine appeared surprised that he didn't know. "Why the photographs of our father. The one in the parlor and the one upstairs in her bedroom. I thought you knew. Florence insisted that I take down all the photographs of our parents and lock them away. She made it clear that if I didn't, she intended to destroy them. She kept blaming him for wasting her life and insisted that she never wanted to lay eyes upon him again. I've been meaning to put them back up, but I haven't gotten around to it yet."

"When did Florence do this?"

"It must have been on Sunday or Monday. Let me think. No, I'm sure it was Monday. The day before Florence passed on. She came back from bird watching and announced that all the photographs of Papa had to go."

"Indeed," declared the rabbi. "So this was after her alleged argument with Fred."

"Definitely," Lorraine said. "We had a terrible row about Fred on Sunday afternoon—the first argument we'd ever had in all these years—and I remember I was about to apologize to Florence in the hope of working things out. I'd had a night to reflect on things, you see. I thought maybe I could gradually convince my sister to yield. But then she started in on the photographs, and I began to fear that she just wasn't right in the head, if you know what I mean."

"I see," mused the rabbi. He tamped out his cigar. "Was your sister prone to such behavior, Miss Eisenstein? Had she ever done anything like this before?"

"That's just the thing, inspector. It was so out of character for her. Florence was one of the most agreeable women you could ever have met. It was more the type of behavior you would have expected from Isaac."

"Your late brother?"

Lorraine nodded. "Isaac was always doing things on impulse—like marrying that dreadful *shiksah*. Florence and I are much more cautious. Or I guess I am. Florence isn't here anymore. Sometimes, I forget that. I imagine that I'll come downstairs in the morning and she'll be sitting at the kitchen table with her binoculars around her neck."

At that moment, the phone rang. It was an old-fashioned rotary telephone of the type now found only in museums. Our host answered it. "Mr. Abercrombie?" she said. "Oh, dear me....I see, I see....Yes. Five o'clock is just fine....Thank you, Mr. Abercrombie." Lorraine hung up the phone.

"That was just Mr. Abercrombie from the lawyers," she explained. "He needs me to sign more paperwork regarding my father's will. It's all so complicated. More papers every day. And the strange part of it is that I don't even want the money that much. I'm happy here. It's not worth the hassle."

The rabbi smiled. "That's a noble sentiment, Miss Eisenstein," he said. "I'm afraid other people aren't as indifferent to money as you are. It's amazing what people will do for the smallest sum. But where were we? Would you mind if we took a tour of the house, Miss Eisenstein? I'd like to see your sister's bedroom and I'd like to take a look at the guest wing."

"If you wish," agreed Lorraine.

She led us up the right-hand staircase and pushed open the door to her sister's bedroom. Florence's wedding dress still hung on the back of the door. Someone had opened the window, but otherwise the room remained exactly as we'd seen it the previous day.

"I take it that this is where your sister died," said the rabbi.

"That's right."

"And you found her?"

Lorraine nodded. "I felt so awful about what had happened that I couldn't sleep. I was hesitant about waking Alfred, but I needed to speak to Florence. We often stayed up late into the night talking, you understand. Sometimes,

I'd sit at the foot of her bed and we'd reminisce about the old times. But that night I wanted desperately to go to sleep with a clear conscience." Lorraine paused and wiped her eyes. "I wanted so much to apologize—to be sisters again. We'd never fought before, inspector. It was too much for me. So I knocked on the door. When there was no answer, I pushed it open and tip-toed into the room. I wanted to wake Florence without disturbing my brother-in-law. But Alfred wasn't there and Florence...."

Lorraine Eisenstein burst into tears. The rabbi assisted her to a chair in the corner. "I'm sorry," she kept repeating between sobs.

"That's quite all right," replied Rabbi Kappelmacher. He left the old woman momentarily and peeked into the walk-in closet. Then he peered through the open window. "Only a few more questions, Miss Eisenstein. I wouldn't ask but there's your safety to think of. On the night of Florence's death, did you hear or see anything unusual?"

Lorraine paused as though she were trying to remember. Then she shook her head vigorously. "Not that I can recall."

"No strange sounds, Miss Eisenstein? Possibly the sound of somebody hiding in the closet?"

"Definitely not. Except for Florence's being that way, nothing was at all out of the ordinary."

"And when you found Florence, you phoned Dr. Scott?"

"No, inspector. Not for a couple of minutes. I was in shock. It wasn't until Alfred returned from the pharmacy that we called the doctor. Or Alfred did. I didn't have the wherewithal to do anything."

"Understandably," said the rabbi. "Incidentally, Miss Eisenstein, when was the last time you actually saw your sister alive?"

"Tuesday morning at breakfast," Lorraine replied. "I'll never forget it, because we didn't speak. We'd had another argument about Fred on Monday night, and we just sat there at breakfast and stared at each other. It was awful. If only I had said something, inspector....If only...."

"Did your sister go bird watching on Tuesday?"

"No," replied Lorraine. "I don't believe so. Why do you ask?"

The rabbi laid his cards on the table. "I'm not exactly sure, Miss Eisenstein. It just strikes me as odd that your sister would go bird-watching on the day before her wedding. I think it's just possible that she may have been looking for something else other than birds."

Lorraine shrugged her shoulders. "Maybe, inspector. I really don't know. You've told me so many things this afternoon that I never would have believed that I guess anything is possible." The spinster stood up and wiped her hands on her overalls. "Would you like to see those other rooms?"

"We retreated downstairs and walked up the opposite staircase into a slightly wider passageway. The layout was similar to that of the corridor on which the sisters lived, except that there were five doors opening on the hallway instead of two. All five doors stood along the far wall. There was also a bathroom to the left of the stairs.

The rabbi poked his head into the bathroom. I looked over his shoulder. It contained an old toilet and a sink, but no bathtub. "Miss Eisenstein, I have an odd question for you. Where did your guests bathe?"

"They used the bath next door to Florence's room. It's the only working bath in the house."

"So each of your relatives must have been up to that bath on the night of Florence's death."

Lorraine thought for a moment. "I don't think so. I remember Cousin Agatha insisted on a bath before she went to bed, but I don't think the others bathed that night. I'm not certain, of course. But I believe that my niece, Gladys, took a bath on Wednesday morning. *After* Florence's death. I don't believe anybody else used the bath at all. There was so much commotion on Wednesday, you understand. Louise and her husband departed pretty early in the morning and Fred didn't stay much later. But I'm not certain. My brother-in-law may remember better than I do."

"Indeed," replied the rabbi. He followed our host into the room at the top of the stairs. It was a small, musty chamber furnished in the same haphazard style as the drawing room. A double bed with a head board, a bureau with ornate carvings, two end tables that did not match. "Whose room was this?" asked Rabbi Kappelmacher.

"Louise and her husband's," answered Lorraine. "It's the only room with a double bed. It used to be my parents' bedroom, but my father moved into the room next door after my mother died."

We proceeded onward to the next room. "This was Fred's room," Lorraine explained. "It was where he stayed when he visited us once as a boy."

The third room had been Gladys's. "It's the smallest of the rooms," the old woman observed. "Between you and me, I figured Gladys was used to it."

"And this must have been where Agatha stayed," the rabbi suggested when we entered the fourth room.

"That's right," Lorraine agreed. "I didn't want her to stay the night, but Florence insisted. She wanted her entire family to be present for breakfast on the day after her wedding."

The rabbi rubbed his beard. "Did she say why, Miss Eisenstein?"

Lorraine shook his head. "Who knows? I think she had some absurd idea about all of us becoming close again—like back in the old days before our brother died. It was just another of Florence's silly notions."

We returned to the corridor and Lorraine made her way toward the stairs. "What about that door?" the rabbi demanded.

"Oh that," Lorraine replied nonchalantly. "Nobody ever goes in there."

The rabbi opened the door to reveal a room no different from the other four except that it lacked a bed. "This is where Louise stayed when she came to visit us as a child," Lorraine explained. "We had the bed removed a number of years ago because Florence wanted to turn it into a study, but nothing ever came of it. Nobody stayed in here on Tuesday night."

Rabbi Kappelmacher looked thoughtfully at the space where the bed had been.

"Is something wrong, inspector?" asked Lorraine.

"Not at all," he mumbled.

We then followed our host back downstairs to the drawing room.

"I do hope that was helpful, inspector," our host said.

"Of course, of course," the rabbi replied absentmindedly. I could sense that his mind was elsewhere. "Miss Eisenstein," he finally said, "I wish to thank you for your time. You've been extremely helpful. I also want to urge you to be very careful. It is quite possible that someone close to you may be...." He left the sentence unfinished.

"Dear me," said Lorraine. "I understand. But isn't it also possible, inspector, that you're mistaken?"

"It's possible," answered the rabbi. "Yet it's always wise to err on the side of prudence. I'll have to ask you not to discuss our meeting with anybody, especially your family."

Lorraine nodded and walked us to the kitchen door.

We were about to leave when the rabbi turned to Lorraine with his eyes aglow. "Did you say that your nieces and nephews stayed here once when they were children?"

"Yes," replied Lorraine. "Way, way back. When Isaac was still alive. They couldn't have been more than twelve years old at the time. He'd bring them up for the weekend. Sometimes, Agatha would come too. It's amazing how close we all were back then and how far apart we've drifted. Thirty, thirty-five years is a long time...."

"Miss Eisenstein," the rabbi asked, "did you and Florence occupy the same bedrooms then that you do now?"

"Yes," Lorraine replied. "Wait a second. No, in fact, we didn't. Good Lord, that's so long ago. That was before we'd closed down the rest of the house. I had a room on the far side of the house back then. In what was called the new wing, even though it dates from the turn of the century. The house itself was built in 1887."

"And Florence also lived in the new wing?" prompted Rabbi Kappelmacher.

"No, she didn't," Lorraine replied decisively. "In fact, she lived in the room that I occupy now. She only switched rooms about ten years ago to be closer to the bath. That was also when I moved into her old room, inspector, on account of wanting to be closer to my sister. It's a very large house, you understand. Larger than it may appear from the outside. Do you think that our changing rooms is significant, inspector?"

The rabbi ignored Lorraine's question. "I must urge you to be extremely careful, Miss Eisenstein," he said. "If anything at all out of the ordinary occurs, please contact me immediately at this address." He handed our host a business card. "Make sure you ask for Rabbi Kappelmacher. We have an arrangement with the synagogue for the purposes of our field work. If you don't ask for me specifically, they'll put you through to the real rabbi."

"I understand, inspector," Lorraine replied. "I imagine your line of work must be very exciting."

"More than you could dream of," stated the rabbi. Then Florence shut the door and we headed down the steps to the Cadillac.

"Do you really think she's in danger, rabbi?" I asked. "Maybe we should contact the police."

The rabbi shook his head and lit a cigar. "And tell them what, Steinmetz? That we have no proof or evidence, but we believe that an old woman who died recently was murdered, even though her own doctor believes she died of self-suffocation. Don't be a *noodnik*. What we need to do is use our rabbinic reasoning to solve this puzzle on our own."

"So what do we do now?" I asked. "We've visited everybody who might know anything about Florence's death—and I, for one, am as confused as ever. I don't even feel like we're making any progress."

The rabbi pulled the car onto the gravel lane. "Do you think Moses felt he was making any progress when he led our people across the desert, Steinmetz?"

"At least he knew where he was going," I mused.

"Don't be a *dumkopf*," retorted the rabbi. "I've had enough *tseuris* dealing with liars. It's enough to give a man a heart attack. If I have to deal with a *dumkopf* on top of that, I don't know if I'll be able to handle it. Now let's get back to the synagogue before they wonder what's become of us. It's almost time to say the evening prayers."

"But what do we do next, rabbi?" I inquired. "You have all your precious facts, and correct me if I'm wrong, I don't feel as though we're any closer to a rational explanation than we were when we started. In fact, I can't imagine being any further from a rational explanation than I am right now. So what's our plan?"

"We go to the synagogue and pray. Then we go home and think. And who knows? Maybe we've rocked the boat a little bit. With any luck, the mills are already set in motion and somebody will bring us a clue of their own accord."

That didn't seem too likely to me, but I was only the assistant rabbi, so I didn't object. I looked down at my watch. It was already five o'clock. As if to confirm the time, Art Abercrombie passed us on the gravel lane driving a red mustang convertible. A much better way to spend one's sixth decade, I couldn't help reflecting, than mucking about in strangers' lives trying to solve a murder.

CHAPTER 13: COUSIN AGATHA PLAYS
DETECTIVE

On Tuesday morning, Rabbi Kappelmacher didn't show up for work. I stopped by his office at nine o'clock in the hope that we could attend the *minyan* together, but Mrs. Billings said that she hadn't seen him. I instantly worried that something was amiss: In the entire time I'd been at the Haddam Jewish Center, the rabbi hadn't ever missed the morning prayers. I raced down the corridor to my own office, planning to call the rabbi at home. I found the following note pinned to my door.

"Steinmetz – I've decided to take the morning off to do some investigating on my own. Please attend to the morning prayers and meet me in my office at three o'clock this afternoon – Kappelmacher."

So the rabbi had ditched me. I found myself both disappointed and personally offended that the rabbi had gone sleuthing without me. I guess I'd come to view us as a team like Holmes and Watson or Hercule Poirot and Captain Hastings. What right did he have to leave me behind this far into the mystery? I couldn't imagine what I'd done to deserve such treatment.

The remainder of the morning passed slowly. I organized the *minyan* and then I taught my "Women in the Bible" course to six elderly widows, including the later Cantor Puttermesser's wife. Yet try as I might to concentrate on our discussion of Rebecca and Isaac's encounter at the well, I found that my heart wasn't in it.

My mind drifted to thoughts of Louise Sinkoff, stumbling around in the dark, suffocating her aunt with a pillow. In my gut, I still suspected Gladys; there was the disturbing evasiveness lurking behind her mousy nerves. Yet Florence's room switch pointed toward the other sister, the blind sister. Louise could easily have remembered which room Florence had occupied during her childhood visits, and it stood to reason that she assumed her Aunt Lorraine slept in the other bedroom. If that were the case, the blind woman could easily have murdered the wrong aunt by mistake.

I passed the early afternoon in my office taking care of the mundane synagogue business that I'd neglected at the end of the previous week. By the time three o'clock rolled around, I could barely concentrate on my work. I even remember the combination of curiosity and apprehension that I experienced as I walked down the narrow corridor to the rabbi's office. At three o'clock on the nose, I knocked on the door.

"Come in," said Rabbi Kappelmacher.

I found the rabbi, his shirt sleeves rolled up, relaxing on his reclining chair. His desk blotter was empty, save for an ashtray that contained the stubs of several exhausted cigars. "It's been an intriguing day, Steinmetz," he observed.

"Where have you been?"

The rabbi grinned. "Right here," he said—leaving my stupefied.

"What do you mean, rabbi? I stopped by this morning around nine and you weren't here then. In all honesty, I'm somewhat offended that you didn't take me along with you on your investigation."

The rabbi laughed. "I've been in this room since six a.m., Steinmetz, except for when I ducked out for a quick lunch around noon. I was in the office when you knocked. I simply chose not to answer. Why? Because I needed some time for my investigation. My *mental* investigation, that is. I've been here all day, using my rabbinic reasoning." Rabbi Kappelmacher chuckled. "Incidentally, my boy, you were welcome to do the same in your office."

So that was the big mystery! I couldn't help feeling overwhelmingly disappointed. I would have rather that the rabbi went out on his own and discovered new clues than that he sat in his office all day contemplating the old ones. I expressed my frustration to Rabbi Kappelmacher.

"Steinmetz," he said, "a man can read the Torah a thousand times and never know the meaning of our religion. By the same token, a man could find out everything there is to be known regarding Florence Eisenstein's death and never put his finger on the rational explanation. The time has arrived to think. If any new clues do turn up, my rabbinic instincts tell me that they'll come *to us*. In fact, I received one when I was out to lunch."

The rabbi opened the drawer of his desk and removed an envelope. He inspected it carefully. I was about to inquire as to its contents, when I heard the door open behind me and turned to see the obese Agatha Grossbart hobbling into the rabbi's office. Rabbi Kappelmacher quickly slid the envelope back into the drawer.

"I've been looking everywhere for you, Jacob," she bellowed. "This place is like a maze. None of the doors have names on them and they all look the same. If not for that woman across the corridor, I could have wandered around down here for months."

The rabbi pushed shut his desk drawer and smiled apologetically." We certainly wouldn't want that, Miss Grossbart," he replied. "I keep pressuring the bigwigs to modernize our offices, but for now this is it—so we make do. And what brings you to my humble neck of the woods?"

Agatha strode across the room as quickly as she was able and waved a manila folder only inches from the rabbi's nose. "This is what brings me here, Jacob," she declared. "Do you remember what we discussed earlier regarding my cousin's death? Well, now I have the evidence to prove it."

"Indeed. And what evidence is that, my good lady?"

Agatha glared at me with hostility. "Can't we go someplace private, Jacob? If you'd like, we could discuss the case over dinner."

The rabbi shook his head and held his watch up to his face. "I truly wish I could, Miss Grossbart, but I have a five o'clock appointment. However, if you'd like, I'm sure Rabbi Steinmetz and I would be delighted to join you for a cup of tea."

"Can't we talk alone?" Agatha persisted.

The rabbi's loyalty, however, proved unflagging. "Not if it's about Florence Eisenstein's death, I'm afraid. It's too risky to speak alone. If you do have evidence to prove the hypothesis you suggested earlier, then by sharing it with me you place both of our lives in grave danger. I'd feel much more comfortable if Rabbi Steinmetz were present as a witness."

Agatha frowned. She'd been trapped by her own logic. There was nothing she could do but accompany both Rabbi Kappelmacher and myself down the block to the East Haddam Diner. She did manage to walk the entire way at the rabbi's side, relegating me to an isolated position behind them. When we'd finally ordered our tea—which the rabbi took with a lump of sugar and for which Agatha substituted a vodka tonic—the woman slammed her folder down on the tabletop and rested her elbows across it.

The rabbi rubbed the bridge of his nose with his fingers. "Well, Miss Grossbart," he said, "I can't wait to hear what your evidence is. I admit that I haven't made much progress myself."

"That's quite all right," Agatha replied. "I told you we're a team and I mean to stick by my word. All for one and one for all. Besides, I understand that you must be very busy with your rabbinic duties, Jacob. I'm confident that you'll have an opportunity to make it up to me in other ways."

The rabbi gulped down half a glass of water. "It is always to be hoped for," he observed politely. "Now what is this evidence of yours, Miss Grossbart?"

Agatha polished off her drink and laid the empty glass on the tabletop. Then she leaned forward as though she were about to reveal a deep secret. "I tell you, Jacob, I've had the most interesting week. When I spoke to you last Thursday, I knew Gladys had murdered Florence—but I couldn't prove it. Now, I can...."

I glanced at the wall clock. It was already three thirty and Agatha had yet to tell us anything at all.

"I'm not sure whether I did right or I did wrong, Jacob," Agatha continued. "That's for a wiser man like you to judge. But I told myself, 'Agatha, there's a murderer on the loose.

If nobody else is willing to do anything about it, you have the responsibility to take matters into your own hands. And that, Jacob, is exactly what I did."

"What did you do already?" I finally blurted out as my frustrations got the better of me.

Agatha glowered at me with disdain. Then she spoke directly to Rabbi Kappelmacher. "On Saturday night, Jacob, I sneaked into the Eisenstein house. I was planning to pick one of the locks with a bobby pin, but as it turned out, the door to the kitchen was unlocked. I imagine there's not much crime to worry about up in Pine Valley."

"Except murder," prompted the rabbi.

Agatha ordered a second drink and rummaged in her purse. She removed a tattered yellow envelope with which she began to fan herself. "Exactly, Jacob. Here I have conclusive proof that Gladys murdered Florence. I don't know if you were present when she said it, but on Thursday night, Gladys told all of us that she hadn't had any contact with Florence since she left for the West Coast.

"She conveyed that similar impression to me," the rabbi agreed.

"Well, look here, Jacob," Agatha declared, handing Rabbi Kappelmacher the envelope. "I spent the entire night on Saturday rummaging through the Eisenstein papers. Everything from the filing cabinets in the library to the old business papers in the drawing room secretary. It was hard going, because I didn't want to wake Lorraine, but I knew that if I searched hard enough, I'd find the proof I needed. And here it is, Jacob. Straight out of Florence's bedroom drawer. Take a look at the date."

The rabbi examined the envelope. I looked over his shoulder. The letter was addressed to Florence Eisenstein. No return address. The postmark was San Francisco, CA, June 3, 2007. Rabbi Kappelmacher quickly removed a folded piece of stationery from the enveloped and together we read the following:

June 1, 2007
Dear Aunt Florence,

I hope that this letter finds you and Aunt Lorraine in good health and spirits. I know it has been many years since we've last spoken, but I sincerely hope that we can put past misunderstandings behind us for the welfare of the family. I have been meaning to write for several years now, but I've never had the courage to admit that I was mistaken about certain matters. Now, however, urgency compels me to write. Due to a series of poor investments, I find that I am in desperate financial straits. Your assistance would do more good than you could possibly imagine. If there is any way that you can help, please contact me at Gladys Eisenstein, General Delivery, San Francisco.

I must explain that while I would welcome your reply at my current address, my roommate harbors strong—and I might add, in my opinion, unjustified—prejudices regarding the family. In fact, it was she who pressured me into certain mistakes in the past. I recently informed her that I might contact you for assistance and this led to an extremely bitter argument. I will spare you the details. Suffice it to say, for the time being I think it best that we correspond in this manner.

Please send my best to Aunt Lorraine.   I would have written to both of you, but I fear that Aunt Lorraine's suspicious nature may lead her to judge me unfairly.   Once again, I implore you that your assistance is desperately needed.

> *Much love,*
> *Your niece,*
> *Gladys Eisenstein*

The letter was hand-written in blue ink. Across the bottom of the page, someone else had written, "Received June 8, 2007. NR." in black.

When he was done reading, the rabbi looked up. Agatha reached across the table and clasped his arm by the sleeve.

"What do you think of that, Jacob?" she demanded. "So much for no contact with her aunt in years. The writing at the bottom, for your information, is Florence's. It's on all of her letters. I figured out that NR stands for No Response.

Most of the other letters in Florence's desk had response dates penned in after the date of receipt."

The rabbi nodded. "This is intriguing, Miss Grossbart. I'll be the first to admit that. But if you'll excuse me, I don't see how this proves that Gladys murdered your cousin. There's a larger divide between lying and homicide. Just because Gladys wrote to her aunt a few years ago asking for money doesn't make her a murderer. It's possible that Gladys lied to us because she was embarrassed to admit that she needed the money."

"I couldn't agree more, Jacob," she replied. "Those were my thoughts precisely. But now take a look at this." She handed the manila envelope across the table. The label along the top read *Gladys—Eisenstein Family—Murder*. "Once again, Jacob," Agatha explained, "I took matters into my own hands. You can judge whether I did right or wrong, but I'm confident that I'll be vindicated."

"I'm sure," said the rabbi.

Agatha smiled confidently. "Yesterday afternoon, after Fred visited me, I went around to the Bargain Motel in Cedar Springs. A dreadful place, if I've ever seen one. My initial intent had been to confront Gladys with the letter. But when the desk attendant tried to ring up her room and told me that she was out, a better idea dawned on me. So I told the maid that I'd locked myself out of my room and I convinced her to open the door to Gladys's room for me. And that's where I found this. What more proof do you need?"

The rabbi opened the folder. It contained a series of newspaper articles. "Granddaughter Cries Murder in Egg Cream Death" read one headline. Another stated, "Millionaire's Granddaughter Accuses Aunts." Most of the articles dated from the 1970s and came from the *Pine Valley Courant*. As the rabbi leafed through the pages, we also came across several much earlier items: Irving Eisenstein's obituary, a photographed copy of Enoch Scott's medical report regarding his death, several letters from Lorraine to her brother, Isaac, on the subject of the will.

"This is it, rabbi," I declared. "If Gladys really did intend to patch up her relationship with her aunts, or even if she forgot all about their dispute, as she insisted at the motel, why bring all of these clippings with her halfway across the country?"

Agatha smiled in my direction. "I couldn't have said it better myself, rabbi. Gladys flew across the country intending to murder her aunt in cold blood. By her own admission, she needed the money. Now if we can only find the poison, we can go to the police."

"My dear lady," the rabbi replied, "I *do* admire your detective work. As a fact finder, your skills are impressive. But I urge you not to do anything premature. These papers aren't proof. They're simply circumstantial evidence."

Agatha looked as though she might cry. "I've done the best I can, Jacob. *You* know she did it and *I* know she did it. I thought we could confront her together and hope she'd crack. Under the weight of evidence like this, she's bound to confess."

Rabbi Kappelmacher sipped his tea. "I don't think that's a good idea, Miss Grossbart," he replied. "Not yet, at least. Gladys may not confess, and then we'll alert her to our suspicions. Right now, she doesn't know we're after her, so we have the upper hand."

"Very true, Jacob."

"What we need to do, my good lady, is to spring a trap of our own. You haven't mentioned this letter and these clippings to Gladys yet, have you?"

Agatha shook her head. "I didn't even tell Fred. We're a team, Jacob. I thought it was my duty to come to you first. I did right, didn't I?"

"You certainly discovered some intriguing information. And I think it was an excellent decision on your part to bring these papers to my attention immediately. I remind you that there's still a murderer on the loose. If Gladys knew you had this information and hadn't shared it with anyone, your life might be in great danger. As it is, I urge you to be careful."

"I feel safe just knowing that you're on my side," Agatha replied. She finished her second drink and ordered a third. "So what do you think our plan of attack should be? Maybe if we can talk the whole family into confronting her, she'll confess."

"I think," said Rabbi Kappelmacher, "that we shouldn't do anything rash. Do you mind if I hold onto these papers for a few days, Miss Grossbart?"

"Not at all."

"I appreciate that. I wouldn't want you to be in danger. I'll store them in the synagogue vault for safekeeping. Anyway, as I was saying, I think the best plan will be to mull matters over for a few days. There's no need for haste."

Agatha appeared to be disappointed, but she nodded in agreement.

"Of course, I'll call you before I do anything," the rabbi lied. "Maybe we can have dinner sometime soon."

The woman perked up. "I'd love that, Jacob. I know a wonderful Kosher restaurant in Maple Cove. They have a patio and it's just delightful at this time of year."

"I'm sure," said the rabbi. He paid the check and we walked out onto the street.

"Oh, Miss Grossbart," he said as we approached the synagogue. "I almost forgot. I needed to ask you a couple of questions. About the case, that is. I think you may know more than you realize."

"Do you? What do you mean?"

"I mean I want you to think back to last Tuesday night. You said you heard someone in the next room and then you went into the hallway and you saw that Gladys's door was open and that her room was empty."

"That's right, Jacob. If I'd only gone downstairs, Florence might still be alive today."

"Now I want you to think back, Miss Grossbart. Did you notice anything on Gladys's bed?"

"On her bed?"

"Like a magazine, for example?"

Agatha pressed her fingers against her temples to concentrate. "Come to think of it, Jacob, there was something on her bed. It could have been a magazine. I'm not sure."

"And how about in the rest of the room, Miss Grossbart? Did you happen to notice a pair of binoculars on one of the end tables?"

Once again, Agatha furrowed her brow and rubbed her fingers against her temples. "There was something on one of the end tables, Jacob," she finally said. "It might very well have been a pair of binoculars. I'm pretty sure you're correct. Do you think that's important?"

"That's the most significant piece of information I've received all day," the rabbi replied. "I think you helped explain one puzzle just now. I believe that we're closer than ever to our rational explanation."

"I do hope so, Jacob," said Agatha. Then she reminded the rabbi to phone her and she walked over to a nearby payphone, presumably to call a cab. I followed Rabbi Kappelmacher back into his office.

I could sense from the rabbi's mood that he had just made an important discovery, but I had absolutely no idea what it was. "Rabbi," I asked. "How did you know about those binoculars in Gladys's room?"

He smiled at me. "Just a hunch, Steinmetz," he replied. "If you used your rabbinic reasoning, you'd see their significance. But we don't have time to discuss this now. We have far greater *latkes* to fry. Have you been putting your rabbinic reasoning power to good use?"

I shrugged. "I'm not sure what you're asking, rabbi. I've been thinking about this business all day, if that's what you mean. But I still haven't made any progress."

"Maybe you're thinking about things the wrong way, Steinmetz," replied the rabbi. "Let me tell you a story that you may find edifying. Cantor Puttermesser told the story much better than I do, but I'll give it my best shot. It was about fifteen years ago, maybe even twenty. The cantor was tutoring a young boy for his bar mitzvah and the youth was highly resistant. He was interested in baseball, not *haftorah*. You know the type. Well, one day the boy asks the cantor, 'How do you now the Torah is five thousand years old? How do you know it wasn't written two hundred years ago and was part of a giant hoax?' Now Sol Puttermesser was a brilliant scholar. He could have provided a detailed explanation of papyrus dating and a discussion of the Dead Sea Scrolls that would have dazzled your socks off. But he didn't. Instead, he asked the boy a question of his own. He asked, 'How do you know what Joe DiMaggio hit in fifty-six straight games and that his record wasn't part of a giant hoax?' And after that, Steinmetz, the boy studied his *tuchus* off. Do you understand what that means?"

I shook my head. "No offense, rabbi," I said, "but I haven't the slightest idea how that relates to Florence's death or anything else."

"The point is, Steinmetz, that if you question one thing, you have to question everything. Sometimes, as in the case of Joe DiMaggio and the Torah, one is better off not questioning at all. In other situations, such as the matter of Florence's death, one is best off questioning everything. Your mistake is that you're easily convinced. For example, how do you know that Agatha found that folder in Gladys Eisenstein's motel room?"

"But where else could she have found it?" I asked incredulously.

The rabbi shrugged his shoulders. "I think she probably did find that folder, just as she told us. In fact, I'm quite confident that she did. But unlike you, Steinmetz, I didn't take her word for it without considering the alternatives. For example, maybe Agatha photocopied those newspapers at the county library this morning in an effort to frame her cousin. It's unlikely, but it's possible."

It frustrates me to no end when the rabbi plays skeptic like that. I'm a firm believer in faith and I don't think one can go through life doubting everything. "So what you're saying, rabbi," I replied, "is that you don't believe anything anybody tells you. Then what's the point of meeting all these people?"

"That's not what I'm saying at all, Steinmetz. What I'm saying is that I only believe things that make sense. If a fact conforms with what I already know, then I'm inclined to believe it. If it doesn't, then I doubt it. As it is, I've found myself doing a lot more doubting than believing this week."

I threw up my hands. "So does this mean that you have your rational explanation? If you believe Agatha about the folder, do you really think Gladys is the killer?"

"I don't know yet. There are a number of pieces of this puzzle that don't fit together yet. But I am convinced we'll have our explanation, sooner or later. And at the rate people keep providing us with information, I'd say sooner. But before I tell you about that, I need to make a phone call."

The rabbi dialed a number and spoke into the receiver. "Gladys Eisenstein?....Yes, that's correct. Rabbi Kappelmacher...I have to see you tomorrow.....Yes....I assure you it's good news....How about lunch at Knobler's Deli? On the Lower East Side....You know it? Perfect.....Does one o'clock work? See you then....Bye."

Rabbi Kappelmacher smiled ecstatically. "Tomorrow, we have the lunch of our lives, Steinmetz. And maybe we solve a murder in the process. But that's tomorrow. Today, I need to share with you the most unusual thing."

The rabbi opened his desk drawer and retrieved the envelope he'd been about to show me when Agatha showed up. Then he looked at his watch. "It's nearly five. We might as well wait for Green, so I don't need to explain myself twice."

As if on cue, someone knocked on the door. A moment later, Marshall Green limped into the rabbi' office.

CHAPTER 14: THE INCRIMINATING LETTER

Rabbi Kappelmacher rose to greet his former assistant. "Marshall Green appears in a synagogue twice in one week!" exclaimed the rabbi. "This is indeed a miracle. If I didn't know better, I'd say it defied rational explanation."

Green blushed. I sensed that the rabbi's references to the lawyer's religious practices made my predecessor uncomfortable. "There's a perfectly rational explanation," said Green. "As I told you over the phone, I was just wondering if you'd made any progress on the Eisenstein matter. I find myself having a hard time concentrating on anything else, knowing that there's a murderer on the loose and that it's probably somebody I know."

"There *may* be a murderer on the loose," replied the rabbi. "I don't want to jump to any hasty conclusions. I don't have any proof yet."

"Then you have your doubts?" Green asked. "I thought you were convinced that someone had murdered Florence Eisenstein."

Rabbi Kappelmacher shook his head. "No, Green," he said. "That was you. You're the one who was convinced that someone murdered Miss Eisenstein. That's your nature. You're easily persuaded one way and then just as easily persuaded in the opposite direction. I withhold my judgments. As far as I'm concerned, Florence Eisenstein *may* have been murdered. It's a probability, not a certainty."

"What you mean to say, rabbi," Green retorted with a smile, "is that you haven't solved the case yet."

The rabbi held up his cigar in front of his face and examined the flame. "That is true, Green," he said. "I have not yet solved the case. However, I received a rather unusual letter today that may prove instrumental in finding a rational explanation." The rabbi slid the envelope across his desk. "I want both of you to take a look at this and tell me what you think."

The envelope was entirely blank. No address, no stamps. Marshall Green opened the envelope and removed the letter, which he rapidly unfolded and placed on the rabbi's desk. It was typewritten in all capitals. Green and I exchanged puzzled looks and then we read the letter together:

DEAR RABBI KAPPELMACHER,
I URGE YOU TO INVESTIGATE THE RELATIONSHIP BETWEEN LORRAINE EISENSTEIN AND ART ABERCROMBIE. ASK ABERCROMBIE WHERE HE WAS ON THE NIGHT FLORENCE EISENSTEIN WAS MURDERED. TIME IS OF THE ESSENCE.
SINCERELY,
AN OBSERVER

I didn't know what to make of this unusual note. I turned to Green for assistance, but he also appeared bewildered. "Where did this come from?" I finally asked.

"Not through the mail," said Green. "There aren't any stamps or postmark."

The rabbi laughed. "We'll make a detective of you yet, Green. That was impressive use of your rabbinic reasoning—or should I now say legal reasoning? They must have taught you deduction in law school."

Green smiled uncomfortably. The rabbi folded the letter back into the envelope.

"You ask a very good question, Steinmetz," observed the rabbi. "Where did this letter come from? While I cannot tell you that, I can tell you how it came into my possession."

"How?" asked Green.

"I went out to lunch around one o'clock," the rabbi explained. "I left my office door unlocked, as I always do. That's one instance where I believe a rabbi has a responsibility to trust people. If you start to lock doors inside a synagogue, I say, you're only a small step away from giving up faith in humanity. In any case, I left for lunch around one and I came back here at one thirty. This note was waiting on my desk when I returned. So I ask you gentlemen, why go to the trouble of waiting for me to leave my office and deposit it on my desk when one could easily deliver it through the mail?"

Green removed his glasses and wiped them with his handkerchief. "Urgency, I suppose. Somebody wanted you to get this note quickly. I imagine one of the staff must have seen who left the letter—either Mrs. Conch or Mrs. Billings or that new librarian you hired after I left."

"I've already asked," replied the rabbi. "Mrs. Billings said she didn't see anyone out of the ordinary in the corridor all afternoon. Of course, she sneaks out to the parking lot for a cigarette every once in a while. The librarian, Mrs. Geist, also claims she didn't see anyone—but she takes her lunch break around the same time I do. And Mrs. Conch, of course, has Tuesdays off...."

"That's right," chimed in Green. "I'd entirely forgotten."

"Well, you're welcome to visit us any time, Green," the rabbi said. "If you stop by often enough, maybe you'll even remember some of the prayers."

Green turned a deep purple. "So what do you make of the letter, rabbi?" he asked. "Do you think there really is something going on between Art and Lorraine?"

"I was hoping you could tell me that," answered Rabbi Kappelmacher. "You work with Abercrombie. What do you think?"

Green frowned. "I don't think so," he said, "except that....No, never mind." The lawyer lowered his eyes and concentrated on his folded hands.

"Except what?" the rabbi pressed. "Don't hold back on me, Green. If ever it was important that we be honest with each other, now is the time."

"Well, rabbi," Green replied hesitantly, "it's like this. My conversation in the car with Art the other night started me thinking. Maybe it made me a little bit more suspicious than it should have. But I've been on the lookout these past few days. Now, I don't know if you remember, but I told you that every year, Florence and Lorraine used to visit Abercrombie about the will. We never went out to Pine Valley; they always came to the office. There are, of course, some wealthy clients for whom we make house calls—but very few. Yet ever since Florence's death, Abercrombie has insisted upon delivering all of the papers regarding the Eisenstein estate to Lorraine personally."

"Indeed," exclaimed the rabbi.

"There are lots of papers that need signing. But there's absolutely no need for Abercrombie to drive out to Pine Valley. Even if there was a need to take the papers directly to Lorraine, it's the sort of task we'd assign to a junior associate. Certainly not the senior partner. Moreover, I've noticed that Abercrombie keeps trying to find excuses for going out there. One day he'll claim to have forgotten to bring a document on his last visit and the next day he'll say he left a folder at Lorraine's and needs to pick it up. He always goes out there around five o'clock in the evening. So yesterday, I performed a little experiment of my own. I called Abercrombie's home at eight o'clock—and there was no answer. Yet if all he needed was Lorraine's signature, it shouldn't have taken him more than twenty minutes. I know that doesn't prove anything, rabbi, but it struck me as suspicious."

"Maybe," said the rabbi. "Or maybe Mr. Abercrombie went to the theater. In any case, somebody wants me to think he's mixed up in murder. As I understand it, if Abercrombie marries Lorraine, she still keeps her money."

"Exactly," Green confirmed. "It was a loophole in the original will. Only the first sister to marry was disinherited. Once the first sister married, the second was free to wed with impunity. But do you really believe Abercrombie's involved in this business?"

"I don't know yet. What I can tell you is that he appears to have been in an excellent position to lie to Florence about the will. I can also surmise that *if* he duped Florence into marrying Alfred by telling her that the will had been broken, then he had every motive to kill her before she discovered that she'd been lied to. Then he'd be free to marry Lorraine and to share in her inheritance. Of course, all of this is pure speculation. I'm much more interested in who wrote this note."

Green twirled his pen between his fingers. "The letter does raise an interesting question though, doesn't it? Where was Abercrombie last Tuesday night? Maybe we should ask him...."

Rabbi Kappelmacher shook his head. "I'm one step ahead of you, Green. I already called him this afternoon. I had to tell him a host of unconscionable lies to find out what he was doing on Tuesday night. As it turns out, he was at home reading. Or so he said. So that doesn't help us at all."

"At home, reading?" mused Green. "It's the alibi the murderer always supplies in detective novels."

"Not the murderer," I corrected him. "The primary suspect. The murderer always arranges an alibi which needs to be cracked."

"In any case," observed the rabbi, "for now we cannot be certain of Abercrombie's whereabouts on Tuesday night."

"The plot thickens," said Green.

"Thins, rather. The more information we have, the fewer possible explanations for it. Eventually, we'll have enough facts so that only one rational explanation can account for them."

"And you think that you're closer to that rational explanation?"

"Closer than I've ever been before," said the rabbi. "I've even made a list of some of the facts in this case which still must be explained. Perhaps the two of you would like to take a look at it?"

We both crowded closer to the rabbi's desk. He opened another drawer and slid a piece of notepaper across the table. Green read aloud:

FACTS TO BE EXPLAINED

1. Florence Eisenstein decides to get married after many years living a quiet, single life. Why?

2. Florence goes bird watching on the day before her wedding. Was she really bird watching or was she looking for something else?

3. Fred Eisenstein claims he never argued with his aunt despite overwhelming evidence to the contrary. He states that on the Saturday before the wedding, they spoke about birds and planned a trip to the Museum of Natural History.

4. Florence lets it be known that she believes her father's will has been broken, but she does not mention the matter to Green on Monday morning. Why would she deceive him?

5. At her wedding, Florence tries to keep Gladys from speaking to the other guests.

6. Abercrombie "explodes" at the suggestion that Florence has been murdered.

7. Louise tells us that she received a series of crank phone calls.

8. Gladys claims that she didn't leave her room on the night of the wedding and she hadn't had any contact with her aunts in years; Agatha says that she heard Gladys leave her room and provides evidence indicating that Gladys had contacted her Aunt Florence last year. What was Gladys Eisenstein doing with a pair of binoculars in her room on Tuesday night?

9. An unknown person writes a letter suggesting that I investigate the relationship between Lorraine and Abercrombie.

"You're forgetting about the room changes," I added. "I think that's important."

The rabbi nodded. "It very well may be, Steinmetz," he replied, "but it's not something that, taken on its own, would be unusual. I'm sure elderly people switch rooms all the time. So while that fact may help solve our puzzle, it doesn't have to be explained. After all, it could just be a coincidence."

I shrugged my shoulders. "Well, it's your list, rabbi," I said. "Personally, I think several of the items on it aren't all that unusual. Especially item number one—which is what started all of this. So an old woman gets married. That happens all the time. Probably even more frequently than old women switching bedrooms."

"You're entitled to your opinion, Steinmetz. For my part, I'm convinced that something extraordinary must have prompted Florence to marry. Only time and rabbinic reasoning will tell us for sure. What's really bothering me is why Florence went bird watching on Monday morning. We have every reason to believe that she did in fact go bird watching. For starters, Mrs. Finchley says that she saw her. Lorraine also said that Florence went bird watching. And I believe Alfred told us that she'd told him about her bird watching experiences when he stopped by the house on Monday afternoon. So I, for one, am firmly convinced that she did go bird watching. I just don't understand why."

"Why not?" asked Green. He seemed to share my sentiments on the subject. Yet it was clear that the rabbi had it in his head that Florence's bird watching was significant and there was no prospect of changing his mind—at least, not without conclusive evidence to the contrary.

"It just seems highly unusual to me, Green," observed the rabbi. "What I'd like to do now is to test your rabbinic reasoning. Both of you, that is, if Green here can put his lawyerly instincts on hold for a moment."

The color returned to Green's cheeks. "What do you mean, rabbi?"

"I mean I'd like each of you to try to provide a rational explanation for all of the events that I've just listed. You first, Steinmetz."

"I don't think I can, rabbi," I stammered.

"Well, try, Steinmetz. If nothing else, it will do you some good. You need all the practice you can get if you plan on becoming head rabbi."

I winced. What a tactless remark, I thought, to make in front of Green.

When I tried to provide a rational explanation, I found that I didn't even know where to begin. The case I finally offered sounded something like this: "Florence Eisenstein's marriage wasn't out of the ordinary. She called up her relatives because she thought she wouldn't live long and she wished to see them—and possibly to make peace—before she died. She told them that she'd broken the will in order to keep them from trying to talk her out of marrying Alfred. She wanted a truly festive affair. Then she argued with Fred because she sensed that he didn't approve of her marriage, and he lied about their argument because he's ashamed. And then, on Tuesday night, either Louise or Gladys learned that the will hadn't been broken and suffocated the wrong aunt by mistake."

"Why Louise or Gladys?" the rabbi asked. "Why not Agatha or Fred?"

"Louise because she's blind," I replied without confidence. "It would be easiest for her to make the mistake. Gladys because of those folders Agatha found and because she left her room on the night of the murder."

"And who wrote this letter?" the rabbi asked, holding up the suspicious note.

"I don't know. The murderer, I imagine. Somebody who wanted to divert your attention. I guess that couldn't be Louise, because she can't use a typewriter."

"They have voice-operated typewriters these days, Rabbi Steinmetz," Green cut in. "They also have typewriters with keys labeled in Braille."

"Then maybe Louise did write the letter," I conceded.

The rabbi chuckled. "That's an interesting hypothesis, Steinmetz," he said. "Of course, among other things, it doesn't explain why Florence went bird watching. How about you, Green? Big *macher* fancy-pants lawyer. You must have a theory as well."

"I'd rather not say," said Green. "I don't like to play guessing games."

"Don't guess then, Green," the rabbi replied. "Think. You're a smart boy."

Green wiped his glasses for the second time. "I suppose I'd have to say that all the evidence points in one direction," he observed. "Similar to the theory you outlined earlier. Art Abercrombie tricked Florence into getting married and then murdered her before she exposed his lie. He must plan to marry Lorraine for her money. I understand he'll need a lot of ready cash if he does seek to self-finance a campaign for the Senate."

"So did Lorraine conspire with him, Green, or is he banking on being able to charm her into marriage?"

"I don't know," Green replied.

"And who wrote this note?"

"I couldn't tell you."

"And how does that explain why Florence went bird watching?"

"I have absolutely no idea."

The rabbi laughed heartily. "That's certainly not a comprehensive explanation then. There's one more flaw in your theory as well. Why marry Lorraine? Why not lie to Lorraine and trick her into marrying, and then kill her and marry Florence?"

"I guess because Florence already had a boyfriend?" Green replied without conviction. "Maybe Florence hinted to Abercrombie that she hoped to marry and he prodded her along."

"Maybe," replied the rabbi. "What is entirely clear is that all three of us agree on the most important point."

"We do?" both Green and I asked simultaneously. I couldn't imagine anything in our theories that meshed at all. I didn't even know the rabbi's theory yet, so I couldn't speculate on whether I agreed with him.

"Yes, we do," said Rabbi Kappelmacher. He smiled smugly and then puffed a cigar. "In fact, we agree on the most unusual of all facts in the puzzle."

"Will you tell us already, rabbi?" Green demanded anxiously. "What do we all agree upon?"

The rabbi pushed an imaginary button with his index finger. "Isn't that obvious, Green? We all agree that Florence Eisenstein was murdered. You'll note that I didn't include this fact on my list. What has amazed me throughout this case is how many times that suggestion has arisen without any conclusive proof. You suggested the possibility to Abercrombie, Green. And Agatha suggested it to me. Very strange. Nobody wants to believe that Irving Eisenstein was murdered and so many people are willing to believe that his daughter, Florence, was. Very strange, indeed."

"Now if you could only tell us who did it, rabbi," said Green.

"In due time," the rabbi replied. He retrieved his jacket from the rack in the corner. "Anyway, I need to get home for supper. Would you care to walk me, Steinmetz?"

"Sure thing," I agreed.

"As for you, Green," said the rabbi, "I'm highly disappointed in you. I would have thought that with your mind, you'd have come up with a more convincing explanation."

Green hung his head. I could tell that Rabbi Kappelmacher had wounded him. "I wish I could," Green muttered. "I'll call you."

"Do that," replied the rabbi. "And feel free to stop by for services on Saturday. You'd be surprised how relaxing it can be."

When the former assistant rabbi departed, I walked Rabbi Kappelmacher into the parking lot. "Don't you think you're being a bit hard on Green?" I asked. "You never cut him any slack."

"He asks for it. I have a great deal of admiration for Green. He would have made an excellent rabbi."

"Rabbi," I asked, "One more question. I'm curious to know how you convinced Abercrombie to tell you what he did last Tuesday night."

The rabbi grinned. "A piece of cake. I played the same role that I played the last time we saw him. It's all about consistency. He believes I think that Green's a crackpot, so I conveyed to him that I still believe Green's as *meshuggah* as could be. I told him that somebody, implicitly Green, thought that he'd murdered Florence, and that to pacify this unnamed individual, whom I otherwise admired greatly, I needed to know what he was doing on Tuesday night. He bought the entire story. It's amazing how willing people are to believe things that conform to what they already expect."

Although I had to admit that the rabbi's tactics had been clever, I felt somewhat uncomfortable with them. When we stopped in front of the rabbi's house, I asked, "Do you think that was fair to Green, rabbi?"

"I doubt Abercrombie will take it out on Green. I imagine he'd like to keep this entire business quiet with the senate race approaching. I also have to admit that Green, although in many ways an admirable man, hasn't always been fair with me. So your answer is yes. I do think I've been extremely fair."

I detected a hint of hostility in the rabbi's voice. I wondered why, but decided I would be better off changing the subject. "Aren't you going to share your own theory of the case, rabbi?" I asked.

His eyes glowed mischievously. "I don't have one yet," he said. "Have a good night. Send my love to Mrs. Steinmetz. You're on your own again for the morning prayers tomorrow. I'll stop by your office around eleven o'clock to pick you up for lunch with Gladys."

Rabbi Kappelmacher started to walk up his front path. After he'd gone twenty feet, he turned around and called out, "And by the way, Steinmetz, I think you're a good man. A fine man and a fine rabbi. I should make a point of telling you that more often."

After this unexpected declaration, the rabbi trotted off toward his front door at high speed. I found myself standing at the curbside, both shocked and elated, wondering once again what I'd done to garner such praise.

CHAPTER 15: THE OLD NEIGHBORHOOD

The rabbi stopped by my office as planned and we pulled into the parking garage across the street from Knobler's Deli at ten minutes to one. Then we navigated the heavy pedestrian traffic—pushcart vendors, tourists, a troupe of street performers juggling bagels—and stepped into the heavy, aromatic air of the self-proclaimed home of "The World's Greatest Pastrami Sandwich." The waitress seated us in a booth across from the kitchen. She was a haggard, strong-jawed woman of indeterminate age who didn't look particularly Jewish.

"I can smell it in the air," the rabbi observed.

"Your rational explanation?"

"Don't be such a *noodnik*, Steinmetz," he replied good-naturedly. "I can smell the pastrami. It's as though I've stepped straight into my childhood."

The waitress arrived to take our order, but we waited for Gladys. In the interim, Rabbi Kappelmacher delivered a sermon on the joys of cold cuts. I could sense the anticipation in his voice. Gladys Eisenstein had barely seated herself when the rabbi summoned the waitress and ordered a pastrami platter.

"Did you have trouble finding the place?" he asked Gladys with one look at his watch and the other at the kitchen.

"None at all. I did have trouble parking, though. Do you know how much a garage costs in this city? Twenty dollars!"

"I'd pay a thousand dollars for a Knobler's pastrami sandwich," Rabbi Kappelmacher replied genially. I do believe he would have too. He savored a pickle and smiled broadly. "Now that's a pickle, Steinmetz! Try one." The rabbi extended the pickle tray in my direction.

"I'd rather not," I replied. "Pickles don't agree with me. How about you, Miss Eisenstein?"

Gladys seemed surprised when I spoke to her. "I'll have to pass as well," she replied. "I remember coming here as a girl. My father used to bring us because he loved the pickles. I couldn't stand the pickles though. What I loved were those murals on the ceiling."

I followed Gladys's gaze. The entire ceiling of Knobler's Delicatessen was tiled with Old Testament scenes: Jonah being swallowed by a whale, Joshua toppling the Walls of Jericho. They were indeed impressive. I could especially understand how the sparkling tiles might appear to a young child.

"I've seen them before," the rabbi said indifferently. "Given a choice between kitsch and pastrami, I'll take pastrami any day." True to his word, he scooped up several slices of meat on a piece of rye bread and indulged himself.

Gladys Eisenstein now looked at the rabbi. "Well?" she asked. "I didn't drive all the way down here to relive my childhood and watch you eat red meat. Red meat's bad for you, by the way. And it's worse for the animals."

"Thank you for the warning," replied the rabbi as he scooped up another bite.

Gladys frowned. "I thought you had important news for me. I thought you told me you had the evidence you needed to break the will."

The rabbi looked up reluctantly from his cold cuts. "I didn't say that, Miss Eisenstein. All I said was that I had some information that you'd want to know about. Are you sure you don't want to order lunch?"

"I don't have time for lunch," Gladys replied. "Anyway, I looked at the menu out front. There's absolutely nothing I can eat here. I haven't eaten any meat or poultry in fifteen years."

The rabbi looked down at our guest with pity. "That's too bad," he said. "Can I at least interest you in a drink? Perhaps some Dr. Brown's Original Cel-Ray tonic?"

"Look, rabbi," said Gladys. "Tell me what you have to tell me so I can go home. I've had a bad couple of days. Somebody broke into my motel room."

"Did they?" the rabbi asked, feigning disbelief. "I hope they didn't steal anything of value."

Gladys shook her head. "I didn't have anything of value for them to steal."

"Then you should be thankful that they didn't take anything."

Gladys glared at Rabbi Kappelmacher. "Yes, I guess I should be thankful," she replied.

"Are you sure they didn't take anything, Miss Eisenstein?" the rabbi asked again.

"Yes, I'm sure. Now what information do you have for me?"

The rabbi ignored her question and posed one of his own. "If your burglar didn't take anything, Miss Eisenstein, how do you know that your motel room was broken into?"

Gladys flared her nostrils. She no longer looked like a mouse, but instead resembled a large Norwegian rat. I feared for a moment that she might lunge across the table and bite the rabbi. "I know because I know!" she shouted. "It's none of your goddam business. Now if you're going to share your information with me, do it. And if you're not, then I'm going to leave."

Two elderly women at a nearby table turned to look at us. I feared that Gladys was going to cause a scene. To my relief, the rabbi reached into the side pocket of his attaché case and removed the folder.

"Are you sure you don't know that your motel room was burglarized because you're missing this, Miss Eisenstein?"

Gladys's eyes widened. She reached for the folder. The rabbi held it to his side, just beyond her grasp. "Give me that!" Gladys cried. "I'm going to go to the police!"

"Relax, Miss Eisenstein," replied the rabbi calmly. "What will you tell the police? That a sixty-six year old rabbi broke into your motel room to steal a folder of newspaper clippings? I don't know what life is like in San

Francisco, my dear lady, but in New York, they'd laugh you out of the station."

Gladys Eisenstein quickly realized her predicament. She flashed the rabbi a look that could have transformed wine to stone. "Tell me what you want and I'll do it," she said. "I just want my file back and I want to be left alone."

The rabbi nodded and ordered a second platter of pastrami. "Aren't you going to taste it, Steinmetz?" he asked. I'd been so engrossed in the ongoing drama, I hadn't even had a bite. I speared a slice of pastrami with my fork and raised it to my mouth. The rabbi finished off the remainder of the cold cuts and smiled contentedly.

"What do I want, Miss Eisenstein?" he asked. "I want to know who murdered your Aunt Florence. And how and why. That's all I want. A rational explanation. So I promise you that as soon as I have that, I'll leave you alone. In the meantime, I have a few more questions I'd like to ask you."

Gladys continued to stare at the rabbi without uttering a word.

"So will you answer a few questions, Miss Eisenstein?" the rabbi asked. "Or do I need to bring this file to the police and accuse *you* of murder? Between this and some other information I have, I believe I can make a pretty strong circumstantial case."

The mousy woman's skin turned ashen. "I'll answer your questions."

Rabbi Kappelmacher rubbed his hands together, as though about to indulge in a rich meal. "I'm delighted we see eye to eye, Miss Eisenstein. Now the first thing I'd like to know is when was the last time you had any contact with your Aunt Florence?"

"I already told you," Gladys replied. "I saw her at the wedding."

"And before that?"

"On the phone, rabbi. How many times do I have to go over this? She called me in San Francisco to invite me to her wedding."

"And before *that*?"

"Good Lord, rabbi," Gladys exclaimed in obvious frustration. "I don't know....1982? 1983? I don't keep track of these things. It's not everyday that one faces interrogation at the hands of the Jewish Gestapo."

Gladys's last remark hit the rabbi like an arrow. For the first and only time in my life, I saw him lose his temper. "Watch your tongue, lady," he snapped. Then he drew several deep breaths and reached into the side pocket of his attaché case. "Are you certain you didn't contact your aunt after 1983, Miss Eisenstein? Sometime in the last few years?"

"I'm sure of it."

I had to admire Gladys's ability to lie with a straight face. The rabbi slid the letter from Gladys to Florence Eisenstein across the table.

"Then how do you explain that, Miss Eisenstein?"

The woman blanched again and started to gnaw at her sleeve.

"I don't like being lied to," the rabbi said coldly. "I think you have some serious explaining to do."

Gladys nodded. "I'd forgotten all about this, rabbi," she said. Her tone was more congenial. "Honestly, I had. It was such a rough time for Amy and me, and she hated my aunts with such a passion after what I'd told her about them. But we needed the money desperately...." To my surprise, the mousy woman broke off her explanation and started to cry.

"You forgot?" the rabbi demanded. "Do you expect me to believe that? You carry around a folder of news clippings relating to your grandfather's death and you forgot about this letter?"

Gladys nodded. "Believe me or don't believe me, but that's the way it is. I guess I blocked it out of my mind entirely."

Rabbi Kappelmacher folded the letter and slid it back into his attaché case. He retrieved another letter at the same time—the letter he'd found in his office.

"How about this note, Miss Eisenstein? Have you seen this before?"

Gladys read the note to herself. "I've never seen this note before in my life. It's typewritten, rabbi. I don't have a typewriter in my motel room. If you don't believe me, you can come and look for yourself."

At that moment, the second platter of pastrami arrived. Rabbi Kappelmacher paused to gorge himself. After he'd consumed about half the meat and I'd picked at a few morsels, which in hindsight were quite delicious, he resumed his aggressive questioning of Gladys.

"I'd like to talk about the night of your Aunt Florence's murder. You told me that you didn't leave your room that night after you retired for the evening."

"That's exactly what I said."

"Not for any reason?"

"I fell asleep reading a magazine. You can keep asking me the same questions over and over again, but I'm not going to change my answers."

The rabbi smiled. "Just like you didn't change your answer regarding when you'd last contacted your aunt, Miss Eisenstein?"

Rabbi Kappelmacher savored another pickle.

"Are you a bird watcher, Miss Eisenstein?"

Gladys's eyes widened. "Excuse me?"

"I asked if you're a bird watcher, Miss Eisenstein. Do you watch birds?"

Our guest pondered this question. I could almost feel her mind racing, trying to ferret out the rabbi's trap. "No," she finally said. "I don't. In fact, I don't think I've ever been bird-watching in my life. It's a senseless bourgeois hobby. The last thing birds need are a bunch of middle-aged men trampling through their habitats. Is there a point to your questioning, rabbi, or are you just interested in what I do with my free time?"

Rabbi Kappelmacher polished off the last of the pastrami and washed it down with a swig of Cel-Ray tonic. "There is always a point to my questions, my dear lady. Sometimes, however, I wonder if there is a point to your answers."

"What do you mean by that?" demanded Gladys. "Are you accusing me of lying?"

The rabbi laughed. "Let's not get personal, Miss Eisenstein. I never accuse; I only expose. What I'm wondering is why you had a set of binoculars on your bedside table if you don't go bird watching."

Gladys pounded her fist on the tabletop. "I didn't have a set of binoculars on my bedside table. In fact, I don't own a set of binoculars. For a man who claims to be interested in the truth, you do an awful lot of accusing."

"Indeed," said the rabbi. "Indeed. Now about the folder that you want so dearly. Might I inquire why you brought this folder with you to New York, Miss Eisenstein?"

Gladys nibbled at the buttons on her sleeve. "I don't know, rabbi," she said. "I just did. And on the subject, I don't understand why I have to explain myself to you. I'm not the one who broke into a woman's motel room and stole her personal papers."

"Nor am I," replied the rabbi.

"What do you mean? Did you have your sidekick here do it for you?"

I suddenly found myself disliking the mousy woman very strongly.

"No," the rabbi replied. "Rabbi Steinmetz is as innocent as I am. If you want to blame somebody, you'd best look closer to home. It was your cousin, Agatha, who brought me this folder."

Gladys clenched her fists. "Agatha? That oversized nitwit! Why on earth would she do something like that?"

"You'll have to ask her," replied the rabbi. "Right now, what I want to know is why you brought this folder with you from San Francisco."

Gladys thought for a moment. "Because they did it, rabbi. Florence and Lorraine. They murdered my grandfather. I did try to block them all out over the years, but when Florence called, I decided that this time I was going to prove it. For poor Amy's sake. When she died, rabbi, I thought about all the times we had to struggle to make ends meet and all the things we had to skimp on and all the vacations we never took—and I determined that I wasn't going to live that way anymore. Of course, I didn't exactly have a plan. I just brought the file with me, hoping something might turn up. I didn't murder my aunt, if that's what you're thinking."

The rabbi shook is head. "Sometimes even I don't known what I'm thinking, Miss Eisenstein. Why don't you tell me why you tried to prevent your aunt from speaking with the other guests at the wedding?"

"I didn't," Gladys declared. "We keep going in circles. Like I said, I thought she was trying to keep me from speaking with the other guests."

"Do you have any idea why?"

"Who knows? Maybe she wanted bygones to be bygones and she feared I'd cause a scene. Not that there wasn't enough of a scene without my needing to cause one."

"So I've heard," mused the rabbi. "It must have been tough growing up in your family, Miss Eisenstein."

"Not much worse than most," she replied. "My parents were actually good people. Cowardly, but decent."

"Do you ever think about the crank phone calls your sister received as a girl?"

This question appeared to catch Gladys off guard. "No, rabbi," she replied after a pause. "Actually, I don't think about them at all."

"But you remember them?"

Gladys nodded. "Yes, I do. What does this have to do with my Aunt Florence and the will?"

"I'll ask the questions, Miss Eisenstein," the rabbi replied. "That is, if you want your folder back. Did you make those phone calls, Miss Eisenstein?"

Gladys paused again. A guilty pause. "No, I didn't," she finally announced. "How many more questions do I need to answer?"

"Only a few more," said the rabbi. "Do you have any idea who did make those calls?"

"No, I don't."

"Are you sure?"

"Very sure."

"Did you know that your sister received a series of similar calls several weeks ago?"

Gladys shook her head. "No, I didn't. I really don't see the point of these questions, rabbi."

"No," the rabbi replied. "I guess you couldn't. But I'm sure you'll be glad to know that I have only one more. Do you have any idea why your Aunt Florence went bird watching last Monday morning?"

I could see the clockwork turning in Gladys's mind. Searching for a trap. I too found myself searching for the rabbi's trap. For the life of me, I couldn't find it. "Maybe," Gladys said after almost a minute, "she was looking for birds."

"Maybe," the rabbi agreed genially. "It's always possible."

He removed Gladys's folder from his attaché case and slid it across the table. She snatched it up and hugged it to her bosom.

"Please feel free to go now, Miss Eisenstein," said the rabbi. "If you remember anything else that you think might interest me, you know how to find me."

Gladys stood up and pushed in her chair. "Red meat kills," she said icily. Then she turned on her heels.

I looked at the rabbi. He was staring at the ceiling, his eyes glazed over in thought.

"Rabbi?" I asked.

"Give me a minute," he muttered.

Nearly fifteen minutes passed before he returned to the world of the living. His eyes gleamed like the jewels on the Torah coverings and his entire body trembled.

"What is it, rabbi?" I asked. "Are you all right?"

"What is it, Steinmetz? It's only the most glorious thing in the universe."

I struggled to grasp the rabbi's meaning. "It's just a ceiling," I observed.

"Not that, Steinmetz. Don't be such a *dumkopf*. Think. Use your rabbinic reasoning. Then think some more, okay? How could a ceiling be the most glorious thing in the universe? I've seen the one in the Sistine Chapel, Steinmetz, and even that didn't impress me terribly. All it is anyway is *goyish* art."

At other times, I would have objected to the rabbi's criticism of Michelangelo's masterpiece. Yet at that moment, I was far more interested in finding out what it was that had caused him to make such an overwhelming declaration.

"Are you talking about the pastrami, rabbi?" I asked.

"No," he mimicked me, "I am *not* talking about the pastrami, Steinmetz. I'm talking about the proof that an omniscient and omnipresent God exists. I'm talking about the order of the universe, the only thing that separates us from chaos and destruction. That's what I'm talking about."

"Do you mean," I asked tentatively, "that you have your rational explanation? You know who murdered Florence Eisenstein?

The rabbi nodded. "Indeed, I believe I do," he replied. "Or, at least, I have a pretty good idea. That's the easy part. Proving it is a different matter entirely. And there are still a handful of smaller questions that need to be answered. So, Steinmetz, what did you think of the pastrami?"

I could hardly believe my ears. The rabbi had just solved the murder and here he was asking me what I thought of the cold cuts. I did everything I could to restrain myself from shaking the rational explanation out of him. "So who did it?" I finally asked.

Rabbi Kappelmacher shook his head. "We still need to test my hypothesis, Steinmetz. I know you well. If I tell you now, you'll give it away before we have enough evidence. Besides, I don't have time to explain at the moment. We still need to trap our murderer."

I thought about pleading with the rabbi, but I knew that it would do no good. On the ride back to Haddam, I devoted my full concentration to the case. If Rabbi Kappelmacher could uncover the rational explanation through rabbinic reasoning, I told myself, so could I. Of course, I couldn't. All of the evidence pointed at Gladys Eisenstein: Her leaving her room on Tuesday night, the binoculars, the lies about the letter to her aunt, the folder that Agatha had discovered. Yet try as I might, I just couldn't piece these facts together into a coherent whole. By the time we arrived back at the synagogue—nearly three o'clock—I was so confused that I began to doubt whether Florence had been murdered at all and we weren't just two suburban rabbis searching for excitement any way we could find it.

"What now?" I asked the rabbi.

"Now we test my hypothesis," he replied. "But before we do that, I need you to do me a small favor."

"Anything you want, rabbi."

I anticipated some service relating to the case.

"Do you remember how to get to Dr. Scott's office in Pine Valley?"

"Sure thing."

"Well, I want you to drive up there and tell him I'm suffering from abdominal pains. Ask him to give you a prescription for a pain killer—anything that might soothe the gastrointestinal tract."

I stared at the rabbi in shock. "You've got to be kidding me, rabbi," I declared with irritation. "*You* gorge yourself on pastrami and now you expect *me* to drive all the way to Pine Valley to relieve your indigestion. If you don't mind my saying so, I don't think that's exactly fair of you."

"I need some quiet time to think," replied the rabbi. "I promise when you get back, we'll test my hypothesis. But right now, I need some pain killers and maybe a good nap. But do hurry up. I want to get to Louise Sinkoff's house before her husband returns home from work."

"I'll go," I grumbled. "But when I get back, I expect to hear a darn good rational explanation. I am the assistant rabbi, you know. I have some stake in all of this."

"Of course, you do, Steinmetz," the rabbi said jovially. "But please hurry. The drive will do you good. You can use it to work on your rabbinic reasoning. In fact, if you come up with the rational explanation on your own before you get back, I'll buy you another lunch at Knobler's."

I watched the rabbi make his way toward the air-conditioned synagogue. When he'd vanished through the glass doors, I walked down the block to my house and reluctantly slid behind the wheel of my car. The rabbi never ceased to amaze me. There we were on the brink of solving

a murder and he eats himself sick. I cursed Knobler's
pastrami and set out for Pine Valley as fast as I could go.

CHAPTER 16: THE BLIND WOMAN REVISITED

A brief visit to Dr. Scott's office procured the necessary prescription and I arrived back at the synagogue at four o'clock. I found the rabbi in his office, smoking a cigar.

"*Nu?*" he asked. "Did you accomplish your mission?"

"Here are your darn pills, rabbi," I replied sullenly. "Just so you know, I had to push my way past that receptionist to see the doctor. She even threatened to call the police on me. It's a good thing you made such a strong impression on Dr. Scott or I'm convinced that woman would have had me spending the night behind bars."

"That would have been a most unfortunate occurrence," the rabbi replied. To my surprise, he removed the bottle of pills from the white paper bag and slid it into his desk drawer. "And all for naught. I'm feeling much better now. It's amazing what a healthy catnap can do. Now we must hurry out to Louise Sinkoff's on the double. I called ahead. This time she'll be expecting us."

In the car to the Sinkoff's, I continued my search for the rational explanation. Yet, having made no progress on the drive to Pine Valley, I'd grown accustomed to expecting very little from my rabbinic reasoning. "Rabbi," I finally asked, "can't you at least give me a hint as to who murdered Florence Eisenstein? If you point me in the right direction, maybe my rabbinic reasoning powers can take over."

The rabbi laughed. "This isn't a game, Steinmetz. This is a case of murder. But just so you don't think I'm being unfair, I will give you a hint. In this case, it will be a useful hint—since I require your help in handling Mrs. Sinkoff."

"You actually need my help?" I asked incredulously.

"Indeed, I do, Steinmetz. I need you to do a little bit of role playing."

"Role playing?" I asked. "So who am I supposed to be? An F.B.I. agent? A private investigator? Maybe even a rabbi? Say, we're not going to tell Louise that her aunt's up for some Jewish award, are we?"

The rabbi shook his head. "Nothing so complicated, Steinmetz. All you need to do is pretend that you're a lawyer."

"A lawyer?"

"That's right, Steinmetz. A lawyer. I want you to pretend that you're Marshall Green."

This was too much. "You've got to be kidding me, rabbi. You can't seriously expect me to pretend that I'm Green. Louise Sinkoff's not an idiot. She's already heard my voice. She'll be able to tell instantly that I'm not Green."

"Possibly," replied the rabbi. "You and Green have similar enough voices. Besides, you hardly opened your mouth last time we were here. It's worth a shot. I want you to pretend that you're Green. Say everything that you think he'd say under the circumstances; do everything that you think he'd do."

"May I ask why I'm doing this?"

"Of course, you may," the rabbi replied. "And I'll even tell you, seeing as I have to if this is going to work. We're going to try to convince Louise that her cousin Gladys did in fact break her grandfather's will. I'll do as much of the talking as possible. All you have to do is back me up. Make up some legal mumbo-jumbo, if you feel up to it. I have a hunch she won't know the difference."

"I'll try."

"That's all I ask," said the rabbi. "And for the record, your performance this afternoon will make or break our investigation. I don't think I can obtain the evidence I need to expose our murderer unless you convince Louise that you're Green and that the will has been broken."

"Why not just have Marshall Green play himself?" I asked. "I'm sure he'd be more than willing."

"I am too," answered the rabbi evasively.

"You don't think Marshall Green is involved in this business, do you?" I asked. "Why in the world would Green want to kill Florence?"

The rabbi remained silent. "What about my hint, rabbi?" I asked. "I thought you said that you'd provide me with a clue to set me on the right track."

Rabbi Kappelmacher let forth a hearty laugh. "You really never do listen to me, Steinmetz, do you? I already gave you your clue. Your clue is that I need you to pretend that you're Marshall Green and to convince Louise that her grandfather's will has been broken. If you can figure out why I want you to do that, you'll have your rational explanation."

"I don't understand," I said.

"If all goes well, you will soon enough," answered the rabbi. "Try to think like a lawyer, not a rabbi. From this moment forward, you *are* Marshall Green."

Having no idea how lawyers think, I approached Louise's with trepidation. I noticed the boy next door seated on the grass with the cat in his arms. When he spotted us, he approached hesitantly. "Hi," he said—clearly nervous. "You're the detectives, aren't you? Samantha Sinkoff told me about you." The boy shifted his weight from one leg to the other.

"I'm not a detective, I'm a lawyer," I retorted with business-like indifference. "Now scram."

The boy bolted across the yard and disappeared around the side of the house. I looked at the rabbi for his reaction. He nodded in approval.

"Now keep that up for another hour, Green," said the rabbi. "I'm placing my full confidence in you. Of course, I already told Mrs. Sinkoff that I'd be stopping by with Green from the lawyers,' so she'll be expecting you."

"Oh, great," I muttered as the rabbi pressed the doorbell.

Mrs. Sinkoff answered promptly. She wore a floral print dress and carried her stick in one hand. "Yes?"

"It's Inspector Kappelmacher," said the rabbi. "And Marshall Green from Abercrombie & Green. You remember Mr. Green, don't you?"

"Of course, I do, inspector. Are you really a lawyer, Mr. Green, or are you also undercover?"

I cleared my throat and shook hands with Louise. "I assure you, ma'am, that I'm a lawyer. It's a good thing, too. I don't understand how anybody can live on an F.B.I. inspector's salary these days. How much do they pay you at the agency, Kappelmacher?"

"Enough," the rabbi warned coldly. He glared at me. I smirked and shrugged my shoulders. Louise appeared to be buying my act. She led us into the parlor and this time she offered each of us a cup of coffee.

"We'll pass," said the rabbi. "We don't have too much time."

"Actually, inspector," I replied, "I'd love a cup of coffee, if it's not too much trouble. Cream, no sugar."

Mrs. Sinkoff departed through an open door and returned with a cup of coffee. In the interim, the rabbi glared at me with displeasure. I smiled back at him. If he wanted me to play lawyer, I was going to play lawyer. In all honesty, I was starting to enjoy being Marshall Green.

"So, inspector," said Louise, once we were all seated, "on the phone you said you had some very good news for me. I've been dying for an explanation ever since. Have you figured out who murdered Aunt Florence or have you come to your senses?"

It struck me that our host was much more composed now than she'd been on our first visit. I surmised that now that she knew we weren't interested in her gambling problems or her husband's embezzlement, we seemed a lot less threatening.

"Unfortunately, I haven't," replied the rabbi. "I've been distracted by another case."

"An interesting one, I imagine," said Mrs. Sinkoff.

The rabbi shrugged. "It's actually down on the Lower East Side. Have you ever heard of the Pastrami Sandwich Gang?"

I bit my tongue to keep from laughing. Louise shook her head. "I can't say I have," she replied. "Anyway, I can't wait to hear my good news. You said you could help alleviate my—our financial difficulties...."

"Indeed," said the rabbi. "Mr. Green, would you like to share the good news with Mrs. Sinkoff?"

Here goes nothing, I thought. I attempted to speak from the back of my throat to make my voice sound deeper. "Mrs. Sinkoff," I said, "I've come to let you know that you are going to be a very wealthy woman. Your sister, Gladys, came to me on the morning of your aunt's wedding with a stack of legal documents. I didn't bother to look at them at the time—I generally ignore legal research done by my clients. Leave it to the experts, I say. That's what we're paid for. But as it turns out, your sister brought us the records of *Billings v. Conch*—a recent court case that overturned the precedent established in *Evans v. Dodge.*"

The rabbi rolled his eyes and motioned with his hand for me to hurry up. "The long and the short of it," I continued, "is that this new case invalidated your grandfather's will. Not just the portion dealing with marriage, but the entire document. As a result, your grandfather died intestate—without a will—and you stand to inherit one third of his assets. In addition, by the terms of your Aunt Florence's will, you stand to inherit one quarter of her third as well."

Louise smiled politely. I expected her to leap from her seat with joy, but she remained quite subdued. "How much money, Mr. Green?"

I leaned forward and whispered an imaginary figure in her ear.

"That is good news," said Louise.

"I hate to say I told you so, Mrs. Sinkoff," interjected the rabbi, "but I told you so. Almost all problems have a way of working themselves out."

The rabbi rose from his seat and propped himself against one of the statues in the center of the room. "Now that Mr. Green here has helped solve one of your problems, I was hoping that you could help to solve one of mine. I still need to know who murdered Florence."

"I wish I could tell you, inspector," Louise replied, "but I'm not an F.B.I. inspector or a lawyer."

"Of course not," retorted Rabbi Kappelmacher. "However, you may have some information essential to resolving this case. For example, you may be able to tell me why your Aunt Florence went bird watching on the day before her wedding."

"I'm sorry, I can't," Louise replied. "I didn't even know that Florence was a bird watcher. I always thought of her as the card-playing, book-reading type."

"I imagine that you're not a bird watcher yourself, Mrs. Sinkoff," the rabbi observed.

"No, I'm afraid I'm not."

"And I imagine that you don't own a pair of binoculars."

"Actually," Mrs. Sinkoff replied, "I do."

This statement caught both the rabbi and me off guard. It struck me as mighty suspicious that a blind woman would own a pair of binoculars.

"You do?" inquired the rabbi.

"They're somewhere up in the attic, I believe. We found them with my father's things after my mother died. I have absolutely no use for them, of course, but Fred told me he didn't have room for anything, so they're still up there somewhere. You're welcome to borrow them, if it's that important."

The rabbi grinned. "No, Mrs. Sinkoff," he said, "it's actually not important at all."

"Oh," our host replied. She didn't seem to know what to make of this answer.

Rabbi Kappelmacher returned to his seat and stretched his arms. "We had the most marvelous lunch today, Mrs. Sinkoff," he said conversationally. "Didn't we, Green?"

"And well worth the cost," I replied, trying to stay in character.

"We dined at Knobler's Deli," continued the rabbi. "Do you know it, Mrs. Sinkoff?"

Our host smiled. "Knobler's Deli. I haven't been there in thirty years. It really isn't my sort of food. And it's such a hassle to get down there nowadays."

"Of course," replied the rabbi. I sensed that he was killing time. "I imagine you went there often as a young girl?"

"Our father dragged us every Thursday night. None of us like the food that much, but he used to say it was like stepping straight back into his own childhood."

"How were the pickles?" Rabbi Kappelmacher asked.

Mrs. Sinkoff scrunched up her nose and displayed a sour expression. "God awful, inspector. I'm not a pickle person. Of course, nobody hated pickles as much as Gladys. Once, when we were girls, she intentionally threw the entire pickle plate on the floor. I still remember how embarrassed I was, inspector."

"Indeed," said the rabbi. "Mr. Green doesn't seem to care for pickles either. Personally, I think they're second only to pastrami. Both gifts of God. Of course, I'm only an F.B.I. agent, not a rabbi, so that's straying from my field of expertise."

"I understand," said Mrs. Sinkoff. She stood up suddenly. "You'll have to excuse me, inspector, but Andrew will be home at any moment. I don't think he'd be pleased to find you here."

"I imagine not," agreed the rabbi. We followed our host to the door.

As we were about to leave, the rabbi nudged my arm. I tried my best to guess what he expected of me. "Mrs. Sinkoff," I said, "I want to congratulate you again on breaking the will. I'll give you a call in...." I looked at the rabbi. He held up five fingers. "I'll give you a call in five days or so to let you know the details."

"Five days," Louise repeated. "That's not so long. Goodbye, Mr. Green. Goodbye, Inspector. And good luck!"

The blind woman stood in the door frame waving at us until we pulled away.

"Well?" I asked the rabbi as soon as we reached the end of the block. "Do you think she bought it?"

"There's only one way to find out, Steinmetz. If she didn't believe your little role play, then she'll be on the phone to Marshall Green's office right now trying to find out if the will really was broken."

"That doesn't help us any," I said. "How are we supposed to know if she called Green?"

"It's very simple, Steinmetz. We merely call him up and ask."

I blinked twice. A week before, phoning Green would have been the first idea to enter my head. After seven days of playing detective, I now found myself becoming a confirmed skeptic. "How do you know Green will answer you honestly, rabbi?"

"I don't. Yet it would greatly disappoint me if he doesn't."

When we reached the business district, the rabbi pulled over to a bank of payphones at the side of the road. I noticed that the neighborhood looked familiar; it took me several seconds to realize that we were only a couple of blocks from Alfred's retirement complex. I watched through the window as the rabbi spoke at some length with Green. When he returned to the car, his eyes were glowing. Without a word, he turned on the ignition and started to drive.

I waited for him to tell me whether we'd succeeded. Instead, he turned on the radio and tapped his thumbs on the steering wheel to the tune of a Mozart sonata.

"Well?" I finally demanded. "Did she call or didn't she?"

The rabbi smiled at me—a thoroughly inscrutable smile. "For the record, Rabbi Steinmetz," he said, "When I say we don't want coffee, we don't want coffee."

"What is that supposed to mean, rabbi?"

"It means exactly what you think it means. Trust me once in a while."

"Do you think I gave us away when I asked for coffee?" I asked in disbelief. I didn't understand how that could blow my cover. Everybody drinks coffee.

"No, Steinmetz, I don't think that gave us away," the rabbi answered ambiguously. "I do think you should listen to me very closely though. There's a murderer on the loose and we can't take any chances."

"So what do we do now?"

"I don't know," said the rabbi. "I say we have a hearty dinner and a good night's sleep, and we forget all about wills and binoculars for a while. Tomorrow, we say our prayers and go about our business. If I know our murderer, and I think I do, we won't have long to wait. Our murderer is bound to get restless. Now how would Mrs. Steinmetz feel about a dinner guest?"

"I'm sure she wouldn't mind," I replied. I'd already explained the details of the case to my wife and she had some questions of her own for the rabbi. "In fact, I think she'd like it a lot."

We stopped by the synagogue for the rabbi to retrieve some papers and to check his phone messages.

"Someone named Agatha Grossbart called for you, rabbi," Mrs. Billings informed him. "Twice. And a Fred Eisenstein phoned less than five minutes ago. He said he plans to stop by tomorrow morning. He said, and I quote, that he needs to speak with you urgently."

"Indeed," mused the rabbi. "I wonder what that could be about."

He emptied some folders into his attaché case and we headed toward my house for dinner. On the way, the rabbi stopped suddenly in his tracks.

"What's wrong?" I asked.

"That Agatha Grossbart," he replied. "I'm just starting to realize how far she'll go to get what she wants."

"I don't understand, rabbi."

"Neither do I," replied Rabbi Kappelmacher. "As God is my witness, neither do I."

CHAPTER 17: FRED CHANGES HIS STORY

Fred Eisenstein's idea of "the next morning" differed somewhat from mine, for it was after noon by the time he made an appearance at the synagogue. I dropped by Rabbi Kappelmacher's office at ten o'clock and again at eleven o'clock, but each time the rabbi called me a *noodnik* and told me he'd send for me when the nephew arrived. True to his word, he dispatched Mrs. Billings to retrieve me. I greeted Fred just as he was settling into a chair across from the rabbi's desk.

"It took me forever to find this place," Fred said. "All of suburbia looks the same. House after house after house—I'm amazed that people don't go home to the wrong families by mistake. And this synagogue of yours," he added with a wave of his hand. "All of these corridors look the same and none of the doors are marked. If I hadn't asked for directions, I could have wandered down here for hours. Even days."

"You wouldn't be the first," I muttered.

Rabbi Kappelmacher placed his watch to his ear. "Mr. Eisenstein," he said, "it is twelve thirty-five in the afternoon. It is no longer morning. But since you are here, I'll gladly overlook your tardiness. Now what can I do for you?"

Fred took a deep breath and exhaled slowly. "What's your racket, Kappelmacher?" he asked. "I called the F.B.I. yesterday afternoon and they said they have absolutely no idea who you are. In fact, the agent I spoke to burst out laughing when I told him the story that you told me."

The rabbi smiled. "Do you think, Mr. Eisenstein, that the Federal Bureau of Investigation reveals the identities of its undercover operatives to anyone who calls them?"

"Look, Kappelmacher," said Fred. "I may not be the richest man in the world or the most successful, but I'm not a fool. I did some checking. I called the National Conference of Conservative Rabbis. I called the United Jewish Appeal. They know who you are. I spoke to a Rabbi Freudenstein at the NCCR who says you performed his marriage ceremony and offered to send me reprints of your article on rabbinic reasoning and Biblical interpretation. You're not F.B.I., Kappelmacher. You're a suburban rabbi. Now, to borrow a Jewish phrase, what's your *shtick*?"

The rabbi sighed. "Very well, Mr. Eisenstein," he replied. "You figured me out. I'm not with the F.B.I. I'm just some meddlesome rabbi."

"Well, what's your racket then, Kappelmacher?" Fred demanded. "What stake do you have in my aunt's death? Did you know that it's illegal to impersonate an F.B.I. agent? You can go to jail for five years or pay a twenty-five thousand dollar fine. Last night, I had an opportunity to read up on the subject."

"Feel free to turn me in then, Mr. Eisenstein," said the rabbi. "And Rabbi Steinmetz too. Do whatever you have to do."

The rabbi's indifference appeared to frustrate our visitor. "That's it? Turn you in? You aren't even going to explain what in God's name you've been doing pretending to be investigating my aunt's murder?"

The rabbi shook his head and lit a cigar. "You wouldn't believe me anyway, Mr. Eisenstein. And to be frank, I don't have time for this."

I squirmed nervously in my seat. Fred Eisenstein started to pace across the small office, waving his arms frenetically. "I don't get you, Kappelmacher," he declared. "One minute, you're mucking about pretending to be an F.B.I. agent on the hunt for a murderer, and the next, you're a suburban rabbi who doesn't care that he might face five years in prison. I think you have a hell of a lot of explaining to do."

The rabbi nodded. "I'll be glad to explain, Mr. Eisenstein. The question is whether or not you'll be willing to listen."

Fred returned to his seat. "I'm all ears," he replied angrily. "I can't wait to hear this one."

Rabbi Kappelmacher leaned forward as though he were about to share a secret. "The truth is, Mr. Eisenstein, that I really am an F.B.I. agent. So is Steinmetz here. And Mrs. Billings across the hall. And even Mrs. Conch, whom you might have seen mopping the corridor. Everyone in this building—with the exception of you—is an F.B.I. operative."

Fred Eisenstein scowled. "What do you take me for? I did my research, Kappelmacher. Do you expect me to believe that the F.B.I. permitted you to marry Rabbi Freudenstein?"

"Don't be a fool," replied the rabbi. "Of course, I don't expect you to believe that. What you never considered is the possibility that I'm not the real Rabbi Jacob Kappelmacher. There is a real Rabbi Jacob Kappelmacher, of course. I met him once about a month ago. He's a delightful man. If you drop by on Saturday, you might even see him. The truth of the matter is that we're borrowing this building from the Haddam Jewish Center to mount a complex undercover operation, the details of which I am not at liberty to explain. The real Rabbi Kappelmacher has been generous enough to permit me to assume his identity for the month. The same is true of the real Rabbi Steinmetz and the real Mrs. Billings and even the real Mrs. Conch. When our investigation is over—and I imagine it will wrap itself up in the next couple of days—we'll return the synagogue to the real rabbi and nobody will be any the worse for it."

I couldn't believe the rabbi's audacity.

"Do you really expect me to believe that nonsense, Kappelmacher?" Fred demanded. "That's the most incredible tale I've ever heard."

"Suit yourself," the rabbi replied indifferently. "Believe it or don't believe it. It's no skin off my nose. Of course, you're welcome to stop by on Saturday and meet the real rabbi. Or to observe that there are no names plates on the doors because we don't want innocent congregants coming down here to search for the real rabbi. Most of the people here only attend synagogue twice a year on the High Holidays. That's one of the reasons why we chose this

community. They have no idea where the rabbi's office is—
and if they can't find it, they give up and go home. Then
they phone the real rabbi; his calls are being forwarded. Not
that any of this matters. I expect to make an arrest in the
Eisenstein case any day now and then I'll be out of here for
good."

Our visitor appeared to be deeply troubled by the rabbi's
suggestion that we were making progress in the case. He
folded his arms across his chest and frowned. I could see
him trying to decide whether the rabbi was an F.B.I.
inspector or a deranged liar. "Do you have any proof to offer
me that you're not just a nutty old rabbi?" he asked.

"I can't offer you proof, Mr. Eisenstein. But I can ask you
a question. Why in heaven's name would I—or anybody
else, for that matter—make up a story like that? And even if
I did, how could I convince Inspector Steinmetz and Agent
Billings and Special Agent Conch to play along with it if
they were only the regular employees of a suburban
synagogue? Think about that for a moment, Mr. Eisenstein.
Mull it over. It doesn't really matter to me either way."

It appeared that the nephew was buying the rabbi's
preposterous story, for suddenly his tone changed. "So let's
assume for a moment that you are an F.B.I. inspector,
Kappelmacher. I can call you Kappelmacher, can't I? Or do
you have a real name?"

"I do have a real name," said the rabbi. "But you'd best
call me Kappelmacher."

"Okay, Kappelmacher. Supposing you are telling me the
truth. Are you really that close to making an arrest?"

"Indeed, I am," lied the rabbi. "I already know exactly
how and why your aunt was murdered. Now I'm simply
biding my time until the agency can get the paperwork in
order."

"May I ask whom you intend to arrest, Kappelmacher?"

"You may ask all you want," the rabbi answered, "But
I'm afraid that I'm not at liberty to tell you. You'll find out
soon enough. I'm sure it will make the local papers. Of
course, you can feel free to ask Inspector Steinmetz for the

name of the person I intend to arrest, but I doubt you'll make much headway with him."

Fred glanced at me and clearly decided that it wasn't worth asking. He suddenly appeared to become unnerved. "Okay, Kappelmacher," he stated. "I believe you. You're on the level. But I don't think you can blame me for being suspicious. This is an awfully strange investigation you're operating here."

"Run-of-the-mill by agency standards. Yet I see why you may have doubted me. But now that we've cleared that up, I want to wish you a good afternoon, Mr. Eisenstein. I remind you that I'm quite busy. I still have a murderer to apprehend."

Rabbi Kappelmacher strode to the door and opened it for our guest. The nephew stood up hesitantly and then sat down again. He took another deep breath and exhaled slowly. "I'm sorry, inspector," he said. "But I need another minute of your time."

The rabbi re-crossed the room and seated himself on the edge of his desk with his hands folded over his knee. "What is it, Mr. Eisenstein? I don't have all day to squander justifying myself to laypersons. As I said, I have a murderer to apprehend."

"Please, inspector," replied a contrite Fred Eisenstein. "I think you'll want to hear me out. You see, I lied to you earlier."

"Lied? I have absolutely no patience for liars."

"Listen to me a moment, inspector. I lied to you because I was ashamed of myself. It was a white lie—or I thought it was at the time. But now it seems absolutely unconscionable, especially when you're about to make an arrest in a murder case."

The rabbi appeared to be highly intrigued. "How did you lie to me, Mr. Eisenstein?" he asked. "If you come clean now, maybe we can avoid criminal charges."

"Charges?"

"For impeding a murder investigation. Obstruction of justice. I believe the penalty is five years in prison and a twenty-five thousand dollar fine. Now what exactly did you lie to me about?"

Fred turned a ghostly white. "I had a terrible row with my Aunt Florence," he said rapidly. "On Saturday. Just like she told everybody. We must have argued for nearly an hour. She said she planned to disinherit me because I was only after her money. But that wasn't true, inspector. I swear it. I loved both my aunts very dearly."

"Indeed," declared the rabbi. He approached the nephew and stared at him coldly. "Why didn't you mention this to me before?"

"I was ashamed of myself," Fred said. "I was ashamed and...I don't know...I'm not a lawyer....I thought maybe my aunt's intention to disinherit me was good enough to invalidate her will....Not that I was after her money, of course, but she was dead and I don't know....Then you started speaking about murder and I was afraid you'd suspect me and—"

"Enough!" Rabbi Kappelmacher interjected. "What I need now are facts, not justifications. Explain yourself to God. What you need to explain to me is exactly what happened between you and your aunt. Is that clear?"

Fred nodded.

"Now let's go through this step by step, Mr. Eisenstein. When was the first contact you had with your aunts upon returning from Europe?"

"On the Wednesday night before the wedding. On the phone. Just like I told you. I didn't lie about that."

"So you expect me to believe you now," the rabbi mused, "when you're already a confirmed liar. Why should I believe you?"

"Because I'm telling the truth, inspector," Fred insisted.

"Very well. We'll give you the benefit of the doubt for now, but I want you to know that I'm taking everything you tell me with a grain of salt. Anyway, back to the facts. Did you fight with Florence on Wednesday?"

"No. Not at all."

"What did you talk about?"

"I spoke to Lorraine about gardening and to Florence about bird watching. She'd seen a sparrow hawk on the Finchley property. Lorraine said she had something to tell me in private. Exactly like I told you earlier, inspector."

"And did you make plans to visit your aunts?"

"I told them I'd drop by on Sunday or Monday. But then there was that business with the prospective investor. As it turns out, he's decided to place his money elsewhere."

"So let me see if I have this right. You went to your aunts' house on Saturday and you had a terrible row with Florence."

"It was just awful. So unexpected. She informed me that she'd broken my grandfather's will, but that I shouldn't expect a penny of the money. She also told me that she intended to get married, but that if I had any decency left in me, I wouldn't show up for the wedding."

"I see," said the rabbi. "So when you phoned your sister's home on Tuesday, you already knew that she was at your aunt's wedding."

Fred shook his head. "No, I didn't. I knew *that* Aunt Florence was getting married. I didn't know *when* she was getting married."

"Of course," agreed the rabbi. "How foolish of me. For the record, Mr. Eisenstein, why did you go to your aunt's wedding if you knew that you wouldn't be welcome?"

"I thought she might have a change of heart," Fred stammered. "Or, at least, I hoped so. Her anger on Saturday was so unexpected. I thought maybe with a few days time, she'd have come to her senses."

"And thinking the will had been broken, Mr. Eisenstein, you wanted to make sure that you obtained your piece of the pie."

"No!" Fred shouted. "I wanted to attend my aunt's wedding because I wanted to see her get married. Because I loved her. It had absolutely nothing to do with the money."

"Of course not," said the rabbi. I could sense that he was growing angry. "Now tell me more about Saturday, Mr. Eisenstein. Did you ask your aunt how she came to the conclusion that you were after her money?"

Fred's hands were trembling. "She said she'd spoken to the lawyers and that they'd helped her to see matters straight and—"

"Which lawyer? Mr. Abercrombie or Mr. Green or both of them?"

"I don't know," answered Fred. "I think both of them. I'm not sure."

"When?"

"When what?"

"When did she say she'd spoken to the lawyers, Mr. Eisenstein? It had to have been between Wednesday night and Saturday morning, didn't it? You've already stated that your aunt didn't mention anything about disinheriting you on Wednesday evening."

"I don't know, inspector," Fred replied. "I really don't know. Does it matter? The point is that we had a terrible row and I stormed off in anger."

"But you didn't call your aunt on Sunday or Monday to try to patch things up?"

"No, I didn't. I was ashamed at having argued with her like that. I was also confused by the sudden change in her attitude towards me. And then there was my meeting with prospective investor. That consumed the greater part of my energy."

The rabbi walked to the window. He gazed thoughtfully into the courtyard. "That is a very interesting story you've just told me, Mr. Eisenstein," he said without turning around. "I only wish you'd shared it with me sooner."

I looked at the rabbi and then at Fred. Both appeared deeply troubled. Even I found Fred's story vaguely disturbing. I sensed that something wasn't right about it— that it called into question facts we already knew.

"I want to make sure I have this exactly correct," the rabbi said. "When you visited your aunt on Saturday, you didn't make plans to go to the Museum of Natural History, did you?"

"No," Fred declared firmly. "I made that part up to make my story more convincing."

"Indeed," replied the rabbi. "And a convincing tale it was. Did you discuss anything else other than Florence's marriage and her plan to disinherit you during the course of your visit? Possibly bird watching or sparrow hawks? I hear they're large birds."

"No, we didn't. From the moment I stepped through the door, Florence was accusing me of wanting her to die so I could inherit her money."

"Puzzling," muttered Rabbi Kappelmacher. "Truly puzzling."

"What's so puzzling?" Fred asked.

"Nothing. I was just trying to understand your motive for lying."

"I already told you, inspector," said Fred. "I was ashamed. That's all there was to it. How was I supposed to know that I was in the middle of an F.B.I. investigation?"

The rabbi smiled. "I guess you couldn't have known, Mr. Eisenstein. How could you have? Anyway, I appreciate your dropping by. Unfortunately, Inspector Steinmetz and I have a lunch date, so you'll have to excuse us."

Rabbi Kappelmacher walked the nephew to the door.

"I hope I've helped clarify matters for you," Fred observed.

"Indeed," replied the rabbi. "Indeed. Good day, Mr. Eisenstein."

The rabbi kicked the door shut with his foot and held up his fist. "I despise liars, Steinmetz. Really, I do. If these people had all told me the truth from the outset, we would have saved ourselves an inordinate amount of time and energy."

"Don't worry about it, rabbi," I replied to calm him. "Now you know the truth. I imagine it helps with your rational explanation."

"I don't need any help with my rational explanation, Steinmetz," said Rabbi Kappelmacher. "None at all. What I do need is a hearty lunch. Are you up for a trip to that new Kosher deli in Cedar Springs?"

I looked at my watch. It was one o'clock. "I'll make you a deal, rabbi," I said. "I'll buy you lunch and you reveal your rational explanation."

"I'll make you a deal, Steinmetz," the rabbi replied. "You'll buy me lunch and I won't nominate you for the *Noodnik* of the Year award."

Now that was an offer I couldn't exactly refuse. So we drove out to Cedar Springs and lunched on what the rabbi proclaimed to be "second-rate pastrami." While we ate, I tried to persuade him to curtail his own falsehoods.

"What are you going to do when Fred shows up on the *shabbus* looking for the real Rabbi Kappelmacher?" I asked.

The rabbi grinned. "Maybe I'll come up with a better explanation, Steinmetz. But you must admit I did a pretty good job for the spur of the moment. Besides, I hope to have exposed our murderer by Saturday."

"By Saturday?" I asked in amazement. "But that gives you only today and tomorrow."

"I'm highly impressed you figured that one out, Steinmetz," said the rabbi. "There's your rabbinic reasoning at work again. But have no fear. I believe I have a rather strong circumstantial case. All I require is a good night's sleep to think matters over and I promise you you'll have your rational explanation."

This news nearly brought tears to my eyes. At least, I now knew when I could expect to have my curiosity satisfied. From that moment on, the "second-rate pastrami" was the best I'd ever tasted.

We returned from lunch just in time to greet an agitated Mrs. Billings pacing the corridor.

"My good lady," asked the rabbi, "what on earth is the matter?"

It took several glasses of water before we managed to coax an explanation from the synagogue's secretary.

"That woman who called yesterday ....Agnes....Angela...."

"Agatha?" the rabbi asked.

"That's right. Agatha. A big woman with a cane. Well, she stopped by about twenty minutes ago. Lord did she look dreadful. Like she'd seen the Ghost of Christmas Past, if you'll pardon the expression. She barged into my office and she demanded to speak to the rabbi. When I told her you weren't in, she got angry...."

"It's all right, Mrs. Billings," soothed the rabbi. "Just tell me what happened."

"She said she needed to speak to you immediately. That she had an important message she needed to give to you. Then she said—I can hardly believe it—that she wanted to tell you how some woman was murdered. A woman named Forsythia Heisenberg—"

"Florence Eisenstein?"

"That's right. I'm not good with names. You know that. Anyway, she told me that she knew all about this murder that's taken place and that she couldn't survive a moment longer with the secret and that she absolutely had to leave a message with you...and...."

"And what, Mrs. Billings? What happened?"

"I gave her a notepad and I told her that if she left a message, I'd be sure that you received it when you returned. She asked me what time that would be and I told her that I didn't know. Maybe two. Maybe two-thirty. When I told her this, she grew hostile again. Extremely agitated. She said to tell you that she'd be at home waiting by the phone for you to call. And then she threw the notepad on my desk and stormed out....and she kept muttering 'bloody murder' over and over again to herself."

"Thank you, Mrs. Billings," said the rabbi. We escorted the distraught woman back to her office. Then we crossed the hall and Rabbi Kappelmacher lit a cigar. The rabbi appeared furious. He ripped the head off his cigar with his teeth and spit it violently into the wastepaper basket.

"That woman will stop at nothing," he said. "Absolutely nothing. She's out of control. Do me a favor, Steinmetz. The next time I call you a *noodnik*, just mention the name Agatha Grossbart, and I promise I'll apologize instantly."

"Excuse me?" I replied. I'd lost the rabbi's train of thought.

"Never mind," said Rabbi Kappelmacher. "I'll just be glad when this business is over. I don't want to see any of these people again, especially Agatha. If it wasn't my sworn duty, I'd abandon this investigation this very minute. It seems I can't get a moment of peace without somebody bringing up the death of Lorraine Eisenstein."

I wanted to tell the rabbi that he'd brought this upon himself, but I couldn't. In any case, at that very moment, there was a knock at the door. Seconds later, as if to prove the rabbi's point, Lorraine stepped into his office.

CHAPTER 18: LORRAINE REVEALS HER SECRET

If the rabbi were fed up with the Eisenstein case, he masked his displeasure well. In fact, he seemed truly delighted by Lorraine's sudden arrival. This, in spite of her somewhat unlikely attire: She was decked out in her gardening outfit, down to the padded gloves and mud-caked overalls. Yet the rabbi made no mention of her somewhat disheveled appearance as he escorted her to a chair.

"Miss Eisenstein," he said. "What a pleasant surprise."

Lorraine wiped her forehead with her hand and gazed around nervously. "Dear me. I'm so sorry for barging in on you like this, inspector, but I just needed to speak with you—to unburden myself. I've been thinking about what you said the other day—that somebody might be trying to murder me—and I'm scared."

Rabbi Kappelmacher pulled his chair up alongside our visit. "I'm very glad you stopped by, Miss Eisenstein. I've actually been meaning to pay you another visit. I was somewhat concerned the last time I saw you that you weren't taking my concerns seriously. I can't impress upon you enough that none of us are safe until your sister's killer is behind bars."

Lorraine removed her gardening gloves. "I know that now, inspector. That's why I'm here. I thought about going straight to the police, but I figured you already knew all the details. Besides, I don't think they'd be as understanding as you are."

"Probably not."

"I would have been here sooner," Lorraine continued. "Only I—"

"Couldn't find my office," interjected the rabbi. "That appears to be a widespread phenomenon. Now what is it that you wanted to tell me, Miss Eisenstein?"

The elderly spinster folded her gloves in her lap. "There was a person in Florence's room that night," she stated.

The rabbi's eyes widened. "Could you repeat that, Miss Eisenstein?"

"There was a person in Florence's room on the night she died," Lorraine said. "I'm sure of it. Or, at least, I think I am. I didn't stop by Florence's room to apologize or to make peace. I lied to you about that because I was afraid...afraid of...."

"Afraid of what, Miss Eisenstein?"

"I was afraid of stirring up old trouble. About my father's death and all those dreadful accusations from the past. I don't know how to put this best, inspector, but I suspected that dear Florence had been murdered long before you did. That very night, in fact. I don't care what Dr. Scott says about it. I'm sure I heard somebody inside Florence's bedroom on Tuesday night. I was on my way to the bathroom when I heard what sounded like a muffled scream and then a series of footsteps. Only they were strange footsteps. First a loud one and then a soft one. So I knocked and when there was no answer, I pushed open the door. But there was nobody there, inspector. Just Florence, poor unfortunate Florence.'

Lorraine broke off her story and began to sob.

Rabbi Kappelmacher rubbed his beard. "When you say there was nobody there, Miss Eisenstein, I take it that you mean there was nobody inside Florence's bedroom?"

Lorraine nodded.

"What about the closet, Miss Eisenstein? Did you think to look in the closet?"

"No, I didn't, inspector. It didn't even cross my mind at the time. I was in shock. Florence was lying there on the bed and I could tell she was dead. Somehow, I just knew it. So I stood there, staring at her for maybe ten minutes. I might have stood there all night if Alfred hadn't come back and phoned the doctor."

"Indeed. It must have been a dreadful shock. But if you'll bear with me, I want to run through exactly what happened one more time. You said you were on the way to the bathroom when you heard this muffled scream. How loud a scream was it?"

"Not very loud," Lorraine replied. "It couldn't have been. I imagine if it had been, it would have awakened the rest of the house. The walls in the old place are like paper, you understand...."

"So you must have been pretty close to Florence's door to hear the scream if it wasn't that loud," the rabbi suggested.

Lorraine nodded. "Immediately across from it. The more I think about it, inspector, it wasn't a loud scream at all. It just sounded loud to me on account of the silence in the house."

"Of course," agreed the rabbi. "And then you went to the door and knocked?"

"Precisely. I knocked on the door and, when there was no reply, I opened it."

"Did you hear the footsteps before or after you knocked?"

"After. One loud and one soft. Over and over again."

"And how much time would you say elapsed between when you heard the scream and when you opened the door, Miss Eisenstein?"

"Hardly any time at all. Maybe five seconds. It all happened so dreadfully fast."

"Why didn't you tell me this sooner, my good lady?"

Lorraine smiled apologetically. "Do I have to answer that, inspector?"

"I'd appreciate it," the rabbi replied.

Lorraine fumbled with her gloves and gazed into her lap. "Like I told you, inspector, I thought Florence had been murdered and I didn't want to open old wounds."

"Is that the only reason, Miss Eisenstein?" Rabbi Kappelmacher demanded. "Tell me the truth, my dear lady. Lives are at stake here. There must have been another reason."

Lorraine, her hands trembling, said softly, "And I wanted to protect the murderer."

"Did you now?" demanded the rabbi. "Why would you want to do a thing like that? Is it possible that you believed you knew the identity of the murderer?"

Lorraine shook her head. She'd started to cry again. "No," she murmured between sobs. "No...."

"Tell me the truth, Miss Eisenstein. I'm tired of being deceived. You did think you knew the identity of the murderer, didn't you? You might as well tell me. I suspect that I already know what you're going to say."

"Dear me," Lorraine said. "Okay. I'm sorry inspector, so sorry. But he's such a dear boy, you have to understand that. He's been under so much stress these past few years. And then there was the way Florence treated him at the wedding. I know it was wrong, inspector. But what would you have done in my shoes? I've already lost a sister. I can't bear to lose my nephew as well.'

Rabbi Kappelmacher paused for a moment to light his cigar. "So you thought it was your nephew, Fred, in your sister's room, Miss Eisenstein?"

Florence nodded and wiped her eyes. "Florence told me how angry he'd been at her on Saturday. Fred can have a wild temper when he becomes angry. Of course, maybe I'm imagining things, inspector. You see, I could have sworn I heard those same strange footsteps on Saturday night."

"On Saturday night?" demanded the rabbi anxiously.

"Dear me," replied Lorraine. "I think it was Saturday. Yes, it must have been on Saturday because I retired early that night. I wanted to plant my gladioluses first thing in the morning. They say spring bulbs should be planted at dawn, inspector. It may be an old wives tale, but it can't hurt trying. My garden needs all the help it can get."

"I'm sure," the rabbi said indifferently. "Now what exactly did you hear on Saturday night?"

"I'd been lying in bed for several hours. For some reason, I couldn't fall asleep. Around midnight, I heard those same footsteps out in the corridor. At first, I thought I was imagining things. I figured I had to be hallucinating. But in hindsight, inspector, I'm certain that I wasn't. It sounds crazy, doesn't it?"

"Not at all, Miss Eisenstein. Please continue."

"There's not much more to tell. I'm certain that whoever was in Florence's bedroom last Tuesday night was also in my house on Saturday night. I couldn't sleep a wink on Saturday, but I was too frightened to leave my bedroom before the sun came up. In fact, I've barely gotten any sleep all week. I find myself lying in bed, listening for those dreadful footsteps.

"And have you heard them again?"

"No, I haven't," said Lorraine. "I've taken to locking all the doors though. I'm terribly frightened, inspector."

Rabbi Kappelmacher rubbed the bridge of his nose between his fingers. "What inspired you to come here today, Miss Eisenstein? You've kept this secret from me for nearly a week. Why share this now?"

"I already told you. I'm scared."

The rabbi nodded. "Fear is a fascinating emotion," he observed. "But I do believe you're still concealing something from me. You forget you're dealing here with an F.B.I. agent. I'm a professional. I observe things. I observe people. I know that you're not the sort of woman to visit an F.B.I. inspector wearing your gardening gloves unless something specific set you off. Now please tell me what happened this afternoon, Miss Eisenstein. My patience is running thin."

No sooner had the rabbi finished his sentence than our visitor burst into tears. She mumbled something several times but I couldn't make out what she was saying. The rabbi placed his hand on her shoulder.

"Please, my dear lady," he said. "I can't understand you when you're crying. Now what is it that's upsetting you so?"

Lorraine composed herself. "Dear me," she said. "I think I'm going mad."

"Not mad, Miss Eisenstein. You've been through a great deal, by your own admission. Now please tell us what's bothering you so much."

Lorraine Eisenstein nodded. "It's nothing really. It's so irrational of me. I was working in the garden this afternoon—transplanting some marigolds—when I heard someone behind me. I turned around and my cousin, Agatha, was standing there. She had her cane lifted. In hindsight, I imagine she was just stretching or maybe she'd lost her balance. I don't know. But for a moment, I feared she was going to strike me. I know that sounds crazy, inspector. And I'm sure it is. I can't stand, but rationally, I'm sure she wouldn't strike me with her cane. Yet for a moment, I thought she was going to—and it was absolutely awful."

Rabbi Kappelmacher patted our visitor on the arm. "There, there, Miss Eisenstein. It will be all right."

"I know," Lorraine replied. "But I hate myself for thinking that. I scared her off, too. I covered my face with my hands and cried out 'murderer!' and Agatha turned around and walked away. She didn't even say a word to me. It was awful. I don't know if I'll ever be able to forgive myself. And to make matters worse, it all happened in front of the woman next door."

"Mrs. Finchley?"

"That's right. I tried to explain myself to her afterwards, but I couldn't. How can I justify calling anyone a murderer—no matter how much I may dislike her? It's unconscionable."

The rabbi seated himself on the edge of his desk. "I need to ask you an important question, Miss Eisenstein. I want you to think carefully before you answer. Can you think of any reason why your Cousin Agatha might want to murder you?"

"Absolutely none at all. I've never done her any harm. I haven't even wished ill upon her—at least, not to her knowledge."

This reply appeared to disturb the rabbi. "Listen to me carefully, Miss Eisenstein," he said. "Do exactly as I tell you, okay?"

Lorraine nodded. Alarm was plastered across her face.

"I want you to return home immediately. I want you to lock all of your doors and I don't want you to open them for anyone. Absolutely anyone. That includes not only your family, but also anyone from the law firm of Abercrombie & Green and Dr. Hiram Scott as well. Don't even go next door to speak to your neighbors. I think I know who our murderer is, but I don't want to take any chances. Am I making myself clear?"

"Do you really think I'm in danger, inspector?" Lorraine asked nervously. "If I am, I'd prefer to stay with you until you catch the killer."

The rabbi shook his head. "I'm afraid that's not possible. Inspector Steinmetz and I have important business to attend to. If what you tell me is true, then we have a murderer to apprehend. But I'm sure you'll be safe at home if you follow my instructions."

The rabbi and I walked the elderly spinster to her car and wished her well.

After Lorraine departed, Rabbi Kappelmacher stood in the center of the parking lot and scratched his beard pensively. "It just doesn't make sense," he said.

"What doesn't make sense?" I asked.

Rabbi Kappelmacher ignored my question. "Everything else makes sense," he said, "but this doesn't make any sense."

"What doesn't make any sense?" I asked again. Louder.

The rabbi crushed his cigar under his shoe. "Agatha's behavior never ceases to amaze me," he said.

"It was she in Florence's bedroom, wasn't it, rabbi?" I asked. "One loud step and one soft step. That's the sound that you hear when somebody walks with a cane."

"I don't understand," repeated the rabbi. "I thought I understood, but now I'm not sure anymore. How would you feel if we drove out to Pine Valley to visit the Finchley woman one more time?"

"If you think it's necessary," I agreed.

"Indeed, I do think it's absolutely necessary."

"I disagree strongly," I replied. "In fact, I'm sure it's not necessary at all."

The rabbi frowned at me. "What on earth do you mean, Steinmetz? I was just starting to have full confidence in you and here you go acting like a *dumkopf* again."

"I'm sure it's not necessary," I repeated. "It's the only fact in this entire case that I'm certain of."

The rabbi threw up his hands. "There's a murderer on the loose, Steinmetz," declared Rabbi Kappelmacher. "I have neither the time nor the patience for your *mishegos*. As far as I'm concerned, you can do as you please. I'm going to drive up to Pine Valley to speak with that *goyish* woman."

Rabbi Kappelmacher shook his head at me and turned to walk to his car. He'd barely taken half a step when he walked straight into Mrs. Annie Pierce Finchley.

CHAPTER 19: THE EYE WITNESS

"My good lady!" exclaimed Rabbi Kappelmacher. "Pardon me, but you shouldn't sneak up on an old man like that."

Mrs. Finchley frowned with disdain at the rabbi. She stood arms akimbo, her hands sheltered by white gloves, as though prepared for a confrontation. If there ever is an ultimate struggle between Judaism and Christianity, I couldn't help musing, no better representatives could be found. "My good man," Mrs. Finchley replied, "where I come from, old men don't accuse old woman of sneaking."

I stepped forward to intervene. "Mrs. Finchley," I observed, "it's so good to see you. Rabbi Kappelmacher and I were just discussing you...."

"Were you now?" she asked.

"In fact," I lied, "the rabbi was so charmed by you last Friday that he's decided to nominate you for an award. A high Jewish honor bestowed upon only a handful of Gentiles."

"What sort of award?" Mrs. Finchley inquired suspiciously. "It won't cost me anything, will it? Because I know all about awards, rabbi. The late Mr. Finchley, rest his soul, was once the National Maritime Preservation Association's Yachtsman of the Year. Some honor that was. They expected us to make a contribution of one hundred dollars."

"It's not that sort of award at all," I assured the old woman. "It's a high honor bestowed upon non-Jews who have devoted many years to cultivating their friendships with Jewish people. Of course, the rabbi has only a limited amount of influence. There are higher authorities to consider. But Rabbi Kappelmacher is determined to see you nominated. Aren't you, rabbi?"

Quite pleased with my white lie, I knew enough to back out of the conversation before I got myself into trouble. Mercifully, the rabbi—calmed somewhat—stepped forward to fill the void.

"Indeed, Mrs. Finchley," he said. "Why don't you accompany me to my office? I was just telling Rabbi Steinmetz that if all goes well, we may be able to honor both you and Miss Eisenstein in the same year. She'll receive the *noodnik*'s neighbor award and you'll get the *dumkopf* prize. I'm sure you've heard of it."

"Of course, I have," Mrs. Finchley replied to my horror. Was it possible that at one point or another, this woman had come across the term *dumkopf?* I feared the worst. "I have many Jewish friends," she replied with a warm smile. "I know all about the *doom-koof* prize. In fact, I always told Mr. Finchley that one of these years, you people would honor us. Of course, I didn't expect such a high honor. I only wish Mr. Finchley were still alive to appreciate it."

I sighed with relief. I should have known to expect just such a response from Mrs. Finchley.

"I'm sure he'd be very proud of you," the rabbi agreed. "Did you know that some of our nation's leading political figures have won this award?" I sensed that the rabbi was really enjoying himself now. "You'll be a *dumkopf* among *dumkopfs*, Mrs. Finchley. I can't think of anyone more deserving."

Mrs. Finchley clasped her gloved hands together. "You're too kind, rabbi," she said. "But I do have another matter to discuss with you. Considering how kind you've just been, I feel it's my obligation to share some highly disturbing information with you."

The rabbi looked gravely at our visitor. "Please follow me," he instructed and led us back down into the belly of the synagogue. When we were finally settled inside his office, he leaned back in his chair with his cigar jutting out from between his lips. "I trust you've come to us in regards to Miss Eisenstein."

Mrs. Finchley nodded. "Yes, I regret to say that I have. You told me to let you know if I thought of anything that might be pertinent to bestowing such an honor on my neighbor. Well, it is with great regret, rabbi, that I must tell you this. But tell you, I must. I don't feel Lorraine Eisenstein is fit to be honored. Not after what occurred this afternoon."

"And what exactly did happen this afternoon?"

Our visitor made a face as though she'd swallowed a spoonful of horseradish. "I'll tell you what happened this afternoon, rabbi. That obese woman showed up again. Third time in a week. First, on Thursday, and then on Saturday, and now today. On Saturday, I became mightily suspicious. I was at the window taking a look at the moon before I went to sleep, as I sometimes do, and I spied that woman sneaking up the path. There was no question about it in my mind. She was sneaking. And then I saw her sneak away again the next morning. I couldn't help seeing her, rabbi. I went out for my morning breath of fresh air and there she was slinking down the path."

"Indeed," declared the rabbi.

"Indeed," echoed Mrs. Finchley. "Then, this afternoon, while I was out on the porch, I saw that same woman once more. Lorraine was working on her flowers in the garden. She was bent to her knees, facing the opposite direction. That's when the fat woman tired to kill her."

The rabbi appeared shocked by this accusation. He scratched furiously at his beard. "What did you say, Mrs. Finchley? Did you say that Agatha Grossbart tried to kill Lorraine?"

"I most assuredly did, if the fat woman is named Agatha Grossbart. Honestly, all of those Jewish names sound the same to me. The fat woman sneaked up behind Lorraine and said, "You'll get the same as Florence," and then the fat woman raised her cane into the air as though she were going to club Lorraine with it. I was so shocked, I overturned my pitcher of lemonade and screamed. A good thing that was, too, because it startled the fat woman. It started Lorraine too. She looked up just in the nick of time. Good gracious, it was just dreadful."

"I'm sure," replied the rabbi. "And I understand that Agatha walked off after that."

"Hobbled off is more like it, rabbi," Mrs. Finchley replied decisively. "As fast as her swollen legs could carry her. She had her cab waiting for her at the end of the drive. I could tell it was a cab, rabbi, because it remained idling while the woman was lurking about. The driver must have been running up the meter. Nobody else in their right mind would waste gasoline like that at over four dollars a gallon."

The rabbi lit his cigar and tamped it out after one puff. He appeared highly on edge. "I don't understand," he muttered.

"I understand perfect," retorted Mrs. Finchley. "You can't pull the wool over my eyes, Rabbi Kappelmacher. It all makes perfect sense to me. Lorraine tried to convince me that there had been some sort of misunderstanding—that she'd thought the fat woman was somebody else. But I know the truth."

"And what is the truth, Mrs. Finchley?" the rabbi asked with complete indifference.

"The truth is that my neighbor and the fat woman are homosexuals. You can't fool me. They always end up killing each other, those homosexuals. I've read about it in the newspapers. It's hard to believe. All these years, I've been meaning to invite Lorraine over for tea and she turns out to be a homosexual. Indecent, I tell you, rabbi. Not that there's anything wrong with what people do on their own time. *Chaqun a son goût*, as the late Mr. Finchley used to say. Each to his own tastes. But I can't imagine you'll want to give Lorraine a high honor now. It just wouldn't be fitting."

"I don't understand," Rabbi Kappelmacher muttered again. "It doesn't make any sense." He stared blankly in the direction of the window.

Mrs. Finchley folded her arms across her chest. "It doesn't make any sense to me either, rabbi. But *chaqun a son goût*. It isn't our place to judge others. Do not judge lest thou shalt be judged."

The rabbi rose to his feet. Suddenly, he spun around to face Mrs. Finchley. "What did you just say?" he asked. His eyes were aflame.

"I said, do not judge others lest thou shalt be judged," Mrs. Finchley replied emphatically.

"Before that!"

"I don't know," retorted Mrs. Finchley. "I think I said that it wouldn't be fitting for Lorraine and me to receive the same award. I said that I'd been meaning to invite her over to my house for tea all these years, but now I'm glad I didn't. One must have some standards in life, rabbi. Don't you think so?"

The rabbi suddenly slammed an entire fist into an imaginary button. "Good Lord, Steinmetz!" he shouted. "Now, I understand. Good day, Mrs. Finchley. You've been extremely helpful."

The rabbi bolted for the door. "Steinmetz!" he shouted. "Hurry up!"

"What in heaven's name?" I demanded.

"We're going to prevent another death, Steinmetz," shouted the rabbi. "Hurry up! We don't have much time...."

The rabbi, still running, turned his head upward and started to mumble incoherently. At first, I thought he was criticizing me under his breath. A moment later, I realized that he was praying.

CHAPTER 20: THE CONFESSION

The rabbi charged into the parking lot with more energy than I would have thought he could muster. I raced after him as quickly as I could. I still didn't understand what had set him off so suddenly. It wasn't until we were peeling out of the parking lot that he said anything at all.

"I should have realized it would come to this," the rabbi muttered. "Some rabbi I am! I was given every clue....Let's just hope we get there before it's too late."

I felt the car start to rattle. A look at the speedometer revealed that we were traveling in excess of eighty miles per hour—in a thirty mph zone. I hadn't realized that the rabbi's Cadillac could travel that fast. Even on the highway, he usually stayed in the right-hand lane and never drove faster than the speed limit.

"Please slow down, rabbi," I begged. "Or, at least, tell me where we're going."

"I told you we're going to prevent another death, Steinmetz," the rabbi replied. "That is, if we get there in time...I knew I should have confronted our killer after that lunch with the mousy woman. How could I have been so foolish? How in God's name could I have been so irresponsibly careless?"

"Where are we going, rabbi?" I asked again. "What are you talking about?"

The rabbi sighed. "We're going where we should have gone several hours ago. We're going to Agatha Grossbart's before we have another death on our hands."

I bit my lip. "Why don't we just go to Pine Valley and warn Lorraine?" I asked. "What do we do if we get to the house and Agatha's not there? What if she's already gone back to Pine Valley?"

"She'll be there, Steinmetz," answered Rabbi Kappelmacher. "That's the one thing I'm sure of. Anyway, it's not Lorraine whose life is in danger."

"Whom do you think she's going to kill then?" I asked. "Gladys?"

"You have it backwards, Steinmetz. Agatha's not going to kill anyone. What I don't understand is why I didn't stop her sooner."

I tried to decipher the rabbi's meaning. "I have it backwards?" I asked. "Do you mean Gladys is going to try to kill Agatha?"

"*Dumkopf!*" Rabbi Kappelmacher cried. "Don't you ever pay attention, Steinmetz? Gladys Eisenstein isn't in a position to kill anybody."

The rabbi turned into the Sunshine Enclave and pulled up in front of Agatha Grossbart's condominium. Without even turning off the ignition, he raced up the steps and pounded on the front door. He rang the buzzer. He pounded some more. Then, in desperation, I tried the doorknob—and to my surprise, the door swung open inwards. I followed Rabbi Kappelmacher into the obese woman's apartment.

At first, nothing appeared to be out of the ordinary. The dining room table was set for a one-person lunch. All was silent except for the murmur of the air-conditioner. With the rabbi in the lead, we examined each room—the living room, the dining room, the kitchen and the two walk-in closets. Finally, the rabbi pushed open the door to Agatha's bedroom. It was there, lying on the double bed with a Bible clutched to her chest, that we found Agatha Grossbart.

The rabbi ran to her side and checked her pulse. He shook his head. "Too late," he said. "Poor, poor woman. What's that passage in Ecclesiastes about reaping what one has sewn, Steinmetz? It seems apropos here."

I approached the dead woman and carefully removed the Bible from her fingers. A hand-written note fell from between the pages. The rabbi snatched it away from me and read aloud:

"To Whom It May Concern,

If you find this note, I will already be dead. I had hoped it would not come to this, but I am overwhelmed with guilt and I can see no alternative. I leave this confession in the hope that you can find it in your hearts to forgive me for what I have done.

I murdered my cousin, Florence. She didn't call me to invite me to dinner; I called her. I'd gone up to the Pine Valley Library one afternoon and I saw her with Alfred—and I just couldn't help myself. I knew that Florence wouldn't be able to marry him on account of the will, so I determined to have him for myself. At first, luck was with me. Florence took sick on the night of our dinner and I had Alfred all to myself. Unfortunately, I underestimated my cousin's interest in dear Alfred. Several times, on the phone, I tried to convince her not to marry him—and when that failed, I determined that I had no alternative but to kill her.

On Tuesday night, I hid in the bedroom. I didn't exactly have a plan—all I knew was that I needed to act before it was too late. I spent several hours in there trying to think of a way to lure Alfred out of Florence's bedroom. Yet luck befriended me once again and around one o'clock Alfred departed on his own—as I now understand, to fill Florence's asthma prescription. I had just had enough time to suffocate my cousin with a pillow when I heard footsteps in the corridor. So I concealed myself once again, this time in the walk-in closet. I watched through the keyhole as Lorraine discovered her sister's death and I was still there when Alfred returned and tried to resuscitate her. I managed to escape when Dr. Scott showed up, and Alfred and Lorraine left the room for a moment to walk him out to his car.

It was only later that I came up with the idea of murdering Lorraine too and collecting a portion of Irving's fortune. I would have gotten away with it too, if that dreadful woman who lives next door to my cousins hadn't seen me this afternoon. Of course, I didn't actually hit Lorraine with my cane. I didn't have time. But I now understand that even if I had and that neighbor hadn't seen me, Rabbi Kappelmacher would have exposed me eventually.

*So now I have nothing. Alfred clearly doesn't love me
and he never will—that, even a woman as determined as
myself can discern. My finances are in a shambles as I
overextended myself on the assumption that I would inherit a
large sum of money. On top of all that, I am a suspect in a
murder investigation—which, I am confident, if Rabbi
Kappelmacher is as wise as I think he is, will soon lead to
my arrest. I can see no alternative.*

*Please try to find it in your hearts to forgive me for what
I have done.*

Agatha Grossbart."

Rabbi Kappelmacher slipped the note into his pocket. He
shook his head sadly. "I've done wrong, Steinmetz," he said.
"I've been so concerned about finding a rational explanation
that I nearly forgot that there were human lives at stake. If
we'd gotten here an hour ago, Agatha would still be alive."

"Maybe this is for the best," I replied, hoping to cheer
him up. "She wanted it this way. What good would it have
done to send her to prison?"

The rabbi frowned at me. He examined the room more
closely and indicated an empty medicine bottle on the
bedside table. "Sleeping pills," he observed.

I examined the pill bottle. "How do you like that?" I said.
"Prescription written by H. Scott, Pine Valley. I guess that
brings our case full circle."

"Not yet," replied the rabbi.

I followed him to the kitchen, where he proceeded to
make a phone call.

"Green?....Kappelmacher here....I require your
assistance....Yes....I want you to call up everyone involved
in the Eisenstein matter and tell them to be at the house in
Pine Valley tomorrow at noon....Use any means
necessary....Tell them you're reading the will or that you're
an F.B.I. agent operating undercover. I don't care. Just make
sure they're there....Lorraine, Gladys, Louise and Andrew,
Fred...also make sure you call Dr. Hiram Scott—he's the
physician who attended to her after she died...and that
neighbor we saw...yes, and Art Abercrombie...And then be

there yourself too, okay? Trust me, it's important....No, Green, that won't be necessary. Agatha Grossbart is already death. I'm calling from her apartment....Thank you, Green." The rabbi hung up the phone. "Did you hear that, Steinmetz? Meet me in my office at eleven o'clock tomorrow. If we get to the Eisenstein place at noon, we'll have plenty of time to return before the *shabbus*."

"What is this all about, rabbi?" I asked. "Shouldn't we call the police?"

The rabbi rubbed his beard thoughtfully. "Of course, Steinmetz," he said. "Call the police as soon as I leave, but don't mention the suicide note. I'm sure they can give you a ride back to Haddam."

"You're leaving me here?" I asked incredulously.

The rabbi nodded. "I need the rest of the afternoon to pray," he said. "Tomorrow, we tell the Eisenstein family who murdered Florence."

The rabbi strode rapidly out of the bedroom and I soon heard the outside door to the condominium shut behind him. I took one more look at the dead woman on the bed—a woman who truly had gone further than anyone would have imagined to obtain what she wanted—and then I went into the kitchen and phoned the police.

CHAPTER 21: THE RATIONAL EXPLANATION

When we pulled up at the Eisenstein estate at precisely
noon the next day, the rows of cars out front suggested that
our guests were already waiting for us. Among the vehicles,
I recognized Alfred Shingle's weather-beaten Buick and the
shiny new Town Car that I presumed belonged to Dr. Scott.
Seven automobiles in all, representing the unique individuals
who comprised the Eisenstein family.

"Are you sure this is necessary, rabbi?" I asked. "Why
not just go to the police with Agatha's note? These people
have gone through enough as it is."

The rabbi shook his head and pulled in behind Dr. Scott's
vehicle. "Nonsense, Steinmetz," he said. "Don't be a
noodnik. We still have a mystery to unravel."

"But it has already unraveled itself," I objected. "You
have your rational explanation."

"Yes, I do," agreed the rabbi. "And you'll have it too, if
you'll be patient enough for a few more minutes."

Before I could protest further, Rabbi Kappelmacher
rapped on the kitchen door with his knuckles. As on the day
of the *shivah* call, Lorraine Eisenstein greeted us with a
friendly smile.

"Good morning, Inspector," she said, and she winked at
the rabbi. "Your officers are already here. They're waiting
in the parlor."

"Let them wait," said the rabbi. "First, I must speak with
your family. Your Cousin Agatha left a suicide note and I
think that they'll want to hear it."

"How dreadful," said Lorraine. She glanced at me,
flashing a look of despair, then led both of us through the
dining room and the library into the drawing room. The
Eisenstein family and their entourage sat around the coffee
table. It was clear that the news of Agatha's death had not

troubled all of the family members equally. The circles around the eyes of Gladys and Fred suggested that they'd taken the news hard. Andrew Sinkoff, in contrast, smiled smugly and chatted with Abercrombie as if nothing were amiss. All heads turned when we entered.

"What is the meaning of this?" Dr. Scott demanded before the rabbi had even taken off his coat. "I have a busy practice to run. How dare you send the police into my office!"

"I'm sorry for the inconvenience," answered the rabbi with a pointed look at Green. "All I did was ask Mr. Green to summon you to the house. The means he used—whatever those might have been—are entirely his responsibility. I'm just a rabbi, you understand. Not a police office or a lawyer."

Lorraine Eisenstein nudged my elbow. "That's an excellent touch," she observed.

The rabbi draped his coat over the back of the sofa. "I'm really not a police officer or a lawyer," he emphasized. "Even if I may have led some of you to believe otherwise." He let the words sink in. Lorraine Eisenstein gasped and covered her mouth with her hands. "I'm just an ordinary rabbi. But circumstances, you understand, have forced me to pretend to be otherwise."

"So you lied to us," growled Andrew. "I knew you were just a meddlesome busybody. Didn't I tell you, Louise, that in business I wouldn't trust that man as far I could throw him?"

Louise crossed her legs and said nothing.

"The reason I lied," continued Rabbi Kappelmacher, "will soon become apparent. There was a murderer on the loose, you see, and I couldn't take any chances."

"A murderer?" asked Mrs. Finchley incredulously.

"Yes," replied the rabbi. "A murderer. I presume you all know about the death of Agatha Grossbart. What you don't know is that she left a suicide note. A confession of sorts."

Rabbi Kappelmacher withdrew the note from his pocket and read it aloud.

"Do you mean to tell me that Cousin Agatha murdered Aunt Florence?" Fred demanded. "But that's impossible. Agatha wouldn't hurt a fly."

"You have it in her own words," persisted the rabbi. "She saw Florence at the library with Alfred and, after a couple of inquiries, discovered that he was an eligible bachelor. Agatha knew the terms of her uncle's will—your grandfather's will. So she figured that if Florence couldn't marry him, she ought to have her fair chance. There was no reason to waste an eligible Jewish bachelor."

"She killed Florence for me?" asked Alfred Shingle in disbelief.

"That's what her note says. At first, she was just curious. It was she who called to arrange to have dinner with the two of you—not Florence who phoned her, as we foolishly assumed. But imagine Agatha's luck when Florence fell ill on the night of the dinner and she had you all to herself. You must have really charmed her. Of course, she didn't count on Florence's deluding herself into believing that the will had been broken and marrying you. She waited in the bathroom on Tuesday night, and when she saw you go down the stairs on your errand to the pharmacy, she suffocated Florence with a pillow."

"So it was Agatha I heard through the bedroom door," said Lorraine. "I knew she was a troubled woman—but murder?"

"When she heard you at the door," continued the rabbi, "she concealed herself inside the walk-in closet. It was only later that it dawned upon her that she could kill you as well and inherit a quarter of your father's fortune. She might have succeeded too, if Mrs. Finchley hadn't startled her sneaking up on you. Agatha came by the synagogue to confess to me, and when I wasn't there, she impulsively took her own life."

A silence fell over the room. Green shook his head; it appeared as though he finally had the rational explanation he'd been looking for. The old woman had been murdered—but the broken will and the row with the cousin had had absolutely nothing to do with it. Suddenly, Fred Eisenstein jumped to his feet.

"You expect us to believe that nonsense?" he demanded. "I don't know if you're a rabbi or a detective or merely an interloper, but I know that you didn't know Cousin Agatha like I did. If you'd have known her, you'd never believe that story. I don't care what she may have written—if she did, in fact, write it. But I do know that she didn't kill anybody."

The rabbi removed a cigar from his breast pocket. He glanced at Lorraine Eisenstein for approval and then lit it with a flourish.

"I never said I believed that story," said the rabbi. "The truth is that I don't believe a word of it. Because it's not true. But it's the story the real murderer wanted us to believe."

"The real murderer?" Green asked. "Do you mean to tell me that Agatha *didn't* kill Florence?"

"Far from it," answered the rabbi. "In fact, the same person murdered both of them."

I admit Rabbi Kappelmacher had caught me off guard here. I suddenly feared that he was going to embarrass both of us to no purpose. I was about to intervene when he turned and threw me a pointed glare.

"That's why I've summoned you all here," said the rabbi. "I think it's time to unmask the real murderer before he—or she—strikes again. You see, this case is all about illusions. Grand illusions and small illusions. Gladys Eisenstein helped me to understand that."

"I don't know what you're talking about," protested Gladys. Here eyes had glassed over and she fretted nervously with the hem of her dress.

The rabbi held up his hand to silence her. "I'll explain myself in due time, young lady," he said. "For there is a rational explanation for everything. But first, I want to review briefly the facts of this case as I understand them. At least, the facts that we can all agree upon."

"Is this necessary?" interjected Dr. Scott. He glanced at his watch for effect.

"Absolutely necessary," replied the rabbi. "The sooner we start, the sooner we'll be done. And I must be home in time for the *shabbus*."

Rabbi Kappelmacher seated himself in a reclining chair and proceeded to outline the facts that we already knew. "By the terms of Irving Eisenstein's will, a trust fund was established for his daughters, Florence and Lorraine. However, if either of them married, all of the inheritance—not just the interest, but the principle—would go immediately to the other sister. The purpose, of course, was to keep either woman from marrying. This is an odd arrangement—certainly not an arrangement in keeping with Jewish law—but Green assures me that it is legal."

"*Evans v. Dodge*," interjected Green wit a nod.

"For more than forty years, neither sister did in fact marry. As far as I know, neither sister displayed any interest in men since Florence's ill-fated romance with the lawn chair magnate many years ago. Lorraine devoted herself to gardening and Florence went bird watching, and both sisters kept to themselves. Until about six months ago, that is. All of a sudden, Florence meets Alfred here at the library and falls in love with him. They date. Maybe they *shtup*. That is a matter of debate. Nothing so terribly out of the ordinary. Mrs. Finchley tells us that Alfred was a frequent visitor to the house and Lorraine confirms this. Florence continues to receive her annuity and makes no indication to anyone that she plans to marry."

"About a month ago, however, Florence starts to demonstrate uncharacteristic behavior. First, she either calls—or is called by—Cousin Agatha. In either case, she agrees to go to dinner with this woman she has despised for nearly twenty-five years, a woman whom she blames for stealing her last gentleman friend and scalding her with hot tea. Yet on the night of the scheduled dinner, Florence falls sick and sends Alfred out to dine with Agatha alone. That, in itself, is mighty strange, considering the episode with the lawn chair magnate."

"The next day she visits Dr. Scott, her longtime physician, who also happens to be a college friend of Alfred's. He places her on asthma medication and advises her to keep well rested. His advice seems to do the trick, for three weeks later Florence is healthy enough to decide that she wants to marry Alfred. He's wanted to marry her for months, even if it meant losing the trust fund, because he has his own pension—and, to be blunt about it, he's something of a romantic. Florence calls both of her nieces and her cousin, and tells them that she has planned a wedding for Tuesday afternoon. She also informs them that she's broken the will and stands to inherit—which, according to Mr. Green, was not the case. All of this would seem to indicate that either Florence deluded herself into thinking that the will had been broken or that somebody at Abercrombie & Green had told her that the will had been broken. Knowing what we know of Florence Eisenstein, it would be safe to surmise that she wouldn't accept such information from anyone—only directly from Mr. Abercrombie or from Mr. Green. Neither of whom, I might add, admit to telling her that the will had been broken."

"Finally," continued to rabbi, "there is this business with her nephew, Fred. Florence announces to everyone—possibly except to Fred himself—that she intends to disinherit him because he's been after her money all these years. He has been, after all, the Eisenstein sisters' only frequent visitor among their relations. At first, Fred denies any knowledge of her plan. He insists he was on the best of terms with both his aunts. But yesterday, much to my surprise, he stops by the synagogue and tells me that he did indeed have a fight with Florence on the Saturday before the wedding. And that seemed to be the state of affairs when Florence Eisenstein died on Tuesday night."

Fred Eisenstein shifted uncomfortable in his seat. Dr. Scott glanced at his watch again. Marshall Green finally broke the silence. "But Rabbi, we knew that much last Thursday when I visited you at your office…."

The rabbi ran his fingers through his beard. "Indeed, we did. But there were several things we did not know then that we do know now. For instance, we did not know that there is a photograph of Alfred in Florence's bedroom that has replaced another photograph. Or that there used to be a fourth photograph hanging on the wall in this very room."

"I explained to you," interjected Lorraine, "that they were photographs of us with our father. Florence grew angry with him in the last few weeks."

"Indeed, you did," agreed the rabbi. "I admit I doubted you at first. It seemed strange to me than an elderly woman would suddenly remove photographs of her father after forty-three years. But Alfred confirmed your story, so I decided that there had to be a rational explanation for her behavior."

"When my uncle fell off the ladder," I observed, "my aunt was furious with him. She removed all of his photographs from her bureau."

The rabbi glared at me and continued. "There are other facts we did not know last week. We did not know, for example, that Mr. and Mrs. Sinkoff had been receiving prank phone calls."

"I don't understand what that has to do with anything," demanded Andrew.

"It has everything to do with the matter of murder," answered the rabbi. "Absolutely everything. These phone calls, I might add, began on the day Florence decided to marry Alfred and ended immediately after Florence invited the Sinkoffs to the wedding. That, you must admit, is a rather peculiar fact."

"What are you driving at?" asked Andrew Sinkoff. "Are you suggesting that I lied about the phone calls? I have Louise as a witness."

"We'll come back to that," answered the rabbi. "There are several other strange facts that need explanation. For instance, there is the letter I received on Monday urging me to investigate the relationship between Mr. Abercrombie and Lorraine. A relationship that might drive Mr. Abercrombie to lie to Florence about the broken will and then to kill her."

Abercrombie's jaw dropped. "I resent that statement," he stammered. "I dare you to repeat it in writing. I dare you!"

"You can dare me more later," the rabbi answered calmly. "Right now, we have a murder to solve. As I was saying, that letter still needs to be explained, as does Cousin Agatha's attempt to kill Lorraine. For just because Agatha didn't kill one sister for love doesn't necessarily mean that she didn't attempt to kill the other sister for money."

"That's preposterous," declared Fred.

"We have Mrs. Finchley's eye-witness account. Tell him, Mrs. Finchley."

"I saw what I saw," answered the neighbor. "I wouldn't have believed it if I hadn't seen it with my own eyes."

"There you have it," declared the rabbi. "Now back to business. I admit that the first question that popped into my head when Mr. Green came by my office last Thursday was, who had a motive to kill Florence? It was apparent who didn't. Lorraine stood to gain nothing from her sister's death. She'd lost a companion and she didn't stand to inherit anything. As a result of Florence's marriage, Lorraine had already acquired her father's fortune—more money than she could possibly know what to do with. The only other person who seemed to lose, rather than to gain, from the murder was Alfred Shingle. He would have gained more by living off the proceeds of Florence's trust fund without marrying her than by killing her for her small savings. As it turns out, she died—or was killed—before she had a chance to include him in her will."

"Others, however, stood to gain a great deal by Florence's death. Or at least they thought that they did. Gladys, Agatha and Louise all believed that the will had been broken and they might have suspected that they would be beneficiaries of Florence's will. Andrew, through his wife, also stood to benefit. Each of them, for personal reasons, was in desperate need of money. And all of them suspected that Florence would soon alter her will to leave all of her money to Alfred, her new husband, thereby making it essential for them to act as quickly as possible. Fred, if we are to believe his first story, did not think that the will had been broken before the wedding. But he might have learned this false fact from one of his relatives after the ceremony. Even if he didn't, he did expect to inherit a portion of Florence's own savings—and her attitude toward him at the wedding may have led him to fear that she soon intended to disinherit him entirely. Alternatively, if we believe his second story, he knew that he was to be disinherited and so had every reason to kill his aunt quickly."

Fred stared at his feet in silence.

"Of course, at the time, I didn't even know that Florence had been murdered. It was Agatha who first suggested the possibility. That was, I now know, just to—well—to interest me in seeing her again. She surmised, you understand, that I was intrigued by Florence's death—and she gave me what I was looking for. When I pressured her to substantiate her claim that Florence had been murdered, she even made up a story about Gladys leaving her room on the night of Florence's death. I had a hunch that Agatha was lying to retain my interest, so I made up a story about a pair of binoculars on Gladys's end table, and she fell for it, hook, line and sinker. For my part, I only learned for certain that Florence had been murdered from Dr. Scott, whose tale of accidental suffocation seemed too neat in light of the other strange circumstances."

"Are you saying that I killed her?" asked Scott. "I was home in bed with my wife when Alfred phoned me. You can ask either of them."

"Please," answered Rabbi Kappelmacher. "There's no need to be defensive. I'm just outlining the facts of the case. I was simply trying to show that Florence had been murdered and that at least four people, including Cousin Agatha, had a motive to kill her. It was only later that it dawned on me that I might be asking the wrong question."

The rabbi paused dramatically and puffed on his cigar. "From everything I learned in my investigation, both Lorraine and Florence lived retiring—you might say reclusive—lives. It would have been easy for someone who hadn't seen them in years to mistake one for the other in a dark bedroom late at night. This might particularly prove true in the case of a blind woman. So the possibility existed that the intended victim hadn't been Florence at all, but Lorraine."

"Are you accusing my wife?" demanded Andrew.

"All I'm saying is that the field of suspects widens somewhat if the intended victim is Lorraine. Not to mention which, considering the terms of Irving's will, the stakes are much higher. Art Abercrombie, for example, might have planned to marry Lorraine after lying to Florence about the will. If Lorraine rebuffed him, that would have given him cause for revenge. I learned from Agatha's snooping that the Eisenstein sisters leave their doors unlocked at night. Anyone can come and go as they please."

"For the last time, my relationship with Miss Eisenstein is purely business."

"But you'd like it to be otherwise?" asked the rabbi.

Abercrombie blushed. "Not at all," he said, half-heartedly. "Well fine, I admit it. I'm interested in Miss Eisenstein. Lorraine. But I've never expressed the interest to her until now. I swear it."

All eyes turned toward Lorraine. "This is the first I've heard of it," she said. "I never imagined...."

Rabbi Kappelmacher smiled at the lawyer. "I'm not accusing you of anything, Mr. Abercrombie. I'm simply showing that you might have had a motive to do in Lorraine. First, you dupe her sister into forfeiting her inheritance, and then, suspecting Lorraine doesn't feel about you the way you feel about her, you become angry and drive down to the Eisenstein estate to have it out with her. You enter the first bedroom you see and find an old woman sleeping alone. Since you expect Florence to be sleeping with her new husband, you presume that the woman in the bed in Lorraine. And, overcome with frustration and rage, you kill her."

Abercrombie shook his head, but said nothing.

"Of course, that is if we believe that Lorraine had rebuffed you. An alternative is that you planned together to dupe Florence into marrying and then Lorraine backed out on you, knowing that you can't reveal your secret for fear of disgrace and disbarment. There is, you see, that letter to be explained. Green, would you care to explain the letter?"

"I wish I could," answered Green.

"Oh, you can," continued the rabbi, "because you wrote it. That's why you brought this case to me in the first place. You thought that Abercrombie had in fact lied to Florence about the will and that he had designs, reciprocated or not, on the other sister. In fact, you thought that Abercrombie had intentionally told Florence not to mention the broken will to you—that he'd come up with some pretext for convincing her not to tell you, but that the real reason was that he knew you'd tell her the truth."

"But why—?" gasped Green.

"Why? Because you were tired of living in Art Abercrombie's shadow. You were tired of waiting in the wings while he dabbled with the idea of running for office. Not that you weren't willing to wait. I remember how you waited for me to retire for all those years before you gave up and went to law school. But if Art Abercrombie had lied to Florence—and the truth is, you suspected that he might have killed her—you wanted to bring him down. Especially if she'd been murdered, and your lawyerly instincts told you that she had been. If you were the one who mounted the investigation, you'd have become something of a local hero. Honest lawyer reveals partner's plot. That's a strong political foundation to run for office on."

Green wiped his brow and turned the color of bottled horse radish. "How did you know it was me?"

"Because the letter wasn't mailed. It was hand delivered. Somebody wanted me to receive that letter as quickly as possible, so that somebody placed it on my desk. Only a person familiar with the synagogue could have found my unmarked office in the back corridor without asking either Mrs. Conch or Mrs. Billings for assistance. There's absolutely no way you can know that particular office is my office unless somebody tells you or you've been there before."

"Okay, okay," conceded Green. "I left the letter. But I honestly thought that Art might be involved with Lorraine and that he lied to Florence about the will. I figured your rabbinic reasoning would dig up the proof that I needed. What other rational explanation can there be for Florence's death?"

"I'm getting to that," answered Rabbi Kappelmacher. "There are still a few more herrings to attend to."

"Red herrings," I suggested.

"If it makes you happy, Steinmetz," said the rabbi, "*red* herrings. There is the business of Fred Eisenstein changing his story to deflect attention away from his sister, Louise. I inadvertently hinted to Fred in our first conversation that I thought the intended victim might have been Lorraine and not Florence. When his sister called him and said that I'd visited her a second time to see if she could tell the difference between Green and Steinmetz, he concluded that I thought Louise had murdered her aunt. Louise most likely deduced that I'd concocted the story about the broken will to make the impostor Green more convincing. It certainly contributed to a fine performance by Rabbi Steinmetz."

"But I knew it was Rabbi Steinmetz all along," protested Louise. "I could tell by his voice. I just didn't say anything at the time because I wanted to ask Andrew's opinion first. He told me not to say anything until we consulted a lawyer."

"That may be true," continued the rabbi, "but you didn't know that *I* knew that you could tell the difference. I didn't know for sure myself until I phoned Green and found out you'd called to ask him whether the will had really been broken. So if Fred suspected that I thought you'd murdered Florence by mistake, intending to kill Lorraine, my visit with the impostor Green would have confirmed his suspicions. Am I right, Fred?"

"I knew what you were driving at," the nephew answered. "All along, you thought it was Louise. I could tell. I changed my story so there wouldn't be any doubt that we all thought that the will had been broken. That way, Louise wouldn't have had any reason to kill one of my aunts more than the other. She would have stood to inherit just as much from each one. At the time, I didn't know that Gladys and Agatha also thought the will had been broken. Why would Aunt Florence have told them that the will had been broken and not me? In all truth, I was so certain that Aunt Florence didn't believe that the will had been broken that I thought Louise was lying to protect herself."

"Understandably," agreed the rabbi. "That was quite noble of you, young man. At the same time, it didn't lead me any closer to a rational explanation of these strange events. Somebody, for one reason or another, had still murdered your Aunt Florence."

"Will you tell us who already?" demanded Dr. Scott. "Or are we going to keep playing this cat and mouse game all day?"

"I'm getting to that," said Rabbi Kappelmacher. "There was one other fact that needed explanation. It was Steinmetz here who opened my eyes to it. When we stopped by Mr. Sinkoff's house last Sunday, pretending to be private investigators, Steinmetz related a story about his grandaunt. A woman who always believed herself to be critically ill. I think the words Steinmetz used were 'on the verge of death.' Steinmetz said to me and Mr. Sinkoff, 'She could go on about her health for hours, the way old people do.'"

"It was all she talked about," I said, "but I don't see what my Grandaunt Sadie can possibly have to do with Florence Eisenstein's death."

"Absolutely nothing at all," replied the rabbi, "except that you reminded me what it was that troubled me about our meeting with Mr. Eisenstein earlier that morning. He'd said he'd gone to visit his Aunt Florence and that they'd talked for twenty minutes. Isn't that right, Mr. Eisenstein?"

"That's what I told you," said Fred.

"And what did you talk about?" the rabbi asked rhetorically. "You talked about some bird she saw and about your trip to Europe. What you didn't talk about, Mr. Eisenstein, was Florence's health. Now doesn't it strike you as odd that an old woman who hadn't seen her nephew in six months doesn't mention her illness? From everything I know about old people—and I'm learning more by the day— I can't help imagining that her illness would have been the first thing she mentioned when she saw you. So either she wasn't ill or she intentionally concealed her asthma from you, Mr. Eisenstein."

"Since Dr. Scott assured me that Florence was suffering from asthma, I couldn't help wondering why Florence would conceal her illness from her nephew. The third possibility is that Mr. Eisenstein lied about his conversation with Florence in our first meeting as well as our second, but I couldn't understand what he had to gain by doing that. So initially, I concluded that Florence intentionally concealed her illness from you."

"This is ridiculous," muttered Dr. Scott. "I'm going to lose the entire afternoon. Why can't you just tell us who the murderer is and let the rest of us go back to our ordinary lives?"

"In a moment, I will," said the rabbi. "Because I now know for certain how and why Florence Eisenstein's death came about. It was actually Gladys who helped me see the case clearly."

The mousy woman ran her hand down the side of her dress. "I *helped* you? I don't understand."

"But you do, my dear lady," continued the rabbi. "You reminded me that all is not what it seems. That sometimes grand illusions are easier to pull of than small illusions."

"What do you mean?" Gladys asked. Her voice was pregnant with alarm.

"I mean that you told me you had no trouble finding Knobler's Deli. That you used to love the tiled ceiling as a little girl. Only when you were a little girl, Knobler's Deli was five blocks away on Norfolk Street, and there was no tiled ceiling. They must have put that in when they moved to Delancey a couple of years ago. You remember the name, not the restaurant."

"What do you mean?"

"Come on, Gladys," coaxed the rabbi. "Or should I say Amy? If you were actually Gladys Eisenstein, you would have known that we didn't have lunch at the original Knobler's Deli."

"I don't know what you're talking about," the girl insisted.

"Well, the way I see it, Amy," continued the rabbi, "is that you lived with Gladys in San Francisco. Maybe you were *shtupping* her, maybe not. You knew that she hated her family. That she resented her aunts because they lived off the money that she believed was rightfully hers, and that she hadn't spoken to her brother or sister since she was a teenager because they refused to try to break the will. In fact, when she died in a motorcycle accident last month, Gladys still hadn't reconciled with her family. Maybe she never would have. Which is why you arranged for her burial and put off calling them. You'd grown to despise them as much as she did. And then came the call from the aunt announcing that she'd broken the will—and you just couldn't help yourself. Who remembered Gladys well enough to say that you weren't her? I assume you and Gladys were similar in appearance. Besides, twenty-five years had gone by. People's looks change a lot in twenty-five years. You knew all of the old family stories, even down to how much Gladys hated the pickles at Knobler's Deli. You had lived with her for a quarter of a century, after all. So you flew out here pretending to be your dead roommate, hoping to claim your piece of the pie. That's why you weren't at all self-conscious about sitting with your relatives on the night I made the *shivah* call. And that's why you had so little difficulty being friendly to your family. Because they weren't your family at all. They were Gladys's family."

"Gladys deserved the money," Amy retorted. "She hated all of you. I was her real family. I'm the one she loved. Why shouldn't I have some of the money? But I didn't kill anybody. No matter what you try to pin on me, I'm not a murderer."

"I didn't say you were," said Rabbi Kappelmacher. "But you helped me solve the case, nonetheless. You reminded me that this wasn't a close family. That many years had elapsed since some of you had seen each other. In fact, that not only Gladys, but also Louise and Agatha, were practically strangers from their aunts—and each other. Nobody even knew for certain that Agatha was actually who she said she was and not an impostor."

"I did," objected Fred.

"Nobody," agreed the rabbi, "except for Fred Eisenstein. He visited his aunts regularly and he kept up with his cousin and, as we've seen, he was very close to his sister, Louise. So we have his word for it that everybody else here is who they say they are."

"Without a doubt," Fred agreed.

The rabbi lit another cigar and scratched his beard for several moments in silence. "I agree with you, Fred, that everybody *here* is who they say they are."

"Do you mean that Cousin Agatha wasn't Cousin Agatha?" asked Louise incredulously.

"No" explained Rabbi Kappelmacher. "Cousin Agatha was Cousin Agatha. Your Aunt Florence, however, wasn't your Aunt Florence."

"Excuse me," said Fred. "But you are out of your mind. I've known Aunt Florence for my entire life."

"That is true," agreed the rabbi. "But you were in Europe for the past six months. You only arrived back in town two weeks ago."

"What are you driving at, old man?" demanded Andrew Sinkoff. "Is this confusion really necessary?"

"There is no confusion," the rabbi retorted triumphantly. "There is a rational explanation for everything. Listen closely. Your Aunt Florence's wedding was an illusion."

"But I was there," objected Green. "I saw it with my own eyes. You're going too far, rabbi."

"Did you see Florence get married, Green?" asked the rabbi. "Are you certain?"

"As certain as I am that I can tell night from day."

"Let us be thankful, Green," answered the rabbi, "that you're not an astronomer. What you saw last Tuesday was an illusion. First, you were greeted by an elderly woman in a wedding gown and veil who told you that she was Florence Eisenstein. You had no reason to suspect otherwise, as you had come anticipating Florence's wedding. Amy, we now know, had never met the woman. Neither had Andrew Sinkoff. Louise can only distinguish people by voice, not appearance. And Cousin Agatha hadn't actually seen Florence in many years."

"But I was there," objected Alfred Shingle. "I married her, for Lord's sake."

"I'll come to that," the rabbi replied. "You remember telling me that Florence didn't speak to you at the wedding, Louise. That you thought she ignored you. Well, that was because the woman under the veil wasn't Florence. If the woman under the veil had spoken to you, you'd have recognized immediately that she was an impostor. Like you did when I had Steinmetz pretend to be Green. You thought Florence was trying to keep Gladys from speaking with anyone else. In fact, the woman you thought was Florence was trying to keep herself from speaking with anyone else. She knew that Gladys couldn't expose her, not having seen her in a quarter of a century, and that somebody else might be able to. That's also why the impostor Florence darted upstairs as soon as Fred arrived. Her veil saved her from blowing her cover. For the life of me, I couldn't understand why Florence went bird watching on the morning before her wedding. Everything I knew of human nature told me that a woman doesn't go bird watching on the day before her wedding. Especially on a morning when she's desperate to call her lawyer to disinherit her nephew. And then it struck me. Florence went bird watching last Monday morning, like she did every morning, because it was just that for her: An ordinary morning and nothing more. She had no intention of getting married and she didn't ever get married. Someone else donned her mother's wedding dress and veil and got married for her."

"I don't understand any of this," objected Dr. Scott. He now appeared to be genuinely intrigued. "If the woman under the veil wasn't Florence, who was it?"

That rabbi puffed on his cigar and waited several seconds, examining the physician perched on the edge of his seat. "That's obvious," answered the rabbi. "The woman under the veil was Lorraine."

"You're out of your mind," declared Alfred Shingle. He stood up and walked toward the door. "I don't have to listen to this nonsense. I know I married Florence. Are you telling me I can't distinguish my own wife from her sister?"

"Not at all, Mr. Shingle," Rabbi Kappelmacher replied. "Please sit down and I'll be glad to explain."

The widower tentatively seated himself on a piano bench in the corner.

"The larger the illusion," stated the rabbi, "the easier it is to pull off. How do we know that you were dating Florence? We have your word for it and we have Lorraine's confirmation. Nothing more."

"But Mrs. Finchley saw me."

"Saw you what? Visiting the house? The truth is, Mr. Shingle, it was Lorraine that you were visiting. The two of you hatched the plot together. Lorraine was tired of scraping by on her annual stipend and she was tired of hoping that her sister would get married. You came around at just the moment when she realized that Florence wasn't *ever* going to get married. That if she didn't act quickly, she would die poor and alone."

"The two of you couldn't control whether Florence got married. Yet it dawned upon you at some point rather early in your relationship that you could trick people into thinking that Florence had gotten married. It was straight out of one of your detective novels, Alfred. Lorraine phoned old relatives whom neither she nor her sister had spoken to in many years and, pretending to be Florence, invited them to a wedding. That explains the Sinkoffs' prank phone calls. Louise would have recognized her aunt's voice instantly. Lorraine had to keep calling until she got through directly to Andrew, and considering his business schedule, that took longer than she'd expected. Lorraine must have remembered the calls Louise received as a teenager and she mimicked them to the best of her abilities."

Alfred stood up. The rabbi motioned for him to be seated again and he reluctantly complied.

"The two of you let the word out that Florence was suffering from asthma so that if she suffocated unexpectedly, it would seem like a death from natural causes. She was actually in excellent health. She didn't tell Fred that she was sick when he saw her on Saturday for the most obvious reason of all: She *wasn't* sick."

"On *Monday* night, the two of you did in fact suffocate Florence with a pillow. She was already dead by the time the guests arrived for the wedding. I'm sure an autopsy will reveal the precise cause of death. The two of you also concocted the row with poor Fred here. It served two purposes. First, it provided Lorraine with a pretext for not attending the wedding. Second, and more important, it provided an excuse for keeping Fred away from the ceremony. You had to. Because as part of the wedding ceremony, Florence had to remove her veil long enough for a kiss. So nobody at the wedding could have been capable of recognizing her. That's why Lorraine insisted that Green here serve as a witness instead of Abercrombie. That's why you called a rabbi from the phone book to perform the ceremony. It's also why you removed the photographs of Lorraine and Florence, side by side, from the bedroom and the drawing room. After Florence was dead, the wedding guests would never remember exactly what she looked like—and they had no reason to suspect that the Florence they'd met and Lorraine were the same person. The idea never entered their heads. Sisters often resemble each other. If they'd seen the photographs, however, they would have known that the woman who briefly removed her veil at the wedding wasn't Florence. People's appearances change after twenty-five years. They don't change in a year or two. It was essential to your plan that nobody who was at the wedding had seen what Florence looked like in old age."

"You added the bit about the broken will as a safety net. It provided a motive for others if anyone became suspicious and it suggested that Florence had gone wrong in the head, helping to explain her other uncharacteristic behavior. Most important, it helped explain her decision to get married in the first place. Yet when Lorraine called Green on Monday, pretending to be Florence, she couldn't mention that she'd broken the will because he would have told her that she hadn't—and Lorraine knew that. Thus, the seemingly inexplicable contradiction that Florence thought the will had been broken two weeks ago and again last Tuesday, but not last Monday."

"There's a problem with your theory, rabbi," objected Dr. Scott. "I told you that I saw Florence and Alfred together on the day she first became sick. She did indeed have asthma. Are you insinuating that I'm part of this absurd plot too?"

"No, I'm not," replied the rabbi. "But I will suggest that you didn't see Alfred and Florence on that day or any other day. I first doubted your story because you said the visit took place on a Saturday. I wondered why Florence would come with Alfred when her sister needed to drive to town to visit the beauty parlor that afternoon anyway. Then I lied to Steinmetz here and told him that I had a bad case of indigestion. When I had him stop by your office for a prescription on Tuesday, it all fell into place. You're a busy man. Dr. Scott. You have a thriving practice. If a longtime patient called you with a problem, I'm sure you'd make a diagnosis over the phone. And if you'd give Steinmetz a prescription for me, I have no doubt you'd give your old friend Alfred a prescription for his lady friend. Everybody does it, but you could lose your license. Of course, if you can convince the rest of these good people not to say anything, I certainly won't."

"Stuff and nonsense," declared Alfred. "Tell him, Hiram."

"I wish I could," replied Hiram Scott. I noticed that Lorraine had started to cry.

Suddenly, Fred rose to his feet. "But if what you're saying is true, why did Agatha try to murder Aunt Lorraine?"

The rabbi's eyes gleamed and he pushed yet another imaginary button with his index finger. "Another illusion, my boy. Nothing more."

"But I saw her," chimed in Mrs. Finchley. "Maybe you can pull the wool over the eyes of the rest of these people, but you can't pull the wool over the eyes of Annie Finchley."

"I wouldn't try," said the rabbi. "You saw precisely what you thought you saw. Cousin Agatha had her cab drop her at the foot of the path and wait for her, as she always did. She came upon Lorraine in the garden working on her flowers. And then she noticed something highly unusual. Something that reminded her instantly of something else. She saw Lorraine Eisenstein's bare arms.   And this shocked her. Because Lorraine Eisenstein's arms aren't scarred. They bear no trace of the scalding tea that burned Florence. It wasn't you that startled her, Mrs. Finchley. It was the realization that the woman in the wedding gown with the bare arms couldn't have been the woman she'd thought she was. Once she started thinking along those lines, of course, she quickly realized that the Florence she'd met at the wedding and Lorraine were the same person. That's why she lifted her cane. It was a visceral response. Agatha was trying to protect herself. What you heard her muttering, Mrs. Finchley, wasn't that she'd do the same to Lorraine as she'd done to Florence—although it must have sounded something like that. At twenty-five yards, you could probably make out only the gist of what she was saying. What she was actually saying was that Lorraine *was* the same as Florence. The same person. And I imagine you heard her too, Lorraine, didn't you? Which is why, as soon as she left, you phoned Alfred and told him what had happened.

"I called the only Mrs. Metzger in your complex early this morning, Mr. Shingle. As it turns out, she *did* attend yesterday's meeting of your mystery book club. You didn't. You were too busy murdering Agatha in her apartment. You suffocated her with a pillow just like you murdered Florence and then you left out the empty bottle of sleeping pills to make it look like a suicide. You also wrote the note— primarily intended to provide me with the rational explanation I was looking for, so I'd drop my investigation. Agatha Grossbart couldn't have written that note herself, of course. She had terrible arthritis. She could barely move her hands. She couldn't even leave me a note at the synagogue to save her soul."

"Meanwhile, Lorraine drove out to the synagogue and told me that story about the person in Florence's bedroom. The person whose footsteps alternated from loud to soft. The idea probably struck Lorraine when she heard Agatha snooping in her house on Saturday night. Lorraine expected that I'd put two and two together and conclude that Florence's murderer walked with a cane. Of course, the only person in the house on the night of the murder who used a cane was Agatha, so Lorraine's story dovetailed neatly with the confession which Alfred wrote for Agatha. It was a very clever plan, I admit. Very clever. In fact, I believe it may have fooled a mind as keen as Rabbi Steinmetz's. Unfortunately, the timing in Miss Eisenstein's story was off. She told me that she was directly outside Florence's door when she heard a muffled scream. She knocked, waited five seconds, and opened the door. I imagine that if Agatha had been in the bedroom that night, those five seconds might have given her enough time to take at most one or two steps toward the closet. No more. After all, she was an obese woman hobbling on a cane."

The rabbi retrieved his hat and coat from the sofa. "And that, my friends, is the rational explanation for what happened to Florence Eisenstein."

"What now?" Alfred asked incredulously. "Are you going to give us a chance to do the honorable thing like they do in mystery novels?"

The rabbi shook his head. "That is for Green to decide. He's the lawyer. Rabbis are for rational explanations. It isn't my job to mete out justice. But I imagine Green's legal system can temper justice with mercy."

Alfred slumped onto the piano bench. Lorraine wiped her tears with a tissue. Green summoned his officers from the parlor.

"Incidentally, Green," said the rabbi. "I believe I've won your challenge. If this business proves rough for you at the law firm, there's always a place for you at the synagogue."

Green smiled. "I'm sure this will pass. It always does."

"Suit yourself," replied the rabbi. Then he turned to me. "Hurry up, Steinmetz," he said. "It's almost the *shabbus*."

"We have time," I replied nonchalantly. "We can even stop for a cup of coffee."

"Don't be a *noodnik*," said Rabbi Kappelmacher, his eyes aglow. "I have only three hours to stop the sun or I'll have to wait until Sunday."

Before I could reply, the rabbi winked at me and darted through the open door.

THE END

ABOUT THE AUTHOR

 Jacob M. Appel's first novel, *The Man Who Wouldn't Stand Up*, won the Dundee International Book Award in 2012. His short story collection, *Scouting for the Reaper*, won the 2012 Hudson Prize and will be published by Black Lawrence in November, 2013. Jacob has published short fiction in more than two hundred literary journals including *Agni, Conjunctions, Gettysburg Review, Southwest Review, Virginia Quarterly Review,* and *West Branch.* He has won the New Millennium Writings contest four times, the Writer's Digest "grand prize" twice, and the William Faulkner-William Wisdom competition in both fiction and creative nonfiction. His work has been short listed for the O. Henry Award (2001), Best American Short Stories (2007, 2008), Best American Essays (2011, 2012), and received "special mention" for the Pushcart Prize in 2006, 2007, 2011 and 2013. Jacob holds a B.A. and an M.A. from Brown University, an M.A. and an M.Phil. from Columbia University, an M.S. in bioethics from the Alden March Bioethics Institute of Albany Medical College, an M.D. from Columbia University's College of Physicians and Surgeons, an M.F.A. in creative writing from New York University, an M.F.A. in playwriting from Queens College, an M.P.H. from the Mount Sinai School of Medicine and a J.D. from Harvard Law School. He currently practices psychiatry in New York City.

Made in the USA
San Bernardino, CA
09 February 2020